Murder
in an
Amethyst Haze

A Juicy Crones Sisterhood Mystery

Hana Cannon

First Edition, January, 2008
Copyright © 2008 by Hana Cannon

Grateful acknowledgement is made to the following sources for
permission to reprint copyrighted material.
"To Mom on Mother's Day: Be a Juicy Crone!"
© by Jean Shinoda Bolen, M.D.
"Swamp Witch," © by Jim Stafford

Published in the United States by BookSurge.com.

Library of Congress Cataloging-in-Publication Data
Hana Cannon
Murder in an Amethyst Haze/Hana Cannon
Juicy Crones who solve mysteries.

ISBN # 978-1-41968521-7
ISBN # 1-4196-8521-x

Cover photo of Magda (Alissa Gloor) and Magdalena (Melisa
Donnelly) by Evan Donnelly. Author's photo by John Dach
Book Design and Layout by ...Jessica & Lynda at ...In Graphic Detail

Murder in an Amethyst Haze is published by www.BookSurge.com

Hana Cannon is an eclectic collection of personae — no doubt that's what keeps her so plump. She came into this particular life in Hollywood, California. Born into a doubly creative family - father an animator and director, mother a designer and creator of wonderful objects - Cannon grew up in a warm and stimulating atmosphere. Traveling extensively in Europe became her education...that and voracious reading. After stints in the magazine business, market research/advertising, and then film production, she has found her spot, looking over the top of her MacBook at the seasons playing out in the trees. *Murder in an Amethyst Haze* is one of the *JuicyCronesSisterhood Mysteries*, which number about a dozen, in varying stages of development. Currently she's involved in turning *Amethyst* into a screenplay, interspersed with taunts from her characters to finish another of their adventures. She, and her audacious characters, live in Sequim, Washington.

Hana@JuicyCronesSisterhood.com

This book is for my sweet,

deliciously supportive family, Abby,

Chris, Piper and her kids, Jason, Melisa

and their kids.

With a 🩷 to Jean Shinoda Bolen, M.D., whose writing provides infinite inspiration. To Cynthia Thomas Dach and John Dach for all they've done to push me forward. To SusanVanGeystel for gamely going where others dare not tread. To Tory Abell for Grandmother Strong Feather. To Linda Connors for taking me into her "sweatlodge." To Ruth Cones for all the "funnymentalist" information, biblical quotes, modeling for Colleen, and gamely reading through a messy first draft. After that Karen Klein pitched in with a truck-load of commas and comments. Didn't use all of them, so I guess I've got some left over for the next book....

Excerpted from

To Mom on Mother's Day:
Be a Juicy Crone!
by Jean Shenoda Bolen

"Be a Juicy Crone!"... realize ... that there is a remarkable phase to look forward to after the active years of motherhood, when a woman is post-menopausal and can become more authentically herself than ever.

A juicy crone has a life that is soul-satisfying. It has to do with knowing who she is inside and believing that what she is doing is a true reflection or expression of her genuine self. It is having what Margaret Mead called "P.M.Z." or post-menopausal zest for the life she has.

This third trimester of life can be a time of personal wholeness and integration; in the active years after fifty, your mother may become more visible in the world than ever before, or she may develop her inner life and pursue creative interests, or she may be the centering influence in a family constellation, or she may make major changes that disturb the old status quo.

This Mother's Day, [or any day] might you send her the unconventional wish that she be free to be herself? Might you even risk saying, "Be a Juicy Crone?"[1]

Murder in an Amethyst Haze....

by Hana Cannon

As dusk settles over the farm a young woman struggles with a steamer trunk. Is she trying to put it on or take it off of the rear bumper rack of the '31 Pontiac? Suddenly the lid of the trunk pops open and a small feminine leg flops out. It's attached to a body draped in a silken skirt. As the young woman grabs for the leg an arm pops out. In a languid eye blink the vision dissolves time: the body is back in the trunk, the straps in place, a small suit case is placed in the rear of the cabriolet, the door slams, a figure, perhaps the girl, perhaps not, climbs behind the steering wheel, releases the brake and the Pontiac rolls down the drive and into the cold, amethyst mists of a moonlit night.

Chapter One

Anthea tiptoed down the market lane to the Celtic rhythms wafting through the air. Her attention caught on a twig circlet of tiny flowers bedecked with beads of amethyst and cobalt and in that distracted moment her nose came tip to hip at the top of a shaggy black leg. A tingle of adrenalin rippled up her arms. Her gaze rolled up to where the shag ended and a blue-green, sweat-be-dewed torso began. As her eyes lingered on this luscious sight a long-fingered hand reached down and drew her chin up, up, up till she and the creature were gazing into each other's eyes. His were as blue-green as his skin, and rimmed with cobalt Celtic symbols. The visage would have been quite fierce were it not for the twinkle in those eyes.

She burst into a hearty laugh as he stepped around her to saunter on between rows of tiny booths.

The stall that brought about Anthea's encounter with the giant faun was Circlettes de Fae. It featured all manner of head ornaments from entwined garlands of leaves to ornate jewels. They also sold pointy little plastic ear tips, which people all over the festival delighted in sporting. The seventh *Annual Esoteric Extravaganza and Faerie Festival* was a feast for the senses. The Juicy Crone relished every nook and cranny, every audacious costume: faeries in flowing gauze, faeries in almost nothing. In one open area there was a contest for the most creative design on a naked pregnant belly. There were nine entrants.

Thea marveled at the faery wings that sprouted from all manner of backs. Wings fashioned from materials ranging from giant palm fronds to ethereal bits of gauze on wiry frames. There were more fauns on stilts, jugglers, tumblers, tiny tots sporting nothing more than little pinion rigs on their backs, a winged ferret in the arms of an ancient fairy crone, lots of kilts and Celtic battle regalia.

Aromas meant to conjure up love potions or healing balms mingled with the heady scents of foods from multiple ethnicities: hearty olde English to sultry Latino, middle eastern faire to luscious salads, and Thea closed her eyes on more than one occasion to travel where the scents would lead.

Beyond the medieval market place was a stage for performers. Between market and stage lay the locus for this pre-season event at the race track just north of San Diego -- a fully tented infield; the canopy lit with tiny flickering faery lights, enhanced with candles on the tables and in sconces on standards around the perimeter of the area. The tables were set for English tea, with lacy cloths and dainty cozied tea pots. Three-tiered glass cake plates piled artfully with finger sandwiches, scones and faery cakes with pink and lavender icing dotted the tables along with little vases of fragrant freesias. Pots of jam and clotted cream snuggled next to each tri-tier server.

A que of anxious querents lined up outside the tent waiting to get to the readers' tables, but the likelihood of a vacancy soon was next to nil. Heads bent over tea cups, tarot cards, astrological charts and not a few crystal balls. Anthea Calzona, who had given one of the featured presentations of the event, *Reality: Where Quantum Physics Meets Quantum Phantasy*, sat across from a new-found friend, Magda Lindal. Lindal, tall, elegant ash blonde in a sea-foam green silk brocade chimsong over matching pants, had presented one of the more titillating workshops: *Spiritual Enlightenment Through Tantric for Sex-agenarians*. The play on words had been the inspiration of Lindal's friend and partner Tran Thic Gwan. It had proved to be a marketing inspiration cum laude.

Two weeks prior to the event Anthea googled the term Tantric Sex and found 1,247,000 listings. Lindal's web-site alone had a bezillion hits. It didn't hurt that the teaser line was "Remember that multiple orgasms are a natural response to the love of the universe, not a result of training.'"

Anthea's seminar that day only lasted three hours. Magda's workshop was a two-day event. On day two Thea had checked it out from the wings, then lingered backstage during the afternoon break, introduced herself and invited

Magda to join her in the "tea shoppe" out on the green when she was finished. By the time Magda got to the venue that afternoon Thea, thrilled by her encounter with the slit-walking faun, had toured the rest of the shoppes and settled down for several hours with querents.. Her laptop was set up for on-the-spot astrological charts and she was also doing Tarot and faery card readings.

As Magda walked into the tent Anthea stood and bowed, greeting her with hands pressed Namasté fashion. Magda returned the salutation and the two women sat down across from one another. From what she'd seen on the stage Thea had the feeling that this woman could well be the next member of the JuicyCronesSisterhood.

"I was surprised to hear you say you've never had your chart done, never had a Tarot reading, never met the faeries of the cards.[2] If you've been doing this circuit," Thea wafted an arm draped in a lusciously cut peach silk sleeve, indicating the collection of readers, "how'd you avoid all these characters?"

Magda just shrugged her shoulders.

"Shall we remedy the situation right now? If you give me your birth date, time and location, I'll have a chart calculating and printing out for you while we order," she patted her laptop.

It appeared to the astrologer that the tantrition diminished before her very eyes. The bold, sensuous, audacious woman she'd seen on the stage before the throng became evasive and seemed to withdraw into a shell that hadn't been there before. The Juice seemed to have drained from the Crone. This woman to whom she'd felt drawn by a vibration in alignment with her own, now seemed to have swung down to below a 200 on the Hawkin's scale of frequencies[3]. In the field of string theory the string of their new-found friendship felt decidedly frayed when, rather sheepishly, Magda pulled her driver's license from her bag and handed it to Thea. "Okay, so now we've got your age, but time and place?" asked the astrologer.

"I don't know about the time, and the place is a little town in eastern Nevada called Dos Lobos. It's just a bump in the road really."

"That's all right. Someday we'll track down your birth certificate, but in the meantime we can kind of work backward. Its what's called an horary chart and its based on using a significant date in your life. We can take something off your biography here." She held up the trifold for the seminar. "Sound reasonable?"

The woman who spoke in fluid, lucid terms on stage now spat dry, brittle word morsels and fragments, "Sure, whatever you say."

"Magda, I want this to be fun for you. We don't have to do it if you feel uncomfortable," Anthea offered.

As they talked Thea input an event from Magda's brochure into her Astro-chart program, but she stopped when she felt Lindal's reticence.

"No offense, but I had a very bad experience years ago and it turned me off on the whole concept; I met a man from Cleveland on a train to New Jersey, and he told me he was on his way to straighten out the Astrologers in India. He insisted on doing my chart on the floor of his compartment with shaving foam. You know? The circle and the pie pieces, and the symbols. He told me I was totally screwed up because my father had been suicidal when I was a kid and the stars said I always thought it was my fault. I told the guy that was crazy. I didn't feel remotely guilty about anything." Magda blushed. "Anyway I gave you my information. It's just that, well, the truth is I don't really remember my childhood, but I'm sure it wasn't all that bad. Besides, if I get it right, its written in the stars. There's not a whole lot you can do about it."

Anthea replied soothingly, "I'm sorry to hear about your experience. Maybe I can give you a different perspective. The idea of the chart is that it's sort of like a map to the life you've chosen this time around. You get to decide which paths to take as you go along. What about the cards?" Thea asked.

"Oh, the cards are usually so depressing I just figure its best to stay away. I try to keep to positive, happy thoughts. But if you really want to..." Magda shrugged a go ahead.

Not the most enthusiastic acceptance of her art thought Anthea, but spirit had led her to Lindal and the intuitive knew better than to ignore her inner guidance system. There was something she was to learn from this relationship. Then again, wasn't that always the case?

At that point the astro-printout began drawing her attention. She became deeply engrossed in the chart until she felt her brow furrow.

Simultaneously she was beset by a huge, loudly buzzing fly that landed smack dab on her third eye. It was so unexpected she almost slapped herself in the head before she remembered her prominent position on the board of PETA. No killing allowed. Not even flies or gnats. Besides, she might accidentally hit a fairy. One of the real ones, not the humans emulating them. The tiny creatures were all over the place today. But then they would be at an event that honored them and their contributions to Gaia. Anthea shooed the fly away but another quickly took its place. "Govno, govno, govno," she muttered to herself. This was not good; having her focus interrupted by a herd of huge blue-bottle flies.

She looked in the direction of the horse stalls, but her gaze was broken by the arm-flapping of Eidola Binder, a tea leaf reader given to the blackest of teas, and thereby the darkest of prognostications. Eidola's concept of making a point never ceased to amaze Thea. It entailed what Thea called a flapdoodle, extensive waving of her exceedingly heavy arms adorned in jangling bangles and swaths of black and gold batik-dyed polyester, with layers of gold fringe. *Not the best look for a woman of such abundant proportions. Stop!* Anthea chided herself. *Judge not lest ye be judged.* One of her great challenges seemed to be to let go of criticism. *Especially of people who seemed to have no taste. Stop!* Oh, those nasty thoughts insisted on creeping in. And it didn't help any when Anthea's gaze dropped down to Eidola's tea table. It was covered with pastry crumbs, an open honey pot, and a schmear of jam left in a dish. No wonder the flies had been drawn to the tent. *Some people just... Stop!*

Anthea shifted her attention back to the flies annoying her, tuned in to a nearby clutch of the fae folk dancing amongst the floral arrangements, whispered "Gabrella, Sylvana, please get these flies over to Eidola. There're still plenty of sweets over there," she cajoled them. She was so into trying not to whine while she wheedled (*I don't do wheedle* – a thought within a thought protested), she almost said it out loud. Catching herself, she waved at the little monsters, (*now there's an oxymoron* she snickered at her left brain), pleased with the outcome as the flies flitted toward Eidola. She sent a heart full of gratitude to the faeries who herded them along.

Magda was perplexed by Thea's seeming departure

from sanity. "Is there something wrong Anthea? Did I annoy you? What was that you said? Something like gabble? It sounded a little on the angry side, and then you just totally spaced out and you keep shooing. And who's Sylvana?"

"What? Oh, no, no." She wasn't about to tell Magda that she talked to faeries yet, or that she had said *govno* which was Russian for shit, and that she had learned how to say shit in 47 languages for occasions just such as this. Brigid, the gypsy grandmother who raised her, had traveled all over Europe and as far as India, and that's the one word she picked up wherever she went. Gran told Thea she found it handy in situations similar to this one. Ones where you want the querent to feel reassured that you are totally engrossed in their problem and some odeous distraction descends just as you've almost found out why your calculations feel as though they're being done with at least one number suffering from <u>mathmaticas dementia</u>. *Great goddess,* she thought, *this whole thing has really stirred up a cluster fluster in my neuro-peptides. It's set my synapses snapping. Pull yourself together Thea. Deep breathe. Come on spirit, flow through me. Remember, we're here to help shine the light.* She interrupted what seemed like a freight train of her own thoughts and actually said, "It's just that something appears to be off with your chart. Are you certain about the birth information you gave me?"

Magda bristled. At least that was the energy shooting at Thea as the Ellen Burstyn look alike huffed, "Are you doubting what I told you? Because, if you are, we can end this right now." That was Burstyn in *Divine Secrets of the Ya Ya Sisterhood* talking now. It never ceased to amuse Thea how she so often saw people as characters in films. Many of them the oldies she'd seen when, as a child, she snuck into the theater to keep warm while her gran gathered provisions in preparation for moving the caravan to the next Romany camping site. Ah, those were real stars, something none of today's celebrities could emulate. Rosalind Russell, Kate Hepburn, Bette Davis. Her friend Cybil was Russelleque, and Mitzy was.... Ooops. Back to center please Anthea.

She patted Magda's hand in a gesture of compassion. "Pardon me, Magda. I'm only trying to get a little clarity here, and the chart is rather murky. Just give me a few minutes to get in touch." She closed her eyes, centered her energy and waved her hands over the printout. It still came back feeling like static on an old radio. She opened her eyes, picked up her Tarot deck. "Maybe a shift of focus will help us after all." She asked Magda to shuffle while centering on the question she wanted to ask Divine Inspiration.

"And just how long do I do that?" Magda was still a trifle chilly.

"Till you feel you've gotten your point across to the cards," Thea replied, calling on all her inner resources to help her sound warm and fuzzy in the face of such skepticism.

Magda did about six shuffles and handed the cards back to Thea. "Is that enough?" As Thea laid out the spread she made sure that her hums and aahs bore decidedly friendly tones, but that same niggling, brow-furrowing tickle crossed her psyche again. She kept her attention focused on the up side cards. "Uumm, this is wonderful. Maggie. May I call you Maggie?"

"Some people just call me Mags. I don't care either way."

"I know what you mean. I'm Anthea but other folks call

me Thea so much I often do it myself. OK, Mags, let's just say
there are a few bumps in the past here," Anthea deftly slid over
the ten of swords with all those daggers in the body. And the
Tower, and the Hanged Man. She'd have to explain that all
sometime, but right now she needed to get this woman's spirits
back to a higher frequency, for she'd observed a phenomenon
here she had noted once or twice before; a charismatic speaker,
a presenter of an ancient art, a teacher of what many would find
scandalous, who was a different creature altogether off stage
and out of her passion.

   That passion apparently emboldened the woman, gave
her the courage to present what to many would be a taboo
subject, and she did it with wit and grace. She clearly had what
Thea called one's inner dragon—firing up ones creative juices.

   One of the high points had been when the rather tall
Magda told the story of an encounter she and her friend, the
diminutive Ruth Gordon, had with a brash young reporter two
decades earlier. Lindal managed to take on the aura of
Gordon despite the fact that she was probably six inches
taller, let alone twenty years younger than the actress. She
certainly got the energy right when she impersonated the feisty
octogenarian.

   As Lindal told it, Gordon, ever the flirt and tease,
loved to shock her interrogators. When asked by the young
man, who clearly thought he was about to knock the blunt
speaking star for a loop, if she missed sex now that she was
beyond that stage in life, the actress whooped in laughter as
she replied: "Still wet after all these years." And Magda
assured the audience that she did not mean she had a challenge
with incontinence. Gordon explained to the young reporter,
just in case he didn't get it, that she was referring to the female

equivalent of "getting it up," and she did indeed enjoy it as often as possible. In case the reporter hadn't heard, she had a bit of a reputation and he better watch out.

Now Magda, the bawdy promoter of ultimate intimacy was retreating, almost shy, pulling back and closing down as though Thea's reading was a threat that would reveal the goddess-only-knew-what deep dark secret.

Anthea gently removed one of the pendants that graced her neck and dangled it over the card throw. "Look here! This Queen of Wands; your time is ripe. Answers are on the way. She tapped the mid-heaven on Magda's chart, "It is odd that your chart implies a late bloomer and we all know you've been blooming for years. Look at your bio," she said tapping Magda's promotional tri-fold. "But this Jupiter trine to your mid-heaven shows that you are about to experience the life-changing phenomena you've been attempting to draw to you throughout this incarnation." She closed her eyes. "I see you on the stage receiving an Oscar!" Anthea was as delighted as if she'd won the statuette herself.

Emerald and sapphire sparkles glinted off Thea's ringed fingers as she waved her hand over the spread. "Look at the way the pendant is confirming it." The pendant swung strongly over the spread in agreement with the vibrations coming off the cards. "Sit back and enjoy the ride, my friend. Your chart confirms that you are on the cusp of pronoia."

"Pronoia? Sounds like some dreaded disease."

"Hardly. Simply put it is the suspicion that the Universe is conspiring on your behalf. It's the niggling notion that others are in cahoots to help you in all your endeavors; the opposite of paranoia."

"Sounds like just what I need. Where do I sign up?" Magda chortled lightly.

"You're already signed if I may be so pun-y." She turned to the chart, "Just look at your Jupiter and the alignment to Venus and Mars!"

"And the down side is???"

"There is no real downside, even though it may feel like it. The pundits and politicians who think they must 'take care of us;' rule by promulgating fear. The majority of us buy into the collective consciousness that life is fraught with misery, that life is out to get us." Thea's own juices flowed now. This was a topic about which she was passionate. Her dragon was dancing. "We're taught to be afraid of everything from bacteria to each other. The media, religion, medicine, everything out there basically promotes life as scary and it behooves those in control to keep us believing that. Well, now is the time to take charge and challenge them all. Part of the paradigm shift we all meditated for and celebrated at the Harmonic Convergence back in 1987."

"And this affects me how?"

"Oh, you're at the forefront. The portal is open. You're ready to step into pronoia, to realize that it is the way we're going to make the shift. With people like you in the media to inform the whole wide world, the shift is already happening. Look." The pendulum practically did loop-the-loops as Thea held it over the table.

"I have no intention of being at the forefront of anything," Magda bristled. "This is already too much stress, having to deal with all these people who just want a thrill. They don't want to get into the spiritual aspect of it. That would be too much work. They all just want the magic part. Over the years promoters and agents and all kinds of people have screwed me over. And don't tell me that twaddle about forgiving them and myself. Forgiving just proves there's something that somebody did wrong, which proves I'm right about how rotten people are. Being pissed at them is getting it out of your system. Ignoring just festers."

"I'm not talking about forgiving or ignoring, I'm talking about gratitude. Gratitude for what those people have taught you. The step up they've provided for you. It's a thank you to them for giving you an opportunity to shift into a new attitude, a new energy."

"Yeah, a major attitude of pissosity."

"Not quite where I was headed. Here," Anthea took another of her pendants from around her neck and looped it over Magda's head, "this is a piece of fused glass with the symbol for a heart full of gratitude. Now you'll have it with you always. It'll remind you to 'Go to Gratitude' any time you're in doubt or discomfort, or feeling lack. So, I think you're ready to get out there and do a new film that will help people understand the energetic shifts that are shaping our lives."

"Thea, I haven't had a good story idea for over fifteen years. There's something wrong with this reading. Anyway, I've long since blown my industry contacts." Magda tried to make it sound sensible but Thea was having none of it.

"Excuse me. Did you see the size of your audience today? That's just the beginning."

"Stop it Anthea. I do not have your daring, your ability to go for the outrageous."

"Moi?" Thea questioned self-mockingly. "I consider

myself audacious its true. Audacious is my favorite adjective. But Magda, when you're out in front of that crowd you're far more outrageous than I could ever be. This coming astrological event," she tapped the trine on Magda's chart, "is going to change the whole way you look at life. You're about to become a flagrant optimist with very good reason."

"You just don't get it, Thea. If you knew the whole situation you'd understand that I have good reason to see the glass half empty."

"You only say that because your inner self knows you're on the cusp of huge success and there's a part of you that is afraid of spilling any of that top half. I'm telling you the glass is brimming... and if you do spill any of it, remember there is someone out there ready and eager to help you refill the glass."

"And I'm telling you Thea, there's too much about me you don't know. This whole thing is just another house of cards about to topple. It happens every time. It just gets down to me being realistic. I will admit I do walk a kind of razor's edge on this whole thing, 'cause like I told you before, I believe in being positive, but my life just sort of slams me in the face with reality."

"How do you feel when you help someone else?" Anthea smiled while Magda furrowed her brow even further.

"I feel great, of course. But that's different."

"And that's because?"

"They deserve it."

"And you don't?"

"When I need help it's so desperate. People have got to be thinking, here we go again, bailing Magda out. And some of them... I get the feeling that they just want me to live according to their rules and then all will be well and they'll never have to help me again."

"There's a vast difference between self-righteous controllers whose way to help you is to show you how to do it their way because they 'know the truth', and people who are simply there to support you, however you choose to go. I can tell you are one of the latter and I'm also here to tell you that you are about to attract more people who live in the vibrational frequency we've been talking about... as soon as you decide to accept it."

"I think you're having a few delusions here Anthea. You don't seem to realize that I'm a flea compared to a person like you. There's no way this flea is jumpin' on this pronoia bandwagon of yours."

"It's not my bandwagon, mi amiga. It's ours. It's what's happening while the rest of the six billion are mesmerized by the horror movies produced in Washington, Iraq, pharmaceutical labs, oil fields, the media. Meanwhile a rapidly growing band of us are focused on shifting the vibrational frequency, upping the energy level. The cards here show you've been on the brink and now you are about to launch, whether you think so or not. You have a very special place in our little army."

"We're back to being scary Thea, and majorly over my head."

"Tish tosh, lassie. You can do it!"

"I don't want to do it!"

"Ah, but you will."

"And just why would I do that?"

"Because it feels so good... almost like a Tantric orgasm on the spirit plane. It's like that feeling you get, your body hummin' in tune with your inner self which has asked for guidance. It lets you know when you're in vibrational frequency with the Universe. And in harmony with your own inner being. The goal is to keep it hummin' at that high vibration. Here, I'll quote you, 'multiple orgasms are a natural response to the love of the Universe.' That's where you're headed."

"So you're equating this high vibe to sex?" Magda almost got caught by a giggle. But she managed to regroup and go for the gloom. "Thea, come on. I've had hundreds of aha or warm-fuzzy or sweet-peace moments. It hasn't made me feel secure. I worry all the time that people are going to see through me, are gonna know I'm a fake. And again, like I said before, there's the whole world situation. How can you not feel bad? with global warming, terrorism, political spinning?"

"Magda, Magda, Magda, the best way to help Gaia and all those you're worried about is for you to take care of you first and your heightened vibration will begin to help everybody else... even people you don't know."

"You're asking too much Thea. I can't see myself doing all this high vibration stuff. No way."

"The thing is, its basically easy. Stay focused on whatever raises your energy level. You already do it. Look at your C.V." Thea pointed to the program that listed Magda's bonefides: "chocolatier, cellist, screen writer, master gardener, and I love this bit... exotic dancer through life. They are a course in the healing power of high vibrations. But of course the best is teacher of tantric sex. How much higher can you get than sharing those vibes?"

Magda blushed, "I've already told you, that was some PR woman who came up with that stuff. It's misleading. Especially the sex stuff. I don't teach sex. I explore its spiritual implications and how the ecstasy that results from genuine sharing has been perverted by men who have feared their sexuality and therefore insisted that women must also fear their urges, and that obfuscates the whole purpose of sexual union."

"Hah! There you are. When you get into your passion, you glow. Your energy could light up this whole pavilion. That's it! You need to focus on these warm fuzzies, get so full of it there's no room for the *shitake*," Thea almost shouted her use of the mushroom for a Japanese swear word. OK, so sometimes she created her own expletives.

"And when you are in the passion of <u>any</u> of these disciplines you are on the brink. The feeling that resonates through your body when that cello is between your thighs, the ecstasy when you sample your latest blend of chocolate, the exhilaration when the first rose blossoms in your garden in spring and you connect to the vastness and beauty of Gaia. Your whole life has been about what I'm now seeing as the 'Sensuous Woman's Guide to Spiritual Awareness.'" Anthea gestured emphatically at each word. "And you are about to realize how it all comes together. All you need to do now is focus on gratitude for this experience of life."

"Great Grandmother, Thea, you should write a book!"

"You're the writer, and it's your life. You've just got to get it on paper, make a movie."

"What I'm getting now is a hugely queasy feeling with a tad of vertigo. I don't do any of that stuff anymore. And a book about stuff I don't even really understand? You're asking too much."

"Ah, but you do. You know it. Now flow it."

"I don't think so Thea. This is too off the wall for me. If anything, I need to try to figure out how I'm going to come up with a bunch of cash to buy the property next door to me before the neighbor puts in a cell tower and destroys the whole neighborhood. I've got practical matters to focus on, not pie-in-the sky like you're talking about."

"Pish tosh. This is your resistance mechanism in high gear. Your inner critic trying to talk you out of it."

"I'm not conscious of any resistance on my part. Maybe a little wary discrimination."

"Discrimination is just your potty-trained paranoia at work. You've been thoroughly indoctrinated, as we all have. You're afraid to let your genius shine."

Magda shook her head in a mixture of bewilderment and awe. "Even if I thought I could do what you're saying, I've got too much on my plate right now."

"Believe me, there is an event about to shift your life." She tapped the ace of swords. "Keep me posted." Thea fastened her pendant around her neck. "This has my website, email and phone. Don't hesitate," she said as she handed Magda her card.

"Likewise to be sure," Magda said as she stood, and scribbled her cell phone number on the trifold flier. They hugged warmly as the twinkle lights blinked off and on. Looking around they realized they were the last remaining guests under the tent.

As Anthea drove back home to LaPlaya that night she wondered if Magda had any connection to the girl and the farm scene she'd visioned just before she headed for Del Mar two days earlier.

Chapter Two

Two mornings later Anthea opened her bathroom door to the sensuous sounds of Bedouin music. She had her stereo system wired throughout the house, set to go on as she entered a room. Now tiny bells, finger cymbals, exotic strings filled the air. She whirled slowly across the room. Daylight filled the space making its own entrance through a stunning curved glass ceiling from which it spilled right down to splash in a pool on the tiled floor.

Around the room orchids, ferns and fronds brought Mother Nature in to decorate. The walls of hand-wrought tile matched the floor in shades of teal blue to green, with little touches of gold in swatches here and there. An exquisite deep purple velvet-covered slipper sofa beckoned her to drape her robe across its voluptuous curves. But not before she placed the lovely little Japanese lacquered tray she carried on the hand carved vanity. The tray contained an amphora of pure vanilla extract, which she had steeped for six months to obtain its essence. Fondly she recalled her trip to Madagascar to pick the vanilla beans.

She draped her silk gown gently on the sofa, stepped out of her faux ostrich-feather trimmed mules and, bearing the amphora with care, she glided across the room to the claw-footed tub. She touched the lever to plug the drain, turned the knobs for just the right mixture of cold and hot water and the swan-necked, burnished-brass faucet spilled its aqua fresca into the huge basin.

NOW! she gently unstopped the amphora and let droplets of the elixir flow into the tub. Vanilla, exquisite pure vanilla aroma filled her nostrils, her every pore, her brain, her spirit. She set the little bottle aside, eased over the edge of the tub and slid down into its warm embrace. Resting her head on the high, perfectly arched back she closed her eyes and in the embrace of this hedonist's delight of sensuosity she gave herself over to the Essence of All That Is, and asked for guidance on how to shine clarity on the vexatious niggling her mind was toying with regarding her new friend, Magda Lindal. Little tweaks kept jumping onto her thought train. What could she do to help the woman get beyond her negative self-image?

When she came out of her meditation, after she did her yoga, put the ferrets back in their arboretum, romped with the dogs and soothed the cats, she was ready for a session with Rosalinda, who insisted her real name was something like A'rzhuld'a' in her native Aztec-Mayan. It was a regal name, or so the woman said. In the fifteen years they'd known each other Rosalinda was as close as Anthea had gotten to pronouncing the name. One never knew with Rosalinda quite where truth left off and epic storytelling took over.

Actually Anthea wasn't sure she knew much of anything about the avowed Aztec-Mayan princess who had been driven off her land by power-crazed village elders when she was about to go through the ritual of becoming a woman. These men knew she planned to demand her rightful heritage as their Orphan Princess and rule over them.

For reasons unexplained she chose to cross the barren

wastelands of Chihuahua bare of foot, after which she forded the Rio Grande with all of her worldly belongings in a basket on her head.

Or there was the version where she escaped the evil nuns at the one-room school and jumped on a train, hiding in the foot locker belonging to a descendant of Pancho Villa. Thus she arrived in Arizona in the baggage car of the Baja Express. That was when she was eight.

Or was it rather that her pregnant mother had snuck across the border through a barbed wire fence with coyotes howling and bore her babe in the nave of a church in San Diego so that the child would be a citizen of the U.S.?

For a woman who seemed to only speak when absolutely necessary, Rosalinda had managed to confuse Anthea with a tome of information, none of which revealed anything about the mujer. Equally vexing was Rosalinda's ability to block any attempts Anthea made over the years to get a vibrational fix on when her comadre was telling her the truth.

The women met while walking on the beach in La Playa, each totally absorbed in her own communication with the sea, or in Anthea's case with the trident king, Neptune. Heaven only knows what Rosalinda called it. Without exchanging a word Thea was not surprised to find the woman with the chiseled features right behind her when she headed up the steps to her house.

The woman with the chiseled features had been there ever since. She took care of everything, but she was not a servant. Anthea didn't do servants. And Rosalinda clearly didn't do subservient. It was more as if the deposed princess ruled the palace and Anthea was allowed to live there. As titular ruler, Rosalinda saw that everything was done. She always seemed to have the right person come in to take care of any job that needed doing. It was this odd mixture of what she did and how she did it that left Thea at odds over how to explain exactly what or who Rosalinda was in her household — in her life.

The point right now was that she was busy creating tiny masterpieces of Aztecan art in nail polish on Thea's toes while they shared some chipotle hot chocolate. Just looking at the designs had distracted the intuitive from thinking about her discomfort at Magda Lindal's odd reading over the weekend. For this she blessed the artist, took a deep hatha breath and got to her dazzling feet. She was headed for the MarVista Inn and a gathering of the clan, a group of vastly divergent personalities of the "beyond retirement" persuasion.

Retirement? A concept that was totally foreign to Anthea. She couldn't imagine what she would do if she stopped reading charts, objects, cards and palms.

Chapter Three

"Hey gypsy woman, how was your esoteric commingling?" Burgess bussed Anthea on the cheek as he joined her on the bench overlooking the beach. The deck of the MarVista Inn was the only place to be on such a sparkling morning as this. "Every bit as glorious as this day," she tugged his Willie Nelson braid.

"Such a Chamber of Commerce photo op day! Mayor Frist must be peeing his sani-pad at the council meeting," Cybil chortled. Anthea smiled, "Ever the elegant turn of phrase cher amie."

Cybil LaCrosse, the amie to whom Thea spoke, was a delicious dichotomy: as tall as Anthea, her hair had turned naturally white long before Streep put it on for Prada. AND, she out dressed the devil herself; but her looks deceived on many an occasion, as what came out of her mouth was as basic and gritty as that of any one of the teamsters who drove the fleet of big rigs she owned.

On the other hand Mitzy MacDonald ran vigorous counter point to Cybil. She enhanced her almost five feet of stature with shoes to elevate: spike-heeled or platformed -- whatever it took. This concoction was topped with a bird's nest of orange-red hair carefully done up each morning with an egg beater, or so it looked.

Combined with Thea's own flowing gypsy look, sandals to show off her artfully decorated toes, a gently drifting cotton-rayon skirt of forest green with an equally soft looking blouse of sage, this day topped by a burnt orange version of her signature fringed scarf wrap meant to tame her mane of peach hair, the trio comprised what Mitzy had dubbed The Juicy Crones Sisterhood. The name struck a chord and they had been collecting sisters from around the globe into a widely spread covey of women who shared experiences, creative new ways to deal with challenges, and just plain sisterhood, i.e. support for one-another in their multiplicity of endeavors.

Now the LaPlaya branch was gathered, as was their almost daily ritual, along with the area's collection of noteworthy sexagenarians who drifted in to the Inn every morning to start the day. Noteworthy if for no other reason than that of being vigorously opinionated.

"You know she's right, Thea. That bag of wind is over there finding some way to take full credit for every bit of it: Catalina laying out there crisp and clear, no smog blanket; the surf shushing on the sand; kids squealing to keep the waves back from their castles," Mitzy longed to puncture the Mayor's balloon, but the magnificent LaPlaya day wasn't lending itself to her political fantasies.

Suddenly Charles, Manager of the Inn, crashed through the dining room door with Hortense hot on his trail, her gleaming motorized Velocity scooter bumping off the door jam, careening into a chair, crashing into a food cart, and banging into a waiter carrying a full tray of huevos rancheros. Phillip, the horrified maitre d', joined the melee just in time to catch the tray on its way toward an astonished customer's lap. Charles managed to stay three steps ahead of the maniac on wheels as she railed and beat at him with her furled umbrella. "He pulled the tube on my oxygen tank," she spewed her venom on him, "you slithering, stinking old bag of permin voop! Somebody trip him!"

Instead Anthea stepped over and turned off the key in the ignition, bringing Hortense winding down to a stop. Then she reached over and untwisted the oxygen tank tube that was caught in the crook end of the hellion's brolly.

"Why do you even have an umbrella Hortense? We don't get enough rain around here to fill an aperitif glass," Burgess moved over and quietly soothed the distraught bumper-car wanna be.

She snipped back, "You know I need it to keep the sun off. I'm sensitive."

Anthea turned to Phillip who was still trying to get his maitre d' feathers smoothed and regain control of his establishment; "How about having Shirley make up a lemonade for Charles," she patted the distraught man's shoulder and eased Charles, always Charles, never Chuck or Charley, onto a stool at the counter over-looking the beach. Charles was a contrariety in her lexicon of movie-star reminders. He appeared debonair in the David Niven mold, but reacted to situations as though possessed by the ghost of Barney Fife.

Under Thea's ministrations, with added support from the other two Crones, Charles/Barney relaxed noticeably, as Phillip bustled off to see to the order and direct the clean up brigade. Charles was fine right up to the moment Shirley, the aging nymphomaniacal bartender, brought the drink out herself, and just as surely Shirley patted his bum when she squeezed past him to place the glass in front of him with a good brush of her buxom boobs. Even as she winked slyly at the 70-

something Christian Scientist, he fought to think loving thoughts about Shirley. She didn't make it easy. She seemed to think she was Marilyn Monroe reincarnated, with a mission to stimulate every male in her vicinity.

After a few moments of soothing, Charles acknowledged that he couldn't quite remember what it was he meant to speak to Anthea about when he came to the dining room. He thanked her for rescuing him and returned to his office to do a metaphysical treatment for himself and the atmosphere of the Inn.

As Burgess approached Anthea she whispered, "What in thunder, aside from her usual plain ol' ornery disposition, has Hortee in such a dither?"

"Oh, she's been watching those broadcasts from Reverend Micah on that Tele-vangel network from the *Temple at Heaven's Portal* down in Escondido. There's apparently some kind of special event for the handicapped next Sunday. They're going to circle the wheel chairs and his eminence will make the rounds laying hands on all their barmy little heads. She's convinced if she could just get down there and get a touch from that Reverend she'd walk tall and breathe free."

"You know as well as I do if she'd just work on her attitude, the stress relief alone would probably lift her out of that chair and put the breath back in those uptight lungs. We need to get her into a higher vibrational frequency."

Anthea turned to where Hortense sat sulking and fuming. "Hey there lady," she smiled politely, even as she uttered the mendacious appellation. But then Anthea was willing to try anything, "look at that glorious sparkle on the ocean, those adorable little kids down there playing. How about getting into that sweet-feeling vibe? How about thinking of all the things you're grateful for: your chair, your oxygen, the meds that keep you going, all the folks making your life easier."

"Hah! You are so full of bullshit Calzona. You try snorting this thing to breathe and sitting in this wreck of a motorized wheelbarrow and tell me how sweet you feel. Those little monsters down there are the problem you know. Too many of 'em, causing all that pollution and warble gloaming that's rune'n my lungs."

There was a united stifling of sniggers at the transpositional phrase, Hortense's specialty. But she didn't notice. She was on a roll. "Just because it's clear out there today is no never mind. Rev. Micah says those little brats propagated by masses of heathens are overpopulating the planet. Pretty soon none of you'll be able to breathe any better than me," she wheezed.

Cybil, ever the logician, couldn't resist, "I'm confused Hortense. I thought he sided with the President that global warming is a natural phenomenon... and, if I'm not mistaken, he's proud of the fact that his father sired 137 children and he himself is working on catching up with that record as fast as he can despite federal restrictions on sex with minors."

Mitzy couldn't stay out of this one: "Yeah, that must be a thorn in his side. No sacrilege intended. His old man was over the one hundred mark in the offspring count by the time he was half Micah's age?"

They were definitely getting Hortense's dander up. "Don't you be castigating aspersions on that good man, you harlots. You're a bunch a' jealous pitnickers. Just 'cause you haven't got any kids."

"You've gotta admit this is a bit confusing Hortense. First overpopulation is choking us all, then we're jealous because we didn't add to the mix?" Anthea smiled, not wanting to correct Hortense on the off-spring count. Thea herself had two and two grandkids. Mitzy had three kids and had lost track of her grandkids, and Cybil had Ralph and his brood. But the point now was to counter Hortense.

"You just don't understand a man of god like Brother Micah. He's got a mission to fulfill. His children are born free of sin, each one the child of a virgin. They will carry on the charge that will heft us Chosen Ones to heaven to sit on the right hand of God while the rest of you all burn down here in hell."

Anthea restrained thoughts of a god-sized group-goosing with all the chosen one's fighting for a seat on those gigantic fingers of the Omnipotent One. "Hortense, his children are all illegitimate. He's never married any of the mothers, all of whom were barely more than babies themselves. Virgins because he only beds virgins, god forbid he have sex with real women. And he doesn't care who knows all of this."

"That is what God obstructed him to do. Be fruitified and multiply. Keep the line pure. You make it sound slugly."

There was nowhere to go in the conversation so Anthea retired. "Burgess, you take it from here."

"Thea, all she wants is to go down there this Sunday. She lives in a world of fear and this gives her hope. You know I'd do it but I've got a long-standing commitment with our board of directors about next quarter's budget for the farm." The farm being Gray Goose Organic Acres, the place where a collection of active oldsters (yes, even Hortense was active in her own way) lived in a converted barn, one of the last still standing in north La Playa.

Actually, they were part of a co-op, along with Anthea's long-time suitor, Will Sutton, who cultivated his own property right next door to the commune. Cybil LaCrosse owned the land next to Will, which he leased from and farmed for her. They sold to upscale restaurants and a chain of local markets within a hundred mile radius, there in southern California. Anyway, Burgess, the guru of Gray Goose Organic Acres, begged Anthea to take Hortense to the *Temple at Heaven's Portal* on Sunday. Despite visions of Hortense chasing her around, beating her over the head with that brolly, and an intense desire to run for the hills, Thea agreed. As he knew she would. She could take the Gray Goose van, with its lift especially fitted out for Hortense's chair. It was settled. Now she had a new consideration; how to cajole her friends into going along with her?

Mitzy and Cybil sidled up. "Don't you ever wonder," Mitzy puzzled, "why Burgess is so caring of that harridan's well-fare?" It was the local social mystery and not even Burgess's father, Sydney, the 98-year-old, internationally renowned flouriste to the rich and famous, knew the answer. Or, if he did he wasn't talking. Surely it couldn't just be because of all the prana Burge inhaled every morning with his yoga. Not even the seven years the garden guru spent meditating in a cave in Tibet, before the Chinese invaded and wiped out the Buddhists, could explain the strange dynamic between Burgess and Hortense.

Even as the Crones were enjoying a moment of tri-lateral cogitative gossip, Thea was having an ah hah moment. Before the other two knew what had happened to them their Sunday was committed to a ride into hell and back. Actually the ride itself was the hell part. Fortunately, Anthea had the virtual organic carrot of curiosity to tempt the duo. She was sure she could inveigle her new friend Magda to join in. And from the little they had heard of the tantric sex instructor/screen writer it was bound to be worth the ride, if only to find out more about her.

Besides, they knew it was what friends did for friends — help protect one another from that flailing umbrella, if not from the Vesuvius of invective that was bound to froth forth from Hortense. Limited oxygen didn't seem to hamper her ability to spew.

Chapter Four

It had been a lovely day on Magda's hilltop in Bonsall. The hired crew had just wrapped up harvesting the last of her avocado crop. She turned the horses back out on the hillside; except for Curry, who had been exceeding his peppery name to the point where she had him quarantined. That day he kicked up a ruckus as Thunder, the Clydesdale, and the dapple gray Arab mare, Zena, chased down the hill through the orchard. Magda had to laugh when they sailed across the corner of the pool followed by Kenai. The golden pup fell in trying to catch up with them.

The rest of the dog pack had all had their turns at this horse play over the years and knew how to sweep around the pool. Magda called, coaxing Kenai to paddle over to the steps. Mephisto, Serena and Groucho, the cats who had adopted her, encircled her feet. She hauled all 85-and-growing pounds of him, plus water weight, out of the pool, only to be nearly drowned in the deluge his world-class shake-out rained on her. Once he got his feet back under him he was off to join the mixed species pack of horses and dogs, leaving Magda dripping wet, with three totally pissed cats sharing her puddle.

She decided to put the trash barrels out on the curb before changing out of her work clothes. As she got the last barrel in place at the end of the cul-de-sac she was nearly run down by one of the new next-door neighbor kids on a bicycle.

When she leapt back away from the kamikaze pilot's attack the girl wobbled, caught her skirt, (yes, she had on a rather longish brown skirt) in the chain and took a header. Her knees left skid marks on the gravel road, and the girl, who appeared to be about twelve or so, bawled to let the world know in no uncertain terms that her dad and God would get Magda for this, "you, you old bat, yer gonna have to buy me a new bike." And then she decided it was time to howl in pain as she noticed she had a worthy stream of blood gushing forth from her wound.

Magda knelt down next to the child and looked directly into her eyes. "You're very good on that bike. You must have hit a rock or I'm sure you'd have made it to the bottom of the road by now." While she held the girl's attention with her praise she took the turkey feather talisman that hung on a thong around her neck and slowly waved it back and forth over the area of the wound. Then she began a very soothing chant. The child quieted down as Magda thanked the Great Father and the Earth Mother for their protection. "What's your name, young road warrior?" she smiled.

"Roberta, Roberta Cantwell," she did one of those little sob-hiccup combos kids do so well.

Just then a huge man came charging down the driveway on the verge of a veritable seizure. He almost knocked over his own mailbox. The one with Clelland Cantwell painted on the side. "Get away from my girl you Devil's Whore. Don't you touch her. Daughter get away from that woman for she spills anymore spells on you. And don't touch that cat. That's prob'ly Satan hisself in that black fur coat."

He yanked Roberta up from the ground, shoved her

toward their property and took a threatening step toward Magda. The littlest one of five more girls standing in the yard in matching brown corduroy jumpers watching it all, whispered rather loudly, "Pa better look out. That gray dog over there looks like he'd just as soon take a bite outta pa if he doesn't back off. Look at those yellow eyes."

Further enraged, "I heard that," Cantwell reached over, grabbed the cyclist's arm and jerked hard, dragging her back in line with the others. Pointing at the little child who'd dared speak out, he bellowed, "An I don' wanna hear no more nonsense about what you see. Nobody else sees that stuff, RaeLee."

"I'm Rhonda. She's RaeLee," she pointed at the biggest girl.

Roberta, realizing she'd lost the advantage of her bloody wound, took up the cry-and-yell attack. "She did something spooky, pa. She said weird stuff and stopped the bleeding." She turned on Magda, "Pa's right, you're a witch. Pa, get the Rev'rend to put a hex on her," not remotely aware of the incongruity of her request. Asking a Reverend to put a hex on a witch, which she wasn't really, but oh well, never mind. Roberta pulled her skirt up to reveal that there was no longer a wound worthy of the crash. "She healed me. It's no fair, pa. Now I can't get Rev. Father Micah to heal me, and I prob'ly won't even have a scar." Roberta howled, "Make her put it back," as Clelland marched his odd little herd up the driveway.

Magda was dumbfounded by this whole scenario. The family had only moved in about a month before. This was not the welcome wagon introduction she had hoped to put on for them. And what was that little one saying about a yellow-eyed dog? None of her dogs was gray or had yellow eyes. And where in creation had the man got his ideas about her, calling her a witch?

She didn't know which was worse; the big bear or the cub with the bike. She'd have to do some serious chanting, maybe call her friend Wolf Tall Trees for some ideas on spirit medicine to defuse the negative energy of this new tribe from next door. She'd start with a cleansing in the sweat lodge right away and began to peel her clothes off even before she was back on her own property. That ought to give the bear something to think about. She grinned, twirled her tank top on a raised fist and, with great restraint, resisted flashing her bra-less boobs at them as she headed down the hill.

The steamer trunk teeters precariously on the luggage rack of the Pontiac. The girl struggles with the body. Tiny as the woman is, the girl has her work cut out. The silky gown that adorns the woman's body hangs down in an amethyst swath. There's a jump forward a few moments in vision time. Something sparkly dangles from the woman's wrist. The loose limbs and the lid challenge the girl to the limit.

Chapter Five

Thea wasn't sure if there was any connection when this premonition came to her, but just about then she also got a nudge from her psyche that now was the time to call Magda and invite her to join the outing to the *New Temple at Heaven's Portal.* After all, Escondido was just over the hill a bit from Bonsall, which wasn't too far out of their way south from Laguna, where they'd be picking up Mitzy. And it would be a chance to get together again with her new friend.

She dialed the hand written number on Magda's trifold and before Thea could launch her pitch Magda was off and running at the mouth, relating the whole story of the prior afternoon, from the arrival of the avocado pickers, and the drop in the market price due to Mexican imports, and that meant she'd have to find a new way to finance buying the strip of land that separated her from the new neighbors for which they wanted over a quarter of a million dollars and it was clearly an issue now that she'd met them: "I tell you, I don't get it. They just moved in a few weeks ago and I feel like they've spent the whole time waiting for the perfect moment to attack. Oh, and get this, one of the kids says she saw a big gray dog with yellow eyes by me. I don't have a gray dog. Anyway, all my dogs were down in the pasture."

"Magda, amica mia, do I detect a note of paranoia? Isn't this something we talked about last week-end? The effects of low vibrations. I've got just the the thing to elevate those vibrations. A whole congregation of people dedicated to helping others get in at Heaven's gate. They must all be filled with the joy of Heaven itself. It's got to be a pronoia event to end all."

"What are you talking about Calzona?"

"It's what I called about. My friends Mitzy and Cybil and I are taking Hortense Greely to *The Portals at Heaven's Gate* on Sunday for a healing ceremony. I wanted to invite you along."

"No way am I going there!" Magda was adamant. "Straight is the way and narrow is the gate, and few there are that find it!" In unison they asked each other, "Where'd that come from?"

Magda felt compelled to explain that occasionally strange quotes seemed to jump out of her mouth. "It's as weird to me as it is to you my friend. Listen — about this place — I don't mean to sound ungrateful, but I guarantee you they wouldn't even let me in the parking lot. I've seen that guy on TV. All prim and proper upscale yuppie. Remember me, Thea? My dress-up clothes come from a little place called Turkish Delight. And you, you gypsy magpie, you won't get past the front door."

"Leave that part to me. I've got an idea. Just say you'll come. You'll be doin' a favor for a wheel-chair bound old woman. I promise you won't be bored."

Somewhat sarcastically Magda relented, "Oh well, in that case, how can I refuse? If I don't go, the boredom factor looms large. After all, I'm stuck here all by myself. Tran won't be back for another week. How could I not be bored?

Thea realized there was more to the icy response than just not wanting to go to *Heaven's Gate*. After the seminar she had googled the event and read more of Magda's bio. It mentioned the exploits of her lover of the last ten years, Tran Thic Gwan, the refugee Thai monk who often co-facilitated her Tantric Sex seminars. From what she knew of Magda, the woman had no room for boredom in her life with or without her young, (only 56), lover around. Magda was still talking and broke Thea's reverie, "...and with the harvest behind me and only three horses, three cats and five dogs for company and my stimulating new neighbors, well, as I said, boredom looms large."

"So I guess that means you'll join us. We'll pick you up at 10:15. I'm anxious for you to meet Mitzy and Cybil. And for them to meet you."

Calzona had hinted that her friends were quite the characters. Magda's interest was peaked. "How about you all come back here afterwards for a bite of lunch out by the pool. If they're anything like you Thea, my new neighbors will be sure we're having a coven gathering. Will you all be riding down on your own brooms?"

Thea laughed, "We'll be in a van to accommodate the center of this coven outing, the ever-charming Hortense. See you Sunday morning. Ciao bella!"

Chapter Six

Sunday morning, as Magda donned a bright red full-length T-shirt with geckos painted on the front, she thought what she really should do was beg off the whole church bit. But the imp in her was eager to see what Anthea could do to get her past dress-code patrol.

When the van arrived she felt almost trumped by the troops' array of garb as brilliant as a field of poppies, which of course Hortense was bent on mowing down with her threshing machine when they let her out for a potty break. It took all of them to get her headed in the right direction and then Thea introduced her cohorts. Now that she saw them all, Magda was really curious how this bunch would pass muster at the Basilica of the Bland.

Thea's peach froth of hair was held in check by her signature Moroccan fringed scarf in forest green, her blouse and trousers (very 1940s, wide legged) were of a flowing cotton-rayon blend in rust and redwood that was as fluid as the former dancer herself.

Carrot topped Mitzy, in Carmen Miranda style, wore shiny red spandex toreadors and an over-blouse of brilliant red poppy print on a background of wheat. Cybil was as close as they got to a yuppie decoy in a silk and challis suit but, being Versace, the shell top dipped in both front and back to what would surely take the breath away from any deacon who dared to question her attire. Only Hortense was dressed to code, but then her attitude was enough to blow her out of the harmony box. "You women gonna just stand around and goggle each other?" Hortense snarled as she returned from her discombobulating trip to the commode.

Magda pointed out the piece of land she'd like to have as a buffer against the Cantwell clan. She explained she really had no business even thinking about such a venture. She didn't have that kind of discretionary cash.

Thea countered that was exactly what she needed to do, envision having the money and to see the way the place would look once she'd got it. "It's called deliberate creation. If you don't get specific about what you <u>want,</u> you're most likely to get what you think you <u>don't</u> want because that's what you're focusing on.[4]

"I don't see things. That's you, Ms Calzona," Magda whined.

"Okay, and no whining. *Crones Don't Whine.*[5] Jean Shenoda Bolen says so." Thea had come up against this problem with clients before. "If you could see it, what would it look like?" This kept Magda occupied only for a moment and then she found something else to worry about.

"So, what is this way you've got to keep us from stirring up the natives at the *Temple?* You going to put them all in a trance so they won't see us? Or do you have some magic Harry Potter cloak we can all hide in?" Magda queried.

"You're not too far off the mark there, Magda," Thea grinned.

Magda didn't have to wait long to find out how Anthea

had dealt with the wardrobe challenge. No sooner was Cybil in the pilot's seat and they were all in the van heading down the hill to the freeway than Thea asked Mitzy to pass out what she found nestled in the boxes beside Hortense's scooter: crushed velvet cloaks in hues from Mother Nature's deep rich pallet; grape purple, wine, olive and verdant forest greens and a lush redwood. Exuberant conversation about the opulence of Thea's gifts took them most of the way to Escondido. That and discussion of what little any of them knew about where they were going... little except for Hortense who was in such a state of ecstatic adoration of the Prophet Rev. Micah Smathers it made listening to her unbearable.

As counter point Thea tuned up the stereo and Mitzy got them all singing along with a concert of folk songs; *Camp Town Races, She'll Be Comin' Round the Mountain* and half way through *America the Beautiful*. As it turned out Magda had a lovely voice and was a natural musician. They kept it going till they entered the parking plaza that looked like one usually reserved for a football stadium.

For Hortense's sake, or maybe it was her own, Thea was grateful the van had a permanent handicap plate. It would be challenge enough just to extract the termagant let alone get her buggy from the rear of the van without the prospect of having to trot after her for a quarter of a mile across asphalt in Sunday shoes.

As they extricated Hortense from the van their tone turned from delighted anticipation to muted curiosity. Surrounded by solemnity they held their collective breath and snugged their cloaks tight around them. The *Portal* of its name seemed more bent on entry to hell than to heaven. The mausoleum-like structure must have been 40 feet high and the carvings covering the *Portal* depicted the Apocalypse in all its gore-y detail. Thea began to wonder what on earth Hortense had gotten them into, and as the leader of the band, she was bathed in a shadowy film of doubt about the potential of Magda's spirit being lifted by this crowd.

A major hushy fuss rippled through the ranks as Anthea, Magda, Mitzy, and Cybil followed Hortense and her oxygen tanks into a Cathedral awash in black, white, gray, brown and navy, on the march to rigid seats. Not literally, but certainly mentally, the congregants held up their crosses to protect themselves against this invasion of colorfully clad women with nary a man or child to proclaim their legitimacy as members of their gender.

The Juicy Crones coterie found a bench. A section at the end was left open for a wheel chair. It had been a long time since Mitzy had been in a church of any sort, and never one of this immensity. "This isn't quite like any pew I remember," she whispered, as Hortense wheezed in and cut her off with as much commotion as possible.

The organ music coming forth from the great pipes was apparently played by an organist hidden away in a pit. On either side of the pit twelve arches fanned out, six to either side, each bathed in muted light. The pulpit was soberly ornate in a very dark and heavily carved wood. The organ music was definitely on the dirgical side until it abruptly shifted to a surprisingly militant *Onward Christian Soldiers.* There was a heavy cadenced stomp to the marching as twelve men in dark wine-red robes, led by a large man whose gray hair and well-worn face did nothing to soften his stern demeanor. Thea couldn't help but think, "Curmudgeon."

"That's Brother Thaddeus. He's in charge of everything," Hortense whispered loud enough to be heard by the Brother himself. The men, all of whom carried Shepherds' crooks, marched across the stage thumping these staffs, herding a flock of children, apparently fearful lest a child stray. As the kiddies entered, the music segued to an odd rendering of the *Jingle Bells* tune with words sung by the entire congregation: "*J.O.Y. J.O.Y. This is what it means. Jesus first, yourself last and others in between,*" repeated ad nauseam in tones that totally stripped any vestige of joy right out of the beloved original.

Cybil whispered to Thea, "You don't suppose they'd be open to questions about whatever happened to the 'thyself' part of love thyself as thy neighbor?"

The song ended, lights faded down and a spotlight irised up on an area high above the stage. An imposing figure in clerical robes, perched on a "cloud," floated down from the heavens above to alight on the stage where the chosen children were allowed to flock around the robed one as he disembarked and strode toward the podium. The hall was filled with 9000 bodies, who had been dutifully holding their breath, waiting for HIM, until Hortense pointed up and blurted out: "There he is! That's Rev. Micah." She was pelted with a barrage of shushes from the worshipers around her, two of whom she deftly bashed with her trusty umbrella before Thea could take it away from her.

"I'm sure you want to hear him speak. Let's just try to keep our cool and remember why you're here," Thea hissed as a pair of burly-looking bouncers disguised as ushers, moved toward them. "You don't want them to make you leave before he gets to the healing part?" Hortense slumped down into her seat and sent withering glares at the ushers.

The congregants settled in, the Shepherds took up their respective posts in the arches around the stage and the little flock nestled down where they could gaze up in adoration while His Eminence the Right Rev. Dr. Micah Smathers droned on for a good 60 minutes about hell-fire and damnation, and all those perverts who were trying to turn our nation away from Jesus/God.

Cybil and Mitzy took Magda's hands as Thea focused her energy to keep them all from sinking into the "pit of despond" which the rest of the congregants seemed to find familiar and thereby comfortable. There was plenty of wailing, sobbing and muttering confirmation in tongues before it finally wound down and Calzona could allow her mind to rejoin the gathering.

While the collection baskets plied the aisles a call went out for all those who had come for a personal laying on of the Smathers' hands to come up on the stage.

Hortense gave Thea a sharp elbow in the ribs, "Calzona, get down there and save me a good place in line."

"Hortense, they've got it all nicely organized. I'm sure they don't want someone on two sturdy legs to go striding down there and get in line. Even if it is as a stand-in for someone as worthy as yourself."

Hortense grabbed for her umbrella, forgetting that Thea had taken it away from her earlier. This riled her further, but she could also see she was losing ground in the lining-up process, so she wheeled around and gunned down the aisle toward the ramp where supplicants were being helped onto the stage. All of this to a reprise of *Onward Christian Soldiers*. They were definitely marching and Hortense was definitely prepared for war.

As the handicapped were led up onto the stage Hortense crashed through the crowd, "Outta my way," she bellowed committing a hit and run to get ahead of a woman with a walker and a blind man. "It's for folks in wheelchairs, you ol' bat." The pilot of the Humvee of wheelchairs smashed her way up the ramp despite the kind requests of an elderly and somewhat fragile usher who tried to reassure her: "everyone will be seen by Rev. Brother Micah. Remember, it's a healing service."

While Hortense was jockeying for position, Magda, Mitzy, Cybil, and Anthea trailed behind in order to retrieve her chair once she had miraculously risen. Or not. At any rate, as they got close to the stage Magda was not totally surprised to see her next-door neighbor's clan standing in a clutch near the edge of the ramp. Well, at least some of them. Magda recognized the five little girls and a woman who must be their mother.

Roberta, the cyclist, and her father appeared to be missing. Never mind, Magda thought as she approached them and exchanged introductions. Sure enough, it was The Mom. The worn but pleasant matron extended her hand and offered, "Hello neighbor. I recognize you. It's a surprise seeing you after what Mr. Cantwell said the other day. Oh, I'm sorry, I'm Mrs. Clelland Cantwell, but you can call me Bonny." Then she turned to the girls, dressed in variations of brown corduroy. Each tried to be a little less present than the next as they did an odd little curtsey: "Rachel, Rhea, Rhonda, Raelene and baby sister RaeLee Cantwell."

Interesting thought Anthea as she focused on each of the girls. All of them clearly Crystal children, children of the Light. Their parents would freak out if they had a clue. The girls knew enough to keep their glow on low beam. They were definitely concealing little smiles, making sure Mother didn't see that they were indeed connecting with Thea, letting her know they enjoyed knowing that she knew their secret.

After Magda introduced her friends, Bonny continued, "And that," she pointed with unveiled pride to one of the hooded disciples, "That's my husband, Mr. Cantwell, Clelland Cantwell, up there. The second one on Rev. Micah's right hand side. The one between him and the Prophet is Master Deacon Thaddeus Orless. He's Clelland's mentor." Her glow wasn't enough to cast any light on the object of her admiration. Magda was just grateful that Roberta didn't seem to be anywhere in evidence. She doubted even church protocol could prevent that child from creating a commotion that would shiver the timbers of the hallowed halls if she spotted the "witch" who ruined her bike and her chances of being in that lineup of supplicants to be healed by the Prophet.

On stage, Hortense's hope over-rode her agitation as she finally found a spot that was acceptable. One or two people threw down their crutches or got up and walked away from their wheelchairs just being in THE PRESENCE. Mitzy scoffed quietly, hoping Bonny didn't notice her less-than-convinced response. But Thea whispered, "It could be a case of their devout belief that Rev. Micah can heal them. The mind is a powerful tool."

However, most seemed to be either mindless or not the faithful believers they professed to be. Their condition unchanged they were told to schedule private prayer sessions with the pastor. This was infinitely clear in the case of an incensed Hortense. "Remember, it is thine unbelief that stands in your way. Come back and we will work together to rid you of those devils within that are keeping you from receiving my help." The Pastor spoke softly with a squinty-eyed smirky smile as he patted Hortense on the head. The way she saw it she got nothing out of her anointing other than an appointment card with a recommended donation ($200.00). As she read that, she almost did lift right out of her chair.

Meanwhile, seeing a job that needed doing, Magda made her way up to help Hortense get back down the ramp. Unfortunately she was spotted by Roberta who darted out of the flock of lambs and ran over to pull on her father's robe. Thea saw her pointing at Magda and urged her own little group toward the *Portal* while she grabbed the keys from Cybil and ran for the exit.

Naturally Clelland spotted Magda. As though hit by a bolt of lightning, he tossed aside all sense of propriety or discipline and shouted out: "That woman's a witch. She's the leader of that bunch of Satan's whores that lives next door to where we just moved in. That must be some of 'em right there with her desecrating our sacred hall." He pointed at the exiting bevy of manless women. "Witches!" he screamed.

Reverend Micah moved to quiet Clelland, but Brother Thaddeus cut him off with hand signals to let Clelland go on. The congregation would have swarmed the Juicy Crones except that they were well trained never to move till their leader indicated it was appropriate. And he was completely focused on Thaddeus. Even though the Master Deacon's voice was mic-ed, no one seemed to hear it. It was meant only for Rev. Micah's holy ears.

Thaddeus hissed a strong direction to the Pastor; "They're in thrall. Let Cantwell juice 'em up. You can give 'em a good sermon at tonight's service about the evil that women like that rain down upon the meek like Clelland and Bonny. It'll ring the sheckles out of every pocket."

Clelland didn't catch the Master Deacon's admonition, but he wouldn't have understood it anyway. Besides, he was too busy ridin' his own thought train, "I'm tellin' ya'all the whole bunch of 'em go running around in skimpy, shabby, witchy clothes."

Cybil pulled her cloak aside and modeled with run-way flare. "This cloak is pure silk velvet from China and my suit is 100% virgin wool challis from Versace, you dolt," she said, barely able to restrain her irritation and her trucker's tongue. What she really wanted was to call him a shithead but she caught Mity's shake of the head. Her friend knew her only too well.

Providentially, thought Magda, Cantwell hadn't heard her because he was busy spouting his diatribe over the audio system and making sure the cameras were covering his pointing finger; "They drive those foreign bio-diesel auto-mobiles. Isn't that against the Patriot Act?"

"Great goddess man, are you saying a Prius is unpatriotic because it conserves fuel?" puzzled Cybil.

He ignored her, "They all got bumper stickers just like back in the hippie days; 'make love not war' and 'war's no path to peace.' An' they hold sacrificial ceremonies."

Magda couldn't restrain any further, "Two weeks ago I had a bar-b-que in my yard for some friends, you imbecile. The most we sacrificed was maybe a few shrimp and some veggies."

"I tell you it's un-natural. They're all women, very perverted. No men there. Only a bunch of faggots and all those naked women."

A quote surprised Magda: "they shall mount up with wings as eagles. They shall walk and not be weary. They shall run and not be faint."

The Crones were momentarily non-plussed, but they had no time to ponder. They chose to honor the admonition and run. By the time Clelland finished his rant, the women were at the door.

The massive portals swung open just as Thea pulled up right in front of the *Temple*. As the quintet made their exit the Divine Rev. Micah made his departure letting loose the spell that had bound the congregants in awe as he ascended with trumpets and harps and of course the organist pounding away down in the pit.

Chapter Seven

At the very moment the music rose inside the *Temple*, lofting the Prophet on his mechanical cloud into the vaulted stone heaven of the sanctuary, Cybil dashed through the *Portal* to the rear of the van, opened the door and let the lift gate down. Mitzy and Magda herded the recalcitrant Hortense in and up went the gate.

"You idiots, I wanna ride shot gun. You can't leave me here backside down?" Tensia, her very apt nickname, bellowed.

Mitzy shut the door with a firm but gentle slam. She and Magda raced to either side of the van, jumped into the mid-section and buckled up as Cybil nudged Thea over to the passenger seat and took control of the pilot position. Before the first congregant came through the huge door, Cybil laid rubber and the van peeled out of the lot.

Even sitting backward spouting curses at the rear window Hortense managed to spit invective at all of her saviors; "You ruined my whole life. It's your fault he didn't heal me. Now I'll be stuck like this fornever. They'll prob'ly banshee me."

Four heads turned to look at her in unison, incredulous, and in unison chimed, "You want to come back?" Before Hortense let loose the murky waters of an explanation no one really wanted to wade through, Magda diverted their attention, "I think what we all need is some good food and I know just the

place to get it. Come on a my house, my house a come on."
And that started them singing oldies whether they were golden
or not.

When they arrived chez Lindal, Magda had Cybil drive
around behind the house so they could unload the motorized
growler close to the pool. "Does it occur to any of you
imbeciles that I might need a shit pot in the house?" she spewed
in agitated Hortense speak.

Magda indicated the loggia. "You can zip yourself right
over there Hortense. It's got all the amenities. Meanwhile I'll
get Hermes to come up from the stables to help you get set up
on a lounge chair. How's that?"

Hortense was hard pressed to complain, but she gave it
a valiant go: "Who's Hermes? Some alien you got stashed
down with the animals?"

"In fact, he is an alien. He's a gorgeous young Greek
scholar with a valid visa. He helps out around here in exchange
for his room and board. You'll be very safe with him"

"I don' know. I disremember when I was a girl travelin' in
Greece, those guys couldn't keep their hands to themselves.
Pinch, pinch, pinch."

"Hortense, he is a strong young man who is going to
help you get comfortable while I get you something wonderful
to eat. Can you try to show a little gratitude?" It was clear
Magda's stress level was climbing rapidly. She had only one
cure for that. She turned on her heels and headed for the
kitchen door.

Hortense shouted: "Thea, what'd you do with my
umbrella? I need it if I'm gonna be stuck out here in this
slathering bun. You know how sensitive I am."

Mitzy almost choked on her stifled snort. They all knew that the umbrella was actually Hortense's alternative to a battle ax. Besides, there was a huge umbrella poised over the lounge chair she was being offered.

By the time Hortense got back from the loggia, Hermes, a veritable Adonis, was plumping pillows on the lounger and adjusting the angle of the umbrella to her specifications. She barely managed to contain her drool as he helped her settle down. Just then Magda returned from the house with a tray of brownies which she set out on the patio table in the shade of another lovely flowered umbrella. She then picked two plump brownies and arranged them on a tray with a napkin that matched the umbrella. Next came a tall glass of something white with beads of cold perspiration dripping down the frosted sides. It looked like a photo shot for Gourmet Magazine. She took it over and arranged it on a little table next to Hortense.

"My god, that looks like milk! Don't you know how intolerant I am?" Hortense grumbled. Mitzy stifled a snicker and whispered that milk had nothing to do with her intolerance. At the same time Magda said, "I'm learning as quick as I can," under her breath. Then aloud she rebutted: "Ah, not just any milk. I got this fresh from the cow this morning. Un-pasteurized and un-homogenized, therefore filled with the very enzymes you need to let you digest it, and fill those fragile bones of yours with real calcium. Who needs Reverend what's-his-name? And boy will it make that brownie hum in your mouth. 76% cacao with raw honey from my own bees as sweetener, raw coconut oil and healing fats from organic walnuts. A brownie to nourish even you right down to your soul! Just get a whiff of that puppy." Magda wafted the dish under Tensia's nose.

Mitzy mused softly, "Soul, what soul?"

Never one to wrap her mind around the concept of manners, Hortense sniped, "That's desert. You gonna give us desert first and rune our appetites. 'smatter, you ain't got enough real food for us all?" Hortense snarked.

"Humor me on this, ok? I happen to believe in dessert first. Get the carbs out of the way. Now, everybody come on, this is a group effort. We've got a lot to do to make sure Hortense doesn't starve." She took Thea aside, "Just to let you know, that's valerian honey in the milk. She should mellow out shortly. And just to make sure, I laced her brownies with a little Mary Jane, as they used to say back in my day.

"And since you've still got the herb in your cupboard today, what do you call it now?"

"A medically prescribed calmative."

"In what country?"

"Ah well, there is that. But hey, its home grown and organic."

She handed Cybil and Mitzy each a wooden trug and sent them out to the garden to harvest. "Mushrooms are down in the little shed by the hothouse there. No wait. Do that last. I like 'em to stay snappy. Round up some of all those pretty colored bell peppers, a couple of Walla Walla sweets, elephant garlic, spinach, mesculin, arugala, squash, slicing tomatoes, basil and oregano. Everything's in the raised beds. Oh, and about six nice warm eggs from the hen house over there by the stable. That ought to do it. We'll be in the kitchen."

As they headed to the garden Mitzy mused, "Takes me back to my childhood."

"You grew up on a farm?" Cybil asked.

"Uh huh. In a little town called Carlsborg, on the Olympic Peninsula."

"You've got to be kidding. I've known you how long and you never said a word. You know I hail from Seattle. You know I live part time up on Whidbey Island. Why didn't you ever say anything?"

"Ah well, that's another story," Mitzy furrowed her brow. Clearly lots of mixed emotions went with that subject.

Back at pool-side, Magda looked at Hortense who was deeply engrossed in watching Hermes swim a few laps while she sipped her icy cold milk and chomped on her brownie. The hostess took Thea by the hand and led her into the house. Calzona marveled at the shifts that took place in her complex friend. From witty and wise to quivering and confused to patient to prickly.

While she peeled and de-veined shrimp, Maggie got Thea going on placing table ware on a tea cart. Then came the bread: home made Italian loaf taken from the freezer, pre-sliced nice and thick, slathered with garlic butter, dusted liberally with fresh grated parmigiano, sprinkled with sesame seeds and popped into an oven set very low. After that the kitchen dervish pulled out the pasta machine, bowls, an 8"x14" casserole which she smeared with organic virgin coconut oil even as she directed Thea in making a large batch of lemonade with the Voila juice extractor: "Three lemons, just peel the yellow, leave the white part, and leave the skins on eight of those apples. They're from my friends in Julian." Somewhere in there she managed to put on a pot to boil the pasta in and set the grater and a huge chunk of Asiago on the tray to go out with the utensils.

"Over there, that wooden bowl," she ordered Anthea.

All the hesitation Thea'd dealt with during the Tarot reading a week ago and earlier this morning at the church was nowhere to be found. This woman was mastery in motion.

The farm maids came in with their haul. "Hortense seems to be napping." Mitzy offered cheerfully.

"All we need now is to rinse, slice and dice all these veggies, and give 'em a quick turn in the sauté pan. You gals can do that and throw together a salad while I make up the linguini," she said, cracking eggs into a bowl. "Oh, there's some artichoke hearts in a big jar up on the shelf in the pantry." She pointed to a glass fronted door. Mitzy found the jar marked "Aug – artichokes, basil, oregano, tarragon, Faragamo extra virgin olive oil." Most of the jars in the pantry seemed to have home made, artfully done up contents.

The meal flowed together like liquid gold. As the others took a huge bowl of pasta and a bouquet of fresh flowers out to the patio, Magda whipped up a vinaigrette and splashed it over the salad which she topped off with pomegranate bits, some Mandarin orange wedges and walnuts.

"All from the garden," she preened. Wheeling the cart out to the patio she hummed a few bars of the *Triumphal March* from *Carmen*. The vibrations were so high Magda figured her feet probably weren't even touching the ground.

As they were eating, there was a rustling in the hedge separating Magda's property from the Cantwells. Squeezing through the foliage came three brown-corduroy clad girls – part of Clelland's brood. They marched boldly over to take up posts by the table. That got Magda's attention and then some. "How the heck did you little imps get through that fence? Now I'm gonna have to get it fixed."

Raelene, the seven-year-old, shook her head, "Nope."

Dogs and cats came from various directions and arranged themselves, one dog and one cat at each girl's side. Thea stifled a laugh. 'Crystals for sure,' she thought. She was clearly the only one to see it when the girls levitated ever so slightly, a kind of giggle-hop. She was also the only one who could see the covey of fairies swarming off near the hedge.

"Don't worry, sweet cakes," she smiled at Magda, "they didn't hurt your fence." She also got a clear telepathic message, please not to tell their dad they'd come over to the witch's house. She thought back to them, "no problemo," and the girls giggled in comprehension. It was interesting to her that they felt comfortable with everyone at the table... even Hortense, who, at that very moment seemed to perk up and twiddle her fingers in a little hidee-ho toward the girls. "Hallooo, faeries. Magda, they musta flew over, haha." Thea always wondered about Hortense.

Mitzy tried to clarify the situation, "Tensia, these are the little girls we met at the Church service this morning."

"You mean at the rip-off service? I didn't meet anybody."

Cybil busily took charge, as usual; fixing plates for each of the girls, skooching everyone around to make room.

Two of the girls were almost as tall as Mitzy, who was very taken with the trio. "So, what's up with you kids? I get the sense from the way Thea and the animals are reacting there is something weird going on here."

Cybil was sure it was something neither the Reverend nor their dad would approve of.

Thea and the girls chuckled in unison. "Well, lets just

say they're 'special' girls. You'll see what I mean when you get to know them better. We're all going to be great friends. That's a promise. Raelene says they do want to be sure none of us says anything to their dad, though."

"Oh great! Now she's gonna start with the telepathy," Mitzy moaned.

"Don't be jealous Mitzy." She turned to the girls, "Mitzy's a singer and she loves the sound of voices. She really wouldn't enjoy it if we didn't talk out loud, would you Mitz?"

Mitzy puffed out a little lip fart at this tiny perversion of the case. "Liar. It's not that and you know it. It's the secrets. You know I have a problem with secrets."

"So we will honor your problem and we promise to speak so you can hear everything, won't we, girls?" They all nodded.

That agreement seemed to open a floodgate whereby Magda and the Juicy Crones found out that the sisters tended to drive daddy nuts with their antics, like telepathically moving things he's about to pick up just as he reached for them, and when he was really nasty they'd make him scared in his own thoughts. Sometimes things just popped out of their mouths, even if they knew it'd make him mad that they knew what he was thinking.

"It's not our fault," Rachel said. "We see things, don't we? They always say to tell the truth. But if we tell 'em, Father gets mad. Lots of times he gets mad at Mom when we tell the truth."

Raelene cut in, "Then she cries. It really makes us sad cause Momma cries when we tell the truth about seeing things, an' he calls us the 'devil's children'. I thought we were his children?"

"He's just a confused man, kids. When he gets upset and frightened by things he can't understand, he says things that don't make much sense." Anthea's words didn't seem to help.

"We send momma happy thoughts as much as we can. But father just gets madder 'n madder."

Anthea handed Raelene her card. "Just in case you need to talk and the quiet way doesn't work," she grinned. Raelene pocketed the card with a glow of gratitude on her lovely little face.

Cybil got right to the point. "So is there some kind of problem with their father? Do we need to call Child Protective Services?"

"I don't think so, Cyb. They know when to hold 'em and when to fold 'em. They know how to protect themselves. Its their Mom they worry about."

Magda jumped in on that note, "What's poker got to do with it?"

"It's not poker, silly goose. There are just some things old dad is better off not knowing," Thea warned the group. "Like I said, they know how to deal with him, but there's no sense getting him mad. At least that's what I get...oops,."

On that note Bonny's voice wafted over the hedge, "Raelene, Rachel, Rondi, you best get on home. Where are my monkeys hiding? You don't want your father to come lookin' for you." The joy drained right out of the kids' faces and they dashed for the fence.

"Now that was a definite diversion. You going to explain it to us, Thea?" asked Magda.

"Not a whole lot to explain. They're Crystal Children.[6]

Very psychic. Tuned into the energy of the planet. They have special talents: some of them see auras, some foretell, some can send out illusions that only the target can see, which tends to make their dad afraid he's going nuts. Some work with the energy grid around the earth. Others are natural healers and can even 'see' what's wrong inside a person so they can heal it."

"On the downside, they don't handle authority well. They see through the 'crap' that people tend to use to sugar coat their thoughts. They tend to cut to the heart of the matter, to see what's really necessary and do it. Teachers'r going to have their hands full as this batch cycles through our archaic educational system."

Cybil gasped, "Holy horse pucky, that's a lot to take in. So you're saying there are other children like them around? Are there websites where I can find out more about them? Do they have a chat room?" Cybil was ready to head for the computer and start googling.

"Sure. You can find out about them on the internet, but the new Indigos or Crystal children don't seem to need the internet. They've got their own web; they connect with each other mentally, especially at night when they get together on the energy grid that surrounds the planet." Anthea was tickled to have turned her friend on to something new.

The group fell relatively silent, munching on their lunch and their thoughts for quite some time. Eventually Magda, still deep inside her head, began to pick dishes up and put them back on the cart. They all pitched in and loaded up, running a strangely subdued version of the Bizet procession back to the kitchen.

As they were humming across the kitchen, Thea had a flash of intuition. She signaled her LaPlaya pals to put their things down on the counter and herded them toward the door just as the phone rang. Magda looked around to see them on their way out and raised a hand to stop them. They hung there, suspended in anticipation. As she listened to the caller, their hostess turned a definite shade of pale and sank onto a barstool. She touched the button and put the phone on speaker, whispering, "Olivia at the ranch," as if they should all know what that meant.

A throaty Ethel Merman-like voice oozed out of the speaker. "Sheriff Willery is here now. He rode out with Doc Saxby. Seems our Wolf just threw up his lunch and keeled over. Heart attack, we guess. He apparently got a squawk through to Gillian on the intercom before he passed out."

"That's plum crazy and you know it, Olivia. Wolf is about the healthiest varmint in the whole state of Nevada. Besides, he can't get sick. He's coming down here. He said he wanted to tell me about his latest tracking gig and hang out, do a few sweats."

"I know it sounds unbelievable Maggie. I think that's why the Sheriff came out lights and sirens. He and the Doc are both puzzled. They're ridin' into the hospital with him. They want to talk to him the moment he comes around. The important thing is Magda, can you come up here?"

"I'm on my way. If I have to drive all night I'll get there as fast as I can."

"Thanks, darlin'. All of us appreciate it. 'Course Wolf'll probably rail a bit thinkin' we're over-reacting. You know how he is."

"I'll go straight to the hospital. I'm sure by the time I get there he'll be pinkin' right up. I'll let you know when I'm on my way. You all take care now. Bye."

"Bye, bye." And that was it. Magda hung up the phone. Thea walked over and drew Magda into a warm hug. "What happened to my high vibration?" Magda sobbed.

"We'll have to talk about that on the way to this Ranch. Which is where?" Thea patted Magda's back.

"Nevada. You'll go with me?" Maggie was a bit nonplussed. "That's great Anthea, but you don't have to do that. It's a long drive. About 95 miles north east of Vegas on Highway 93."

"Eehmm," Cybil didn't want to interfere but she felt a bit of urgency. As her old friend pulled away from her new friend, she put forth a plan, "If it's OK with you, I'd be happy to have Jeff get hold of Burgess. They can fly down to Palomar; we'll drive over and give Burgess the van and Hortense, and we can fly on up to wherever the closest strip is to this ranch. It's got to handle a Cessna Citation," she said, turning to Magda.

"That's probably going to be Las Vegas," Magda murmured, still somewhat dazed, first by the news about Wolf and now by the offer that was being made by a woman she'd just met.

Mitzy had a contribution as well, "I'll give Lulu a call in Vegas and we can pick up a vehicle to get to this ranch. Do we need off-road or what?"

"No, no, just big enough we all fit. Does this mean you're all going?"

"What are friends for Ms. Lindal?" Cybil asked as she reached for her purse and began to dig around for her cell phone. "Jeff can visit with some of Mitzy's show girl friends while we go to see Wolf. He'll love that."

Magda turned to Thea, "Are we back to pronoia?" she queried.

"In spades!" Thea put her arm around Magda's shoulder and gave her a firm side hug. "I'll have Rosalinda pack up a bag to give to Burge to bring down. Mitzy, you want her to go put something together for you?" The Multi-Level-Mogul of Health Supplements nodded, "She knows the usual from my stash of products. I brought my thermal bag with me today, so just have her get the bottles from the door on the fridge, and the box on the sink counter." Mitzy lived in a state of nutritional high alert.

"Cybil, I'm assuming you've got what you need on the plane. Anything else?"

"No. It's all there. I will give Henry a call though just to let him know what's happening. He's such a worry wart." Henry, Cybil's alternate life-style partner lived in a state of hyper attentiveness of late, knowing that his contract was soon up for renewal. "I don't want him to fret." The thing that jeopardized his position the most was his insecurity... an unappealing attribute to Cybil's way of thinking. Ah well, she mused. What she said was, "First I've got to get on to Jeff and have him get the plane ready. Mitzy, will you take over coordinating with Burgess to connect with Rosalinda. You know. What Thea said. Then he can meet Jeff at John Wayne Airport. Eh?"

Mitzy saluted and they each went to separate corners to make calls on their cell phones. This was a well-oiled machine. Magda got the feeling they'd done this sort of thing before.

While the calls were going on Magda finished up in the

kitchen and then went off to pack up her own bag. By the time she got back the calls were done and the next challenge was to get the comfortably stoned Hortense into the van. Fortunately they had Hermes to take care of that difficult little piece of baggage. It was also fortunate that Hermes had a sense of humor because Hortense may have seemed to be out of it, but she worked the situation for all she was worth; snuggled up and clinging to the young Greek, not letting go as he tried to secure her in the van seat, sneaking in a pinch or two on those firm young buns. She mumbled something about ripe cantaloupes. He murmured sweetly, softly to her in Greek and cajoled her into thinking she was about to have a nice little "ride" with him, alone. He also gave her another little piece of the herbally enhanced brownie.

As they drove to Palomar Mitzy was determined to coax a bit of back story out of Magda. "So tell us about this fellow Wolf? Who is he in your life?"

Thea tried to make it sound a little less like an interrogation, "We want to make sure we don't put our proverbial slippers in our delicate little mouths when we meet him," taking care to reassure Magda they weren't just being nosey.

"Rescuer, teacher, fling, business partner and always a very dear friend, even though I only see him a few times a year."

"Whoa, whoa, whoa. Let's back up here and get a little clarity, starting with the fling part." Mitzy firmly believed in pleasure before business.

Anthea retracted a bit, "Let's just get the part about

your history."

Highway 395 wound out of the avocado and orange orchards, past horse ranches, on to the burgeoning sprawl of tract homes till it intersected with Hwy 15. Magda remained evasive. "I'm not trying to hide anything. I just don't remember my past. The only parts of me I can tell you about are the ones in my bio. That was all researched and written by a public relations firm Tran hired when I was asked to do the Tantric Sex lecture series, working with Gillian of course. She's been running the website school for us for years. I give her Tantric info, she runs the e-school."

"Harrumph," snorted Hortense, apparently not nearly as out of it as they'd hoped.

Magda thought to herself that in her pre-memory-loss years she must have been brought up to be polite, since she did feel compelled to tell them something. "Since you've all been so kind and supportive I guess I should explain. I have a kind of gigantic mental block. I don't know what went on in my life before I was about 19 or 20. And there've been lots of other gaps in my memory banks since then."

Not even Thea knew quite how to respond. It did make the queer feeling about Magda's chart inevitable. They'd have to clear that up later. It was also obvious this whole issue was one Magda was uncomfortable with. Timing would have to be assessed and Calzona knew she'd have to do an event reading. Or not? In the meantime they'd have to deal with trying to prevent hurt feelings. Since compassion was a concept well beyond Hortense's grasp the next remark was inevitable. "Mammary banks, what kinda bull puckie is that? Nut case is what she is," she mumbled twirling her finger at her temple, "she's deluding the question. I wouldn't trust her far as you could throw me," and she fell back into her stupor. Mitzy swatted at her but it made no difference.

Magda looked a bit perplexed, "I'm not sure what she meant, but I'm not trying to be evasive. I don't know anything about my family. I don't really know who I am. I just don't know. I have these things called fugue moments, where I do things, where sometimes I'm another woman and I don't recall any of it later."

"What about this Wolf? Doesn't he know? You say you've known him most of your life." Mitzy pushed.

"No. And that's all stuff I don't want to go into. Just trust me. I do not know. Nobody does."

"Would it help if one of us talked to him? Maybe you just haven't asked the right questions," people often commented that Cybil should have been a lawyer.

"It's ancient history. We've been through it all over the years. Oh, don't get me wrong, there are great portions of my life that are very clear to me. It's just, I get these queasy feelings when people get into trying to get me to remember. Can we maybe do this later? Right now I'd sort of like to focus on Wolf," Magda smiled a weak and totally ineffectual smile.

"Yeah, what about this Wolf?" Hortense came out of stupor long enough to start humming the theme from Peter and the Wolf.

"And what does Tran think of your old friend?" Mitzy asked.

Thea often thought that there was a tact gap in Mitzy's sensitivity banks.

"Mitzy, you're almost as bad as Hortense." Cybil said.

Fortunately by then they were nearly at the airport.

Chapter Eight

The timing was that of a ballet choreographed by Balanchine. The van pulled onto the tarmac at McClellan-Palomar airport just as Captain Jeff was taxiing the Citation, with its Great Goddess dragon-fly logo, into place. Burgess emerged from the plane and made his way over to the vehicle where everybody managed to get a hug before they started moving luggage to the cargo hold of the plane. A still "happy" Hortense in a modicum of arousal from her stupor seemed to think Burge was Hermes and she was totally content to have him drive off with her leaving the Juicy Crones behind and asking him to talk alien to her.

After introducing Magda to Captain Jeff Carlson, Cybil took the controls, did the tower talk bit and taxied out onto the runway. As the others buckled into the plush club seats, Anthea tried to reassure Magda that all of this may seem a bit overwhelming, "but it's just a piece of the puzzle. We're all doing our part to complete the grand, if ever changing, cosmic design."

"Sometimes you go a bit overboard, Calzona," Mitzy chided.

Thea snipped back, "I really do see us all as doing our part to heal the planet by learning what Spirit shows us through our individual lives. We're all components of the process. We need to ask ourselves, what am I learning out of every experience? It adds to our totality. It's called the entanglement matrix of physical expression."

"You're drowning us here, preacher woman." If Thea was in meta-workshop mode, Mitzy was in the mood to challenge her perch on the podium. She had a need to make sure that Anthea, whom Mitzy'd known off and on for forty years, didn't get too big for her britches. It was left over from Mitzy's house-mother days. Anthea had been one of the first chorus girls she took under her wing when she managed the showgirl boardinghouse in Vegas. They'd been going at it ever since.

Magda thought maybe if she said something she could stop the bickering. Little did she know how much they enjoyed their verbal tennis matches. It was her nature to keep the peace. But it wasn't giving her any peace at all. "Thea, I don't feel good about this."

"This what, Magda?" Thea was confused. She was still on the part we each played in the cosmic design.

"I'm just not comfortable with all these people I don't even know helping me out. I mean, its not like doing the dishes. This is major and I'm not at ease asking people for help." Not only was Magda uncomfortable with asking for help, she was uncomfortable admitting that she was uncomfortable.

"Well you didn't ask. We just shoved our noses into your beeswax. I'm sorry you have a problem letting us help you, but we happen to love doing it. We're a bunch of nosey women who get great joy out of meddling in other people's lives. So now your dilemma is how do you stop us from experiencing the joy of helping you?" Anthea was determined to make this point. "And if you're thinking we shouldn't be meddling you don't understand the first Do Not rule of creative dynamics: don't should on others even if you insist on shoulding on yourself."

Totally flummoxed Magda stammered, "No-no-no, I don't think you're meddling and I don't want to interfere with your joy. It's just... I know how people get dragged into situations with people like me and then they're stuck."

"You only get stuck if you're doing something you don't want to do. Can you imagine one of us doing something we don't want to do?" Thea spread her arms to include Cybil and Mitzy.

"See, I keep putting my foot in my mouth," Magda whimpered.

"No whining. Remember? Juicy Crones don't whine. They get busy. What would Wolf tell you to do? I'm sure he'd say, 'Be still. Listen to the Great Spirit."

Hah, finally something connected for Magda. "You're right, Thea. That's exactly what he would say. It's eerie, like I could almost hear him."

"Good. Then do it and see if he has a message for you." Magda followed Thea's instructions, got very quiet and seemed to have slipped into a trance with her eyes wide open.

Mitzy sucked in her breath and hissed,. "My god, she isn't dead is she? Is she having some kind of stroke or something? Maybe its one of those fugue thingies?"

Thea shushed her, "Mitzy, land sakes, she's just listening for Wolf to guide her."

"Yeah, but with her eyes staring like that?"

Just then Magda began speaking in a foreign language, but not one that Thea recognized. The intuitive surmised it was whichever one of the 170 aboriginal American languages was native to Wolf. After a few moments Magda came back into her body and said, "There's only one possible answer — follow the trail."

Mitzy jumped in as usual, "Thea, stop that. Now you've got her telepathing. What trail? What are you two jabbering about? No secrets, remember!"

Thea soothed, "Don't know yet. Be patient. I think we're all about to learn from your friend Wolf, Magda."

"Oh, that would be terrific. As soon as he's feeling better we'll all go out on a quest. Sometimes he takes me out into the wilderness for a week at a time to work on being still, listening, connecting. We live on shoots and berries and grubs. He can stalk a buck and have it ready for dinner without the animal ever knowing he was there. Except he always asks permission of the animal before taking it to become one with us."

"Right. You go out there to learn survival techniques from a native? You gonna fess up about this Wolf person... who he is in your life really?" Mitzy was a veritable terrier when her curiosity was piqued, especially if there was potential romance to be unearthed.

Cybil was too busy at the controls to swat Mitzy, which is what she wanted to do. Magda handled it well, "You're trying to make it something it's not... and what if it was anyway. But I'm not going there, Mitzy. Tit for tat, lady. You asked me about me. Well, I think it's only fair to know about you," she smiled that oddly weak, ineffectual smile of hers. At least Thea hoped it was just ineffectual and not outright insincere. There were those disturbing images of girl-body-car lurking in her psyche.

Sensing that they weren't going anywhere without winning Magda over, Thea volunteered Cybil's participation, "You want to know about us, you've got to hear how Cybil won her trucks in a fixed poker game, and built an empire out of bootlegged parachute silk."

"Cut that out, Anthea Calzona. Magda, don't you believe her. I'll tell you how it really was." And with that Cybil related her story starting with the fact that she'd been born and raised in the Seattle area. Her mom worked in a parachute plant during WWII. It went belly up when the brothers who owned it fought over nylon versus silk. Mom Ethel got paid in an endless supply of silk. Cyb's Nanna had always told her daughter and granddaughter, 'if it ain't quality, don't mess with it! "I'd rather have one pair of silk panties than a dozen cotton underdrawers," was one of Nanna's favorite homilies.

That's how Nanna and mom came to make luxurious underwear out of that stash of parachute silk. Cybil learned the technical aspects from them, but she was better at the business part of the enterprise. Partly this was learned from Nanna's brother Philbert. Cybil became attached to him when she was little and he regaled her with stories of his exploits in the Klondike gold mines or racing dog sleds across the tundra. As she grew up his tales turned to his gambling days and pretty soon he was teaching the precocious teen poker with a professional flare. As much as she learned common sense from Nanna she learned focus and the business end of competitive poker from Uncle Phil. "And that's how Silhouettes by Great Goddess was born?" Cybil concluded.

"So what's this part about your business being founded on a fixed poker game?" Magda wanted to know.

"Do you really think I had to fix it?" And along came

part two of the story. When she became a Viet Nam war widow with a baby boy to support Cybil got serious about the gambling and took on a hotshot who made the mistake of letting the pretty young woman play endless rounds of poker with him while he drank his way into a stupor. She won his trucking company. Since he was a chronic drunk she reckoned she'd removed a menace from the highways and saved a few lives in the process.

Granted the company only had two trucks and drivers. But even that meant serious overhead. However, she got right in, doing ride-alongs till she got the hang of handling the rigs and then driving some shifts herself. That way she could keep them on the road more hours per week without upping her bottom line.

Eventually she bought another truck, then hired a husband-wife team, the first on the road, and set about expanding. To date she had about a hundred and thirty trucks doing long haul.

"And that's how you end up with a corporate jet and plenty of spare time to fly around with losers like me?" Magda asked somewhat sarcastically.

Mitzy whipped off her scarf and waved it around in the air. Thea laughed. "That's what Mitzy does when one of us forgets about the attractor factor and slips into a low vibration. Any time you want a MacDonald scarf dance, all you gotta do is get down and pitiful."

Now Magda got a little testy, "Everything comes back to this Law of Attraction with you, doesn't it? You make it sound so easy. Well, you may be here to help me, but I assure you there's nothing you can do in this case. I do not go out there and intentionally create these horrible situations in my life. But when they do happen I don't believe you can get all airy-fairy and think it away."

The energy in the cabin of the jet was definitely heating up. "You're absolutely right. First you've got to dig up the old kung pow, what it is that keeps you hooked on the misery. Then you go to work clearing all that old programming out. The trick is to find the balance between uncovering your addiction to the problem and keeping yourself on a higher frequency. It's quite a tightrope walk. Having the right friends along helps."

"Oh, well thank you so much friend. I do feel better knowing you see me as an addict," Magda shot back.

As she'd said about the Crystal sisters, Thea knew when to hold 'em and when to fold 'em. No more pointing out Magda's self-defeating attitude for now. Maybe if she shifted the focus to someone else's challenges the atmosphere would lighten. "Cybil? You got any addictions."

Cybil laughed. She loved having a captive audience. The warmth of pride energized her. "Bragging is one of my favorite sports. So, I guess addiction to work is one of mine. I imagine it comes from my childhood, when we were so poor. There's probably an underlying fear that I'll be poor again. There's a whole long philosophical discussion possible here. I know Anthea teaches workshops in dealing with your addictions... usually to pain, or misery or something that keeps you running around in the same circles that hold you in the place you insist you don't want to be in. Fortunately, for me, I have the attitude that challenges come to me to be vanquished." She tootled a little snippet from the *Ride of the Valkyries*

"And I guess I'm addicted to turning every hand into a winner. Somehow I always find the flaw in the situation and turn it to my benefit. Its not just the trucks and the bras. You gotta count in the Volkswagen import business which is morphing into electric conversions. And the construction company up in Port Angeles, Washington. We rushed a team to New Orleans after Katrina and now we're building a school in a small community in Alaska, along with an eco-village on the Olympic Peninsula. We're working to set up teams world-wide helping locals build homes that will stand up to Mother Nature at her nastiest. Oh, don't get me started on global warming and what I'm trying to do in that department. And don't let the jet distract you. I'll explain how we off-set for fuel consumption and what we're researching to further reduce our carbon footprint. So I guess you could say I'm driven by my addictions to amass, to not be poor."

"Good heavens Cybil, how do you manage all this from a little town in southern California?" Magda was incredulous. Well, at least it took her mind off her own misfortunes.

Cyb patted the laptop at her side. "Actually I live part time on Whidbey Island, just west of where we're going.. It's the computers, teleconferencing, and all sorts of electronic wizardry, my friend. The whole world truly is our village. So you see, its not such a big deal to help little ol' you. That's another of my addictions, helping people out."

"That story just makes me feel unworthy of all your time and efforts, and this..." Maggie forlornly indicated the plush interior of the Citation. She looked like what Anthea called emotional road kill. So pathetic no one wanted to hear her story lest it infect them all.

Further diversion was needed. First Anthea urged Magda to stand and follow her through a series of BrainGym[7] exercises and then she asked Mitzy, "what about you? What do you suppose you might have been addicted to that your shortness ended up lording it over all those statuesque chorus girls. How did that happen?" Thea always knew how to charge Mitzy's battery.

"That was just it. I was never gonna be tall and willowy. I suppose it started out with me being addicted to the pain of feeling pathetic around all those incredible girls. So I put myself where I could wallow best. The only thing is it turned out to be just where I needed to be. I got to, like Thea says, lord it over all those girls. And then I grew into the position, and became a kind of mentor and a mother figure for them. It all turned out in the end. I'm really quite proud of my girls. Well, women now. You'll see what I mean when you meet Lulu Haynes in Vegas. And I assume you already know Thea was one of the first to live under my iron rule in what came to be known as Flapaflapaflapa house. A bevy of long legged beauties, most of whom were emotionally younger than they thought they were. First time away from home, many from sheltered backgrounds, some escaping from the inner city. If my short little ego couldn't join 'em, I sure got to bask in their glory.

"That went on for thirty years. The only other thing I've done is organize a group of women in Sunshine Village, the retirement community where my mom lived. I got 'em to turn the tables on their philandering husbands by showing the ladies how to stash away a little of their monthly household stipends and invest it in multilevel marketing, then having lots of fun and basically ignoring their silly spouses. The funny part was that the guys were so guilt ridden they became convinced the women were getting their extra cash from turning tricks in the neighborhood. There were some interesting dynamics at work there. The fact that they each did very well financially and became independent for the first time in their lives... much to their husband's chagrin, upset quite a few households.

"That's sort of when the JuicyCronesSisterhood got started. Those women were the ones who asked me to stand for election when our illustrious mayor was caught taking bribes and ended up in jail. Yep, those women got Madam Mitzy, elected. That's what the papers dubbed me, Madam Mitzy. By the time the next regular election came along the local political machine figured out how to take advantage of my past... kind of a Swift Boat operation to blow the madam out of the bay. I didn't feel like spending the time or money to go after 'em. If the locals were so stupid as to believe all that garbage, well let them have garbage desert. There! NOW, I've confessed. Will you tell us about yourself?" Mitzy tried not to sound annoyed. But really, she had been willing to reveal all and Magda was still hanging back.

"It's not that I don't want to so much, it's that I can't."

"I think we need a little clarity here, Magda," Anthea encouraged her gently when what she really wanted to do was shake the woman like a rag doll.

"Maybe when we get to driving up Hwy. 93 it'll help my memory." Magda sounded like she really would try.

"We are coming into Vegas now ladies. Please fasten your seat belts," Captain Carlson's voice came over the speakers with the first words he'd said since Palomar Airport.

"Perfect timing Lindal. But you're not off the hook," Mitzy assured her.

Chapter Nine

     They landed in Las Vegas and were met by a shuttle driven by none other than Lulu Haynes, former protégé of Mitzy MacDonald. The leggy show girl had arrived as a naïve teen from Maine, just before Thea left, back in the '70s. Lulu, still willowy and lovely, though obviously in her late middle years, was now a successful entrepreneur, with four auto rental franchises in Nevada. There was a rousing reunion between the 6-foot tall Lulu and the 5-foot short Mitzy. When they got to the office Lulu brought out a collection of "class" photos with all the girls holding Mitzy overhead. It was a tradition MacDonald relished as much as she hated it, being somewhat phobic about heights.

     Mitzy had remained at the house till she retired, which meant there were lots of these girls-to-women who still thought of her as their surrogate mom. Lulu was gracious and generous, traits she attributed to her years under Mitzy's tutelage, "there's no way I'll ever repay you, mom. Please, just take it for as long as you need it." "It" was a sparkling burgundy colored top-of-the-line Mercedes SUV with a satellite dish,[8] (per a request from Cybil in case they needed to go on-line), a full tank of bio-fuel and 2 huge hampers of gourmet sandwiches with all the trimmings, including champagne. Lulu also handed Mitzy a gas company credit card. "Bring it back full. And don't fuss. It's a family thing I do. Makes me feel good. Now go on, scoot. You've got a long drive ahead and it's getting dark"

On the drive north, as they were about to get somewhere on the Magda-Wolf front, Thea had another flash of the vision, just like the first part only more detailed: *the young woman struggles with the body. The sparkling item from before appears to be a pendant, which comes out of the lifeless woman's hand in the tussle. Other figures seem to be in frame. Is there a struggle going on with them?*

This time there was no way Calzona could hide the fact that she'd slipped into an intuitive moment. Well, several moments. She still didn't want to let on what she'd been seeing. Not until she got a better fix on Magda's involvement in the dark little scenario. She knew how easy it was for people to misinterpret when the visions were this vague. With Magda being so fragile right now, it seemed the better part of wisdom to pretend she wasn't sure what it was all about. Cybil and Mitzy had been with her long enough to know the signs. But they also knew to respect her lead when it came to telling what she'd seen. "Don't push it, Mitzy" had been Thea's plea on more than one occasion.

Thea's main concern, and the reason she didn't tell Magda what she was seeing, was she couldn't get her mind around how Lindal was connected to the visions. There was the chance that Magda might be the victim in the sighting, except that the car put it in a '30's period, and she clearly wasn't dead. But she wasn't sure the body was dead. Perhaps just unconscious. Past life situation or holographic projection? wondered Anthea. She knew she needed to figure out how Magda fit in, if in fact she did at all. Unfortunately things had been too busy to really go inside and ask Source for some good clear direction.

Tequila sunset colors glowed on the sandscape as they headed up Hwy 93 on the east side of Nevada. It was soon going to be dark and they'd arrive at the hospital in Dos Robles within the next hour and a half. Once they got involved with Wolf, there'd be no time for asking questions. Anthea was going to have to force the issue now. With the grace of the dancer she had once been Thea did a verbal dip and turned to Magda. "I know you feel hesitant, but please friend, help us get to know a bit about this fellow who seems to be a major character in your scenario, so we'll know how to support you."

"It may seem like I'm trying to hide something from you all, but I swear I'm not. Wolf Tall Trees is a Native American. He's always claimed he isn't sure which tribe he comes from. I'll tell you about that part some other time. Right now I guess the important part is how he came into my life. It's simple. One day, when he was about 20-something, he was out honing his tracking skills. That came to be what he does in life... track... for the Sheriff, for the FBI, finding lost children, he can track anything in any kind of circumstances. This time he was after a coyote that'd been getting into the hen house at the Ranch. He came across me lying unconscious in a ravine next to the highway. He figured I must have walked away from a car accident, though there didn't seem to be any car around" Suddenly Magda stopped her story and interjected a total non-sequitur: "yea though I walk through the valley of the shadow of death, I shall fear no evil, for thou art with me." It seemed perhaps this was a fugue moment. Nobody dared disrupt her at that point. And then she picked up where she had interrupted her story, as though she hadn't made that abrupt detour. "There wasn't anything around to indicate anything about me. To this day, like I told you before, I have no memory of who I am or where I came from. I was still out when Wolf took me to the brothel where he lived as ranch-hand and all-around man of the house. From all I've been told, I came around some seventy-two hours after my arrival. I had a broken leg, some messed up ribs and a head wound. Those women at the brothel poured all their pent up maternal instincts into taking care of me. I owe my recovery to them. Well, I owe my life to Wolf, but the women took good care of me."

Cybil was dubious. "You really can't remember anything about your family or your home? Where you came from? What about hypnotherapy?"

"I've tried it. Believe me, I've tried everything, but I just get blank walls."

"And never any sign of a purse or a wallet? No one came asking if you were a missing person they were looking for?" Cybil's practical mind was determined that there was a logical way to get this mystery solved.

"Like I said, there were no clues on me when Wolf discovered my body. He's used his contacts over the years, done everything he can, but no luck. I also have to warn you that I may turn weird on you now and then since I still get occasional moments where I don't know who I am and I might not know who you are. They're called dissociative fugue moments. The only way I have managed to maintain over the years has been through the kindness of the women at the Ranch who have kept track of me during wandering moments, days, weeks. That's why I didn't want to get any more people dragged into helping me. And of course Wolf, who could always track me down if I got too far afield. I already feel I take too much from people. It makes me very uncomfortable since I don't seem to have any choice."

"Ah, Wolf" was the collective thought.

Chapter Ten

It was dark when they arrived in the little town of Dos Lobos. The main drag was lit with replica 1890's street lamps. The store fronts were movie vintage 1890's western town. Hitching posts separated parking spaces from the covered wooden side walks.

Cybil was intrigued: "How' does such a small town end up with a kicky style?"

"Oh, it just sort of happened. When the Ranch clientele grew, we kept growing. We added the restaurant, some cabins, classes and work shops."

The concept whirled round in each of the crone's heads. A brothel with classes and workshops?

"We had a set designer, an art director and a construction coordinator, all regular clients from Hollywood. They decided it would be fun to fix up the town. They brought the store fronts from a few back-lots in tinsel town, along with a crew to make it all fit together. A producer friend found a way to use it as a location and write it all off. The town council could hardly say no to that sudden influx of cash and all the free remodels. The folks who'd been tryin' for years to get us shut down kinda softened when they found out a movie was gonna get shot here."

By the time the Juicy Crones were up to speed on the

particulars of Dos Lobos they were pulling into the parking lot at the hospital.

Cybil was impressed with the building. "This is a fair sized facility for such a small town."

Magda pointed to the dedication plaque at the entrance, Clarence P. Vail Memorial Hospital. "Very grateful stock broker from San Francisco. He was a long-time visitor to the Ranch. His foundation was instructed to build it if he 'died in the saddle' as he put it. He did. We got the best hospital in eastern Nevada."

The nurse at the intensive care station greeted Magda with a warm hug. There was no change in Wolf's condition, she reported. Still unconscious. Under the circumstances they could see him for a few minutes. The Juicy Crones all filed in to lend Magda support as she tried to grasp what had happened to her old friend.

Off to the side of the room Sheriff Pete Willery held up the wall. He was a ramrod straight 5'10", in pretty good shape. Checking him out Mitzy figured he had to be about 70. He had thick white wavy hair neatly cut, a square jaw and a cleft in his chin. His badge was prominently displayed on his vest and his shoes required no shine as they were roughout roping-heeled boots. Hanging off his wide leather belt with the silver Nevada-champion-bronc-buster buckle was his honest-to-goodness six shooter.

His side kick, Doc Saxby was surprisingly tall for a country Doctor at 6'4". Somehow Thea thought of Doc Stone in Gunsmoke. She wanted Teddy Saxby to fit that mold, small, feisty. This one was lanky and a bit lumbering. He did have a rumpled mane, with appealing touches of gray.

Magda was genuinely grateful that at least Wolf had his old friends close by. Doc assured her they'd stay right there till he came around to tell them what happened, because they all agreed it was very odd that Tall Trees had a heart attack. He had always been so robust, living outdoors a good deal of the time, climbing trees and mountains. He never went anywhere without his ancient medicine bag with a cure for anything that ailed. This just didn't make sense.

As the old friends talked Thea took Wolf's hand. She immediately got vision spurts: *protect Magda... danger; then in sped-up time a vision of an Indian digging a pit. At first it seemed like a grave, but it kept going, way too big for a grave. And the figure doing all that furious dirt tossing was a young man.* What on earth was that all about?

She came back from her moment of reverie to find Magda trying to cajole her nurse friend into letting her have a room in the hospital for the night. "That way my friends can be on their way back to California," she explained.

"Nice try amiga, but you know as well as we do that Wolf would want you to go to the Ranch and reassure the other women there." Reluctantly Magda agreed with Thea.

Somberly they drove out into the foothills. The sage brush cast squat shadows in the light of the full moon. About fifteen miles outside of Dos Lobos Magda directed Cybil to turn in under an ornately carved entrance way that proclaimed in huge letters *Touch of Love Spa and Institute of Tantric Sex.* To the side was a directory listing the facilities: restaurant, saloon, guest cottages, conference center, massages, couples lessons.

When they got to the Ranch proper, a building straight out of the era the art director had used to fashion the town, they were greeted by the current Madam, Olivia Smart, a strong featured, straight-backed octogenarian very proud of her title. It wasn't like anybody really was a madam anymore, but Olivia seemed to like the way it sounded, "Madam Olivia." Gillian Weaver was the web master of their international school for tantric sex. Their website was one of the first ever registered in the category, and one of the busiest to date. Several women moved into and out of the parlor, but they seemed too busy to stop and chat. They had guests to register and guests to get situated. Gillian and Olivia opted to take charge of Magda's friends.

Madam Olivia had saved two of the little cabins with two rooms each for the quartet. "I'm quite certain you'll be comfortable." No one disputed that. The furnishings for the whole place were tasteful antiques, amazingly plush and comfortable for the period. Some of the comfort had to be attributed to the lounging couches and other adornments that must have come from a Turkish harem. The décor was pure Victorian oriental voluptuousness from an era that professed to distain such voluptuousness.

Once she had seen them back into the parlor after getting themselves arranged in their rooms, Magda headed for the kitchen where she launched a search for hot chocolate fixings. Out came the whipping cream, the vanilla, the honey, and from deep in the pantry came her stash of the darkest of Italian cocoa powder. Whipping and stirring she had the sauce ready within minutes. Pushing the tea cart laden with big cups of the chocolate, a mound of whipped cream, a plate of wonderful little cookies, spoons and napkins, she made a grand entrance. While Gillian helped Magda serve, Olivia regaled the new guests with tales of days gone by. Apparently she'd been there considerably before Magda arrived on the scene after her accident.

Magda interrupted her. "Before you go any further with the reminiscing Olivia, could you just tell us exactly what happened with Wolf today?"

"There isn't much to tell darlin'. Gillian, you know more than I do."

"He must have known something was going on because he flicked the intercom switch and I picked it up in the reception center. All I heard was 'Mags, I de..' then it sounded like he was retching. And then there was the sound of something dropping on the floor and a moan. We ran right out there and found him comatose on the floor next to the intercom. I called Doc and he and the sheriff got the ambulance crew headed out here, and there you have it. I did CPR till the ambulance got here."

Magda nibbled on a cuticle, "It just doesn't seem possible. Had he been ill at all lately?"

"You've got to be kidding. He just got back from about a week in the wilds of northeastern Washington somewhere. Camping out he said. I don't know exactly where, do you Olivia?"

"Not a clue. But you know how he was if he was on a tracking assignment. He never said a word. All very hush hush with these government jobs. Maybe he got something like west Nile virus or hanta or something."

"You know how unlikely that is. He's totally in touch with the elements and creatures, big and small. He'd know if there was anything like that going on and he'd take precautions," Magda reminded her.

"Did anything else happen that might have set off this

attack of his?" Cybil, ever the practical one, wanted to know.

"Not a thing. It was a pretty mellow afternoon. Like I said, he'd just come back from that trip up to Washington. These two men showed up, dressed like city guys, dark suits and such. And they asked for Wolf. Wouldn't come in here. Just wanted to talk to him privately. Something about a sister missing for many years. They went out to his place and after awhile they drove away. About twenty minutes later we got the call from him," Gillian looked disconsolate as she related this event.

In the midst of this relating Doc called to tell them he'd got all the results back and everything indicated Wolf's system was actually quite sound. He hadn't come around yet, but his vital signs were good. Doc thought perhaps he was doing his restorative rest thing, or whatever it was the shaman part of Wolf called it. "You know how he does that native stuff when he's feelin' punk."

"You mean when he gets still as can be and connects with his animal guides to ask for direction?" Magda asked.

"Yeah, like that." Doc replied.

When Magda got off the phone Anthea felt the urge to redirect the conversation, heighten the vibrations, "Ok, there's not much more we can do about Mr. Tall Trees at this point. Can we just turn it over to Doc and the Universe and get to focusing on something in a more productive vein?" That was all it took for Olivia to launch the legend of Wolf rescuing the girl in the ravine.

Chapter Eleven

Back in those days Ruby was the madam who ran the house. She was a short, powerful woman with a train-load of charisma, savvy and authority. It happened about midday that she was over-seeing clean-up after the noon meal. She looked out the kitchen window when Wolf's dog, Cactus came tearing into the back yard, kicking up a major fuss. Very unusual for the Husky-Wolf who was normally as placid and reticent as his human counterpart.

Madam Ruby sent some of the girls out to see what was wrong; they yelled for her to "come quick," which she did. And there arose in the distance, coming slowly toward them, a magnificent image worthy of a Curtis photograph. The young Indian brave, Wolf Tall Trees, his ebony braids down either side of his bare bronze chest, riding bareback astride his paint pony Buck. Where was Wolf's shirt? Where was Buck's saddle blanket? And what was stirring up all that dust along the horse's trail? As he rode into the yard they could see he had fashioned a travois from a couple of branches he must have gleaned from the sparse stand of aspen that struggled to survive in the wash about two miles north of the Ranch House.

He had used his horse blanket for the travois and tied that on with strips torn from his shirt. And on the cleverly crafted conveyance a young woman, a girl really, lay cradled and unconscious. Her leg was bound and strapped to more branches in a crudely constructed splint. Her head was bound 'round with strips of his shirt to protect what must have been a rather nasty gash on her brow.

"Room seven," Madam Ruby called out, and three of the girls ran back into the house to make it ready. Wolf swung his leg over Buck's back and slid to the ground, padded softly over to the body, lifted her gently, gently, ever so gently, and then he carried her into the house and up the stairs to room seven. The girls had the covers thrown back and the bed was ready for its new occupant.

Wolf told the women that he had found her while he was out riding the property line next to the highway. At one point where it skirted a ravine the fence was broken and down below he found the girl. She had no personal belongings on her.

His first thoughts were to get her to the Ranch and then call the Doc to come take a look at her and decide if she needed a hospital. It could be she was in no condition to travel; that bringing her in the way he had may have done more damage than good, but he couldn't leave her. There were hungry coyotes and wild dogs running in packs out there. He had asked his spirit guides and then followed their instructions, and that is how he ended up bringing her to his lady friends at the brothel.

Doc Saxby and Deputy Willery came out from town. The Sheriff back then was Wiley Fox, who felt he had much more important matters to attend to than looking after some accident victim off the highway who was hanging out at the bordello. He was running for re-election in the mighty metropolis of Dos Lobos, population 847 by the 1960 census. Demographics: mostly male desert rats, the few women who gravitated toward sparse living, and a few others who were bound and determined to clean up the god-forsaken town. Not that anyone was running against Sheriff Fox, but he still claimed he had to watch his reputation. This despite the fact that the women at the bordello were potential voters. He was sure they were in his pocket and didn't require his courting their votes. He even went so far as to pretend a disdain for them when he spoke to the town folks. Part of his good, gospel-toting image. His patronage of the women's services was definitely on the Q.T. No, it was the god-fearing, bible-thumpin' women in town he had to cater to. All by way of saying it made sense to send his new young depa'tee, Pete Willery, out with his pal, the freshly minted new Doctor, Teddy Saxby, who had just returned to his home-town from medical school.

When they arrived the girl was still drifting in and out of consciousness. While Doc checked her out the deputy took the story from Ruby. Second hand, because Wolf had disappeared as soon as the girl was set up with the women in attendance. All they could figure out was that she must have been in a car accident somewhere up the road and managed to wander south on foot. Maybe she didn't get hurt till she fell down the ravine. Without a car there didn't seem much chance of figuring out who she was or where she came from, or what had happened, till she came around.

In the meantime Saxby said they should bring her in for x-rays, but he was worried about her head. She might have a concussion. He thought Wolf had done a magnificent job on splinting the leg. Saxby'd cleaned and bandaged her head wound, then palpated where he'd found some serious bruising. It felt like one of her ribs might be broken. But there wasn't really anything to do about ribs other than bind them to keep 'em still and let them heal. As for her head and leg he'd check into sending an ambulance if he could get one to come up from Poteen, but they'd have to pay for the driver and use of the vehicle both ways unless they wanted her to stay in Doc's house. There was no hospital for 45 miles. Only the office Doc had inherited from his own Doctor-father, with his antiquated x-ray equipment and a spare bedroom. No, Ruby insisted, they'd find a way to pay the ambulance, but they wanted to bring her back to the Ranch to recover.

And so she did. She had indeed been concussed and once she came around the women took turns keeping her awake until Saxby gave the all clear that she was out of danger of swelling her brain. But she couldn't tell them a thing about who she was, how she got there, or where she came from. It was all a mystery to her. The Deputy had checked out the scene and cruised the highway for miles in both directions. No sign of a car anywhere, he told Ruby.

"There you are, that is how she came to us," Madam Olivia sat back in satisfaction, her plump hands crossed over her robust tummy.

"Oh my," said Cybil and Mitzy in unison. Thea was lost deep in concentration. Did this fit in with the visions she'd been having lately? How?

"That is an amazing story, Magda," Cybil said patting her new friend's hand. Mitzy was too awe-struck to say anything more. Which was a most unusual response on Mitzy's behalf.

And then she had a thought that would not stay properly in the closet where it belonged. "So how soon did you put her to work to pay her way? Teach her these tantricks?" Mitzy had a very hard time keeping disdain out of her voice.

Visions of sexual slavery danced in her head. Thea reached over and tugged the scarf from Mitzy's neck and twirled it over-head. "Negative energy?" she said.

"Oh, stuff it, Calzona. You may be right, but stuff it." Mitzy didn't like being caught at her own game.

Mme Oliva on the other hand, hadn't a clue what they were talking about. She just wanted to make Ruby's treatment of Magda clear, "Oh, land sakes, no, no. She's the one taught us all about Tantric Sex. But that wasn't right away. No, at first, as soon as she could stand up, the girl insisted on pitching in, housekeeping and such. When we found out what a fantastic cook she was, oh my," this said by Mme. Olivia as though Magda wasn't even in the room.

Gillian had to get in on the tale, "I wasn't here back then, but I've heard there were clients who'd actually come out just to eat on occasion, and that's how the kitchen grew into a restaurant. Had to add that whole wing. And the odd thing was she didn't have a clue where she'd learned her cooking."

Oliva looked a bit forlorn. "You know how you ask a woman, 'did your momma teach you that?' She'd just shrug her shoulders an' go on cookin'. The number one item on the menu back then was home-made fat noodles, spatzle she called 'em, with goulash. She'd tell us all about it in some foreign language. Then a client told us it was Hungarian, so we sort of figured maybe she was some kind of refugee from Hungary. It wasn't too long after those freedom fighters tried to break out of the Russian stranglehold. Except she didn't have an accent on her American, and she'd have been too young to have fought."

Anthea looked at Magda, "Sounds like that gave you a pretty clear picture of some link to a Hungarian heritage. I wonder what it was?"

"Yes, the goulash, the Hungarian talk along with her name being Magda." Olivia. mused.

"Well now, there's a question: how'd Wolf know your name was Magda?" Cybil puzzled.

"Oh, we never really knew if it was her name for sure, but Wolf said it that first day. She moaned it out on occasion when she was still not fully conscious. Or in her sleep, after Doc let her go back to sleeping that is. She'd say things like, 'Magda, oh dear Magda.' Other times it was 'it's all my fault.' Those were the only things till she came to and we found out she couldn't remember, so we called her Magda and it appeared to suit her just fine."

"Okay, but it's a long way from cooking goulash to Tantric Sex. I think we're missing a few links." Mitzy wouldn't let that bone go un-chewed.

Olivia turned to Magda. "Well, Maggie, remember how you sort of started asking questions about our work?" As soon as she'd said it Olivia sucked in her breath and held it. She remembered this was forbidden territory.

"Sorry Madam, but it's all a blur," Magda said as tears welled up.

"Well, is it all right if I tell 'em?" Olivia held out the olive branch. "You may as well say yes. I can see how these women are. They won't leave it alone 'til you do." Magda conceded, though she didn't look exactly thrilled to be in the spotlight this way.

Olivia told them how Magda began to make suggestions about how they treated their customers. "Subtle things about touch, weaving a web of prolonged ecstasy, something bizarre called Kama Sutra positions, how it was spiritual, but also an eastern science thousands of years old, and that the clients didn't need to know all this, they just needed to be coached in the action."

"Some of the girls were sure their clients who preferred it rough would just laugh at them, but Magda showed them how to sort of tease the guys into it. They were amazed to find out that they could actually get pleasure out of this prolonged pleasing of their partner... but it took a long time to train them. There were ups and downs, but Magda stuck with it.

"And after awhile some of our clients were bringing a different sort of friends along, and then a few brought their girl friends, and eventually they brought their wives. But that was a long time coming. What man wanted to tell his wife he'd been learning new techniques for loving her from a bunch of women in a brothel in Nevada?" Olivia was pleased with her recitation.

"I'll bet that didn't happen till after the love generation matured. I mean where you got couples coming. I suppose if you'd been a commune in Berkley it wouldn't have been a problem. But a brothel in Nevada?"

"You're sure 'nough right about that Cybil," Olivia replied. "Like I said, our guys were lots more rough and tumble truckers, ranch hands, traveling sales men at conventions in Vegas, guys like that. Anyway, somewhere in there it just sort of became this place where these men wanted to come and learn what it was we were doing. And then some women heard about it and they brought their boyfriends or their husbands, and there you have it. We changed the name from *The Bunny Hutch* to *Touch of Love* and built the little cabins and the center and, well you can see what's happened."

It didn't bother Magda to tell the next part, but that was probably because it wasn't about her. "By the time the internet came along, Gillian turned up in their lives. An escapee from Silicon Valley. She got them going, set up an on-line store front, started selling books on Tantric Sex, and a variety of stimulants and mood-setting accessories. They were the first Tantric site to go on-line. Drop shipping from all over the world. Now she has them involved, posting, blogging, chatting, answering questions," Magda related the story as any proud mother would.

"You keep saying they. Where are you in all this on-line sex?" Cybil asked.

"Oh there's a lot of stuff that happened in between, with me phasing in and out. You've seen the bio. I'd gone off and done that other stuff. In those times I didn't know who I was, sometimes I had a different name. And then I'd remember this place. Thank god they let me come back, till the next time". And with that she shut down.

Cybil turned to Thea. "Are you all right? You've been very quiet for a long time?"

"Just soaking it all in and letting my inner Source process it. Time for some serious dream work ladies. It's after mid-night." With that Anthea was up and headed for the door.

They all turned in feeling rather up-lifted. All except Magda, who said she always felt miserable when people spoke of the past, since she didn't have one. Thea wanted desperately to say, "Excuse me. What the gollywhompers was all that we just heard?" But she knew it wouldn't do any good... yet. It wasn't easy for a devout optimist like Anthea Calzona to get an equally devout pessimist like Magda Lindal up to a higher vibrational track.

Chapter Twelve

The next morning they were all up before dawn, refreshed and ready to go to the hospital, certain that Wolf would be alert and eager to see Magda. But such was not to be. When Magda called to let the hospital staff know she'd be there shortly, Doc came on the line and she knew it wasn't good news. She sat down in a Victorian wing chair and waited for what she didn't want to hear: "Mags, he slipped away about twenty minutes ago. I was just going to call you."

Distraught and in total denial, Magda was adamant that she had to go right away to see him. She was sure there was a mistake, even though Doc Saxby told her he had been there and there was no denying it. Wolf's body was on its way down to the morgue and he didn't think she really wanted to go there. "Wait till we can get him fixed up and we'll bring him out to you. We'll help you bury him in that family plot out back. Willery and I will take care of everything here. Since he died in the hospital and I was there, we won't have to do an autopsy so I'll be able to bring him out by this afternoon. Is there anything you need from town? And what exactly have you got in mind? I'm sure some of the old timers from 'round about will want to be there. Just tell me and I'll let 'em know."

"Whoa, Doc! Hold your horses. You're goin' too fast. You gotta let me think about this a bit. It's such a shock right now. But one thing's for sure, it's got to be as traditional a ceremony as a bunch of pale faces can put together. We need his medicine bundle, turkey feather, that stuff. It's got to be out on Red Devil Butte. He always went up there to think on things and get together with his spirit guides. I'm sure he'd say they were waiting out there for him now." With that she broke into sobs, dropped the phone and dashed off for the kitchen.

The others followed, only to see her whirling about unable to get a grasp of what to do. Anthea took her in a loving embrace and headed her out the back door for some fresh air. "I think what we've got to do now is what you said: go through his things, figure out what he would want to take with him. It won't be easy, but you'll feel better once it's done."

That only set Magda off more. Thea administered a gentle verbal slap, "Stop this! Right now. This is not what your friend wants from you. He expects a lot more. You've got work to do, Lindal. Show us the way." And with that they were off across the yard, past the barn and into a clearing where a structure of arched poles covered with hides, embellished with hand prints and other native symbols, stood eerily backlit as a waning moon and the rising sun created a chiaroscuro in the morning sky. Looking at that moon slipping feather-like, tauntingly off to the west, a bare hint of what it had been during the night when it had led them to the hospital and hope, it sent a shiver through Magda, but then she squared her shoulders and opened the door to Wolf's empty dwelling, took a deep breath and stepped into her friend's world.

The Wikiup was a work of art, impeccably constructed, large, a monument to the man who had built it. When she took that decisive step a transformation overwhelmed her. As though to assuage her grief, Magda went into hyper-drive.

The first thing she did was head for the phone to call the Sheriff and tell him that, in case he hadn't heard, they'd be having the ceremony on Red Devil Butte at noon the next day, and told him Doc had assured her the two of them would arrange to get the body to the ranch today so they could prepare it.

Then she called the local paper and had them run a banner about the ceremony on the front page. She said she would pay for it as an ad if she had to to make sure it was front page. But Ed Smiley, the owner/editor of the Dos Lobos Gazette, fumed, "Absolutely not!" He'd take care of it. Wolf was a local celebrity!

Oh, he'd hate that, Wolf would, thought Magda. But she held her tongue. The man meant well. Besides, to be fair, Smiley must have been in a bit of shock as he apparently hadn't yet heard the news. After all, he and Tall Trees had gone toe-to-toe on most of the important political issues in the county for as long as anyone could remember. Now who was Smiley going to do battle with?

Next it was time to tackle Wolf's personal things, and figure out how to dress him, and what to send off with him. Magda knew she had to collect Grandmother Strong Feather, the titular head of a group of Native Americans and hangers-on who were into native traditions in the area. But that would have to wait till tomorrow morning. It required a horseback ride out to where the clan had a collection of teepees.

Meanwhile, she said, "We've got to find his turkey feather, and his knife, and bow and arrows, and he's got some ceremonial buckskins and moccasins in the closet, and," she stopped and took a deep breath. "No, wait, he hardly ever wore the moccasins, usually just went barefoot. The better to stay in touch with Mother Earth." She held back tears thinking she'd never be able to tease him about his bare feet in city restaurants again.

Mitzy gave her a little hug. "Slow down woman. You need to keep breathing, and let yourself think clearly. A quick BrainGym session. Come on, breath and move. Follow me." And Anthea eased her friend through a series of moves aimed at relaxing and concentrating, and drawing in cognitive connections with All That Is.

When they finished she reassured Magda, "You'll find everything you need. This isn't exactly a huge place with a lot of cubby holes." Indeed, it was one room,. total efficiency: bed, desk, wood stove with two cook plates, a sink and a back door, "to the out house and the shower," Magda explained when she saw their inquisitive looks.

Shelves with arrangements of odd items. "His trophy case. He didn't call it that, but... its stuff from some of his worst cases: a bomber who blew up Jewish temples, another one who did Family Planning centers. A kidnapper who buried his victim live in a box. Wolf found her still alive, but just. These were all the worst guys. Most of 'em are in prison now." She picked up a notebook and leafed through it. "His cases. He always wrote them up for reference during trials." Magda was devastated by her reminiscence.

"Remember, you can tune into Wolf's spirit and ask him to guide you, Magda. Just trust." Thea began to tune in herself, asking for guidance.

"Trust. How can I trust him? He died on me." Magda plumped down on the bed and let herself be overtaken by sobs again. The other three women encircled her and began to hum the tune to 'You are the wind beneath my wings'. It was an estrogen-flowing, oxytocin moment, a tend-and-befriend interlude that no man could ever understand. Then they all leaked a few tears of release to clear the air.

Magda looked up at them. "You're right. Lets get this act together."

As they went through his things to find the proper talismans for the ceremony, they came across a journal covered in bark and leaves and written in some kind of code that they'd have to tackle later. Odd, Magda didn't remember Wolf writing much of anything but his tracking, notes and those were all in spiral binders. Where were they? Hah! They found the stash. They also found a small deer skin covered box containing a leaf of tobacco in a plastic Ziploc bag. Odd, he never smoked. An amethyst pendant too feminine for Wolf; a scrap of amethyst satin, again strangely out of character for Wolf; and an emblem off an antique auto. Cybil was into vehicle restorations and recognized it immediately, "'31 Pontiac. Wonder where the rest of it is?" There was also a map of Washington State with the word hippies written in the border. "Lets just keep all that in the box. We can deal with it later. What we've got to do now is get back to preparing for the ceremony."

Magda got busy choosing items for those who would come to celebrate Wolf's life. Things they could pick out to keep or to add to the bonfire of release. She found the Stetson she had given him on his 65th birthday. It had "Old Fart" stitched into the hat band. It was what he had taken to calling himself at that time. The band itself was beautiful. It had porcupine quills and pieces of flint. She was torn. Keep it, or send it off with him?

The Crones assembled the tokens for the release ceremony along with Wolf's flute, a couple of drums and several rattles. It all went into a large hand-woven basket that Cybil and Thea carried between them back to the Ranch House.

Later that morning, Sheriff Willery called and asked the women to meet him and Doc at the Wikiup. Upon their arrival at the Ranch, the women found out why. They showed up, not with a coffin bearing Wolf's body to be laid out in the foyer, but with an urn... Sheepishly Doc had to try to explain the second shock of the day: Tall Trees had been accidentally cremated.

The man tried to tell the tale with as much compassion as he could muster, but later they all had to admit it must have taken every bit of self-control Doc had to keep from bursting out laughing. That kind of nervous laughter that can break through in stressful times and often leads to hysteria.

"There was a mix-up and the wrong body went to the mortuary with a toe tag directing immediate cremation due to potential contamination – actually it just stunk of the polecat perfume that had apparently been lovingly deposited by some varmint out there in the foothills. It laid out there a few days ripenin' up 'fore Cozy Rockwell noticed Hardy hadn't been in for vitals for a few days."

"For those who don't know," he nodded with deference at the three women from California, "Hardy was a luckless prospector lived with his 'uncommon law wife,' as he called her, Cozy, who is anything but. Prickly as a cactus that one is. Anyway she said she didn't have no money for such tom foolery as funrals, but she wasn't about to dig a hole for him herself. The men of the town could do that she reckoned. Or they could drop him off a cliff — but make it far 'nough away from her camp so she didn't have to smell him. Anyway I got the Mayor to agree to use some of the town's beautification funds to hurry up and cremate Hardy. We sent the papers down and that's when the morgue attendant at the hospital, Feeny Filbert, apparently in the throes of celebrating the end of his DUI probation, got things a bit botched. He confessed he'd had a bit of a tipple or two through the night, and when the notification came down he got it messed up and Wolf went over to MacClennon's Speedy Crematorium where the instructions for rapid rendition were quickly followed."

This news sent Magda into a funk, or was it a mini-fugue moment? She seemed to be totally out of it. Worse yet Mitzy and Cybil were afraid Thea was having a sympathetic spiritual exodus from their presence. Doc managed to rouse Magda with a serious whiff of good old fashioned smelling salts.

Thea came back of her own accord. "All right friends, it's time for me to explain a bit of what I've been getting in my vision sessions. I just had another one, and my spirit guides are telling me to go ahead and explain what's been happening. " She didn't tell them that she'd been instructed only to reveal this latest vision for the time being. With her eyes closed Thea watched the scene and related what she saw: "*The setting is a barn, a farm. There seems to be a struggle involving two boys wearing shiny jackets: letterman style, with an odd emblem — the body of an old woman, half in half out of a trunk, which rests precariously on the luggage rack of an old car. A gorgeous amethyst pendant dangles from the arm of the body, a long-haired girl wrestles with the trunk lid trying to get the woman in, or is it out? I've been given that it's a '31 Pontiac convertible.*"

"Wait a minute," Mitzy said. Digging into the treasure box, "Look at this." Cybil reached across, took the Pontiac emblem and the map. "It looks like he's written a note here on the edge. "It says '31 Pontiac. No serial number. No plates. Magda.' He must have taken that trip to Washington to track down something about this Pontiac."

"We'll get back to that. What else is in there?" Mitzy was in rat terrier mode. She and Magda were about to get into a scuffle over the artifacts when Anthea pulled out a tiny blue book.

"Hah!" Thea said holding up a bank book, "Just out of curiosity, what was that amount of money you joked about manifesting way back there in Del Mar when I first met you?" she said looking at the back page. Sometimes she wondered about the perversity of her inner guides. For spirit beings they seemed inordinately nosey. This bank book was none of her business. And what made her remember that snippet of Magda's insistence on poverty consciousness at this very moment?

"What are you talking about?" Magda was puzzled. Thea handed it to her and nudged her to open it. Magda slapped at it and it flew out of Thea's hand. Mitzy picked the book off the dirt floor. Lettered boldly on the cover was the name, Magda Lindal. Mitzy gently handed it to Magda who, feeling a bit guilty for even wanting to know what was inside, flipped to the last page of deposits, to the ending balance.

"Oh, my God, $425,000, the amount I'd need to buy that land beside my house." She reacted as though she'd been hit in the gut. Collapsing inward, she began trembling and sobbing.

Thea eased over to Magda and directed healing Reiki energy at her. "You see how the Universe works? When you ask, and you do what Source leads you to do, well, there you are. You apparently asked with enough emotion and expected it on some level." Thea beamed.

But her smile quickly faded as she realized what Magda was about to say. "This is not amusing. I don't want money. I don't want the land now. Every time I look at it I'll think, 'I'd rather have Wolf back'. Besides, I get a feeling I'm not really Magda at all. I'm an imposter.. I don't know who I am. The Lindal thing was my producer's mother's maiden name. I had to have a name to join the writer's guild. Who am I? And what have I done to deserve this?"

"Monkey Mind, you're side tracking again. How about instead we have a little moment of gratitude for what your friend did for you? What he thought of you? The name he apparently gave you. Come on, hold the pendant and think Gratitude."

Magda swatted at Thea. "I do not want to thank him. I want him to come back. And now I'm gonna wonder who I really am and worry about what he did to get all that money?"

She turned on the men, "Have either of you got any idea? Doc? Sheriff?"

The two men just looked rather hang dog. "Do either of you know anything about this car business?" Magda was ready to pound on somebody. She got no response. "Why would he do a thing like that? I've got to find out. I've got to find out what Wolf has been up to all these years!"

"What we need is to move on where we can," Anthea took the amethyst pendant and asked it, "is the car a vital sign in this process?" The pendant swung briskly to and fro. "That's a definite yes!" she told the ensemble. "Does this car still exist?" Again she got an affirmative. "Is it near here? Hah! yes!...Can you lead us to it?" The pendulum swung around in a circle before it went back to the affirmative.

"What's that all about?" Mitzy barked.

"I think I need to change tools. Here Magda, you hold the pendulum. Mitzy, hand me my tote please." Thea dug around in her ubiquitous tote bag, well, really more like a port manteau made of Guatemalan hand-woven cloth.. She scrabbled for a few moments before coming up victorious, with a pair of dowsing rods. She held them with her hands straight out in front of her, closed her eyes and did a little hum-chant. The rods began to quiver. "We're in tune," Thea said opening her eyes. "Magda, get that paper and a pen and draw a quick map of the area around here with the cardinal points, the house, the barn, this building. Anything else, Mags?"

Magda shook her head trying not to cause the pendulum to move. She felt a strange responsibility for the lovely pendant. Thea held the rods over the hastily drawn map and asked Cybil to turn the paper clock-wise. After a moment of this slow rotation, with Thea holding the rods over the map, they dipped down. "Looks like we're supposed to look in..." she squinted at the map, "the barn." To Magda's surprise the pendulum in her hands swung in the affirmative.

Then she realized what had been said. "The barn? That's ridiculous. We've all been in and out of that old building a thousand times over the years. There's nowhere in there to hide a car," Magda remonstrated.

"Well, I believe the rods and the pendant agree. They both say go to the barn. Come on everyone,." and off Thea went following her dowsing rods, Magda and the pendulum swinging off behind her with the other women and two men and the urn following right behind.

It was a mystical little parade that made its way out to the old barn. Well, it wasn't really so old. Wolf had remodeled it using the wood from the original structure. Fortunately, he included good lighting along with plank flooring in the reconstruction.

Inside the door, Magda flicked the switch to reveal a very well kept building. It was abundantly clear that there was no car inside. Wolf's truck was off in the side wing along with his '53 Indian cycle. But the rest of the space held a work shop, a tractor and a lot of gardening gear. No Pontiac.

Anthea asked the rods again and they lead her straight across the open space to the ladder that went up to the loft. "Okay, now what do we do?" Cybil wanted to know. "Climb up into the hay loft and check it out for car parts?"

"Don't be silly, Cyb. I've moved tons of hay in and out of that loft over the years. There's no car anywhere in this barn," Magda insisted. But the rods said otherwise. Anthea followed as directed and there, in an alcove behind the ladder the rods dove down. Magda's pendulum agreed. They all ended up in a small corner that had only a work bench standing rather oddly alone. The rods were pointing straight down. "That's ridiculous. There's nothing there." Magda was totally discombobulated.

"Magda, hold the pendulum over the work bench," Thea directed. It swung mightily.

"This is it! Sheriff, get that pry bar and that shovel. We may need to dig after we pull up these boards," she said as she shifted the bench to the side.

Sheepishly, Willery looked to Saxby, who shrugged his shoulders and nodded consent. "Alright ladies. I guess the jig's up. Doc, hand me that bar." The Doc complied and Willery quickly revealed a trap door that the two men clearly knew all about. If they hadn't been so intent on finding out what lay below, the Juicy Crones would probably have shredded the men then and there and thrown them out for the coyotes that howled away in the foothills each night.

Sheriff Willery led the way down the stairs, flicking on another light switch to reveal a subterranean garage with a hydraulic lift upon which sat a pristine 1931 Pontiac, fully restored. Except for the emblem which was still in Wolf's deer-skin box.

The Sheriff clearly knew all about the car. "But like it said on that map you read Ms. Cybil, no serial number on the frame or on the firewall, no plates. No registration papers. Nothing. We did everything we could to try to find out where it came from way back when. No luck."

Slowly the Juicy Crones circled the gleaming burgundy cabriolet. It had Magdalena painted in gold letters on the front door. "Almost like my name," whispered Magda.

By then they'd come to a steamer trunk on the luggage rack on back. The Sheriff stood between the women and the trunk. "I don't think you gals wanna look in there."

"Well, think again, cowboy." "You better believe we do," Anthea and Cybil challenged him in unison. And so he lifted the lid on the trunk. Inside rested not the skeleton one would expect, but the body of a small woman, in a long skirt, a gypsy-like blouse, a work boot on one foot, a piece of the amethyst-colored satin in her hand. The body appeared to be oddly well preserved. When Anthea remarked about it, Doc Saxby assured them it was due to Wolf's preparations and the naturally-controlled climate in this sub-desert hideout.

Thea decided she had to reveal the rest of the visions

she'd been seeing since before she even met Magda. And so the clairvoyant related the three previous sightings, fragments though they were.

"Why didn't you tell me? I can't believe you. How could you not tell me? You and Wolf. See, I was right not to trust anybody. Paranoia rules." Magda was just a few decibels below full shriek.

"Calm down Magda. I couldn't tell you at first because I had no way of knowing it had anything to do with you."

"And later, when you knew?"

"I didn't really know until today, till we found those things in the Wikiup that fit in with what I'd been seeing."

"But you suspected?"

"Yes, I did. But I felt I needed more information before I said anything. It was all too vague. I wanted to protect you until I knew for sure."

Magda was totally riled up now. She didn't know where to direct her anger. "Hah, pronoia, I suppose? And Wolf?" She turned on the two men, "Was he trying to protect me, too?"

Doc reached out to try to soothe her, "That's exactly what he was trying to do, Mags."

"Don't you 'Mag's' me, Doctor Theodore Saxby." Magda would have swatted him except that he still had the urn with Wolf's ashes under his arm. "You knew about this all these years. And you..." she grabbed the pry bar off the bench and was about to clobber the Sheriff. Mitzy got the tool, but Magda flailed on hysterically. Her imagination had taken hold and was bouncing off the walls with her arms swatting out of control. Her mind leapt back to the conclusion that she must have killed the old woman, and that was what Wolf had been protecting her from finding out.

The Sheriff tried to reassure her, "There's no reason to think you had anything to do with it... other than... maybe you were driving when the car went off the road. But the old woman was already dead. The Doc here even did an autopsy."

Magda was not convinced, "Let's face it Doc you don't see all that well. You've got those floaters in your eyes.. Nobody understands why the Sheriff lets you go driving around when you can't see. And he lets you carry a side arm. Everybody in the county's scared some day you'll make one of those volunteer deputy arrests of yours and accidentally shoot some poor idiot you've mistaken for a real crook. You probably missed some signs. She was suffocated, or something like that. I tell you, I've got this feeling sure as I know that sun's about to set I was responsible for that woman's death. I mean, no disrespect, but Doc, I think we need to have a bone fide forensic pathologist check her out. And then I think Willery outta throw you in the hoosegow just on general principles"

At that point, the Doctor about boiled over back at her. "Magda Lindal, you watch too much TV. They won't find anything I didn't. I was forty years younger. I could see just fine. Don't you go casting aspersions on my character, woman!"

Thea had to stop this before her friend actually did get herself arrested for no good reason. "Enough Lindal! Sheriff, don't pay any attention to her."

The Sheriff raised his hands in the time-honored calm down fashion, "Don't worry, Ms. Calzona. Remember, I was there. I know what happened."

"Well, would you mind filling us in on this great 40-year

old secret?" Magda sniped.

"Cool down there, little lady. You got to remember we were pretty young in those days. Green behind the ears," he mixed a few metaphors to flavor the stew, "Thoroughly dedicated and sure we knew more than any of the old coots around town. Doc'd just got home from med school. I'd only been a dep'ty for two months. Ol' Sheriff Fox couldn't have cared less about the girl, the old woman, none of it. He wanted it kept quiet. According to him, we didn't <u>have</u> crimes, beyond drunkenness and a little mayhem on payday, in this neck of the desert. No, there couldn't be any serious crimes committed in his town. The girl had probably been transporting her dead granny's body to her final resting place when a tire blew out and they went off the road.

"We had to admit it was a possibility. But ol' Wolf, he had this powerful feeling that the woman was a victim of some crime and the girl was in danger if the perps found out she was still alive. He asked us to keep quiet about it while he tracked the car and the women back to wherever they came from. And that suited old Fox just fine. Nobody knew who they were, nobody was looking for them. The broads from the ranch, no disrespect, Magda, the women were covering the tab on your care so there were no charges going against the county coffers. The Sheriff just wanted it all to go away. So we helped pull the car out of the ravine and move it over here. Like I said, Doc did an autopsy just to be sure."

"It was my first chance to do a crime autopsy so I was extra careful. I did it all by the book and then some. Then Wolf and I put her back just the way she'd been. There was no sign of any kind of violence on the old woman Magda. So you just get that notion out of your head," Saxby tried to reassure her.

"Well, I'll think about it. But none of that explains how the car got to Nevada. Or where it came from. Or how it came to be named Magdalena, like me, or was it her? And who was she? And if she's Magda, then who am I?"

"Can't tell you much about any of it, except the Wolf-man asked my permission as the law man at the scene that he be allowed to 'bury' the body along with the car since nobody was laying claim to either one..

"After he restored it. The car, that is. There was an old meat locker out back of the barn. You remember? Where he used to put the deer after he went hunting. Anyway he put her in there till the car was ready. Actually, he told you gals in the Ranch House he needed to do some structural work on the barn and for you all to stay clear till he said it was safe. After a day trying to dig the pit he gave up and rented a back-hoe, installed the hydraulic lift so he could get it down here and then, pardon my telling you, but Magda, you know he knew a lot of that Indian lore stuff. Well he knew how to preserve the body. And that's what he did. And here it's been all this time."

"Over the years he spent many an hour with the old woman, talking to her spirit, asking her for guidance about what happened. He said what he got always seemed fuzzy, like her spirit was drugged. But he swore he'd keep at it and some day he'd find out who did it," Sheriff Willery seemed relieved to get the story off his conscience.

There wasn't much more anybody could say. It was getting late and both men needed to get home to their respective spouses. Magda lovingly took the urn from Doc and placed it in the driver's seat of the old Pontiac. Somehow it seemed appropriate. Solemnly the group made its way up the stairs leaving the two old friends in the car to commune.

As the men drove off, the Juicy Crones huddled and plotted. They weren't about to let either of the men know what they were planning to do.

Chapter Thirteen

Actually, the women themselves didn't really know what to do, for all their huddling and plotting. They just knew that they had to do something. As the dust settled behind the departing duo, Magda walked up the drive way, put her head down and, with a very determined gait, headed straight for the main house and into the kitchen. She was in deep-think mode. Tran would tell her to meditate. And the way she did that was to cook! So there she was in her sanctuary once again, (any kitchen was a sacred place to Magda Lindal). She thought about that name business, but what could she do? What was she supposed to call herself? She'd been Magda Lindal most of her known life. Even during a period when, so she was told, she'd been married to a local rancher, she insisted on keeping "her own name." That's what they told her. She didn't remember ... it was one of those fugue periods.

What wasn't a lost memory for Magda was a knowledge of where everything was in this kitchen. She had set it up all those years ago, and refined it on each visit to the ranch. After all, this was as close to home as anything she'd ever known.

The Juicy Crones filed in and awaited instructions. They came soon enough. Deftly Maggie pulled out a salad bowl, a small bowl for mixing the dressing, got a loaf of Italian bread out of the freezer and popped it in a moderate oven.

She never seemed to plan what to do, just let something inside of her (what Thea would call her inner being) guide her hands, her actions. Before any of them knew what was going on she had them washing and chopping some crisp Fuji apples, celery, chunks of hearts of Romaine, putting it all together in the big bowl. She poked around in the fridge and came up with a chicken breast left over from an earlier meal, on the shelf a huge jar of dried cranberries, some fresh dill, and, of course, walnuts. Clearly the women of *Loving Touch* had learned how to stock their larder from Magda.

What Magda turned out was a hearty variation on a Waldorf salad. She dressed the whole thing with a vinaigrette made by whisking the Himalayan crystal salt[9] Anthea carried in her port-manteau into a bowl of gravenstein-apple cider-honey vinegar with a very mild cold-pressed extra virgin olive oil. All of this she fluffed into a creamy emulsified state which she drizzled over the salad and then tossed lightly. That and the bread hot from the oven, with raw sweet butter, were more than enough fare for the ensemble.

Mme Olivia added the crowning touch. With great flare she presented a few lovely bottles of Veuve Cliquot to toast Wolf, which they did with gusto.

"Now, we've got to figure out what to do next," Magda said as she urged them all to eat up. "First thing is the ceremony, even though there isn't really time to get it together the way I'd like to. And we need to figure out about our mystery woman." Thea suggested they wait on that issue. "Just focus on Mr. Tall Trees."

On that front, Magda had a laundry list of things she was sure would go wrong the next day. Like Smiley turning up like some kind of desert-rat paparazzi. Or the Mayor trying to turn it into a political forum. Or the Widow Lipton weeping all over the urn in some dramatic attempt to claim Wolf as her own when in fact he'd done his best over the years to steer clear of her.

Suddenly Olivia had a flash of remembrance. It was about Wolf's unexpected trip to Washington State. She'd had a funny feeling about it. It wasn't like when he got his normal tracking jobs, but she couldn't put her finger on why. The information did nothing to steer Magda into a higher vibration. She was back on her own dreary track, "I'm sure it had something to do with that car and the old woman. I think that's the key to who I am. You heard Pete. Wolf wanted to find out about all that stuff. I think he wanted to find out why I killed her."

"Magda Lindal, you are one of the most stubborn women I've ever met. You are not a killer. My spirit guides would tell me. I guarantee it!" Thea snarled. This was totally not helping with her own practice of staying in the higher vibration.

Once the heat level lowered in the room, Mitzy had a question, "Is there some reason you never talked about this with Wolf? Asked him to help you find your origins? I mean it's what he does, er did."

"I already told you, he did try to find out, but it went nowhere. And I didn't push it because, you know, I hate to ask anybody for help. I see that look on people's faces. 'Oh, oh, here she comes again, needy Magda'."

"Some day we're going to have to figure out why you have this insistence on unworthiness. But for that you're going to have to do some remembering," Thea pointed out.

"Yeah, like I forget on purpose!" Magda growled back.

Thea was unfazed. "We all forget. It's part of this trip to the physical plane, this dis-remembering who we really are and then working our way through to remembrance. We come into the physical to experience the senses and part of the price at the gate is to leave our true awareness behind."

"Thank you so much Guru Calzona, but that's on a mystical plane. I'm talking practical, day-to-day who-am-I stuff? And don't go tootin' off on the esoteric malarkey again. You know what I mean. What I need is some good ol' physical plane answers. Like who were those boys in the vision, and why were they trying to stop me? And by the way, that report of Docs said she died of natural causes. Well, if that's the case, then I'm telling you I caused the natural causes. I feel it in my gut."

"I don't mean to be critical, but since you're dead set on this physical-plane view of things, you might want to reconsider that you've been basing your responses on information I'm getting from the esoteric world," Anthea wanted to make sure she didn't get blamed for any misunderstandings that might arise through her revelations of visions she received while in trance state. "Everything seems to point to what Wolf was onto when he went to Washington. But it's a big state and nothing here tells us exactly where he went. Mitzy, is that map still there in the bottom of the box?" Mitzy pulled out the well-worn map of Washington.

"This is why I wanted to keep that thing handy. Do you mind if I draw on this, Magda? I really think it will give us what we need."

Magda nodded, "Go for it. Wolf's not going to complain," she jibed somewhat snidely.

Thea asked for the pendant they'd found in Wolf's treasure box. With the map spread out on the floor, she drew diagonal lines across the map and then held the pendulum up over the whole map, not unlike she'd done with the diagram that led them to the car and to Magdalena. She asked the pendulum to guide them to the area where Wolf went on his trip to Washington. The amethyst nugget swung back and forth a few times until it settled in a north south diagonal. Thea centered on the south-west end of the diagonal and got a "no" from the pendulum. She held it directly over the north-eastern end of the diagonal and got an affirmative. She hunkered down over the eastern section of the map and asked again for guidance. That was probably as narrow as they were going to get for now. "Methow Valley. Looks like its somewhere up against that range of hills."

Cybil corrected her: "The Cascade Mountains."

"So, what do you think ladies? Are we off to Washington after the ceremony?" asked Thea.

Cybil raised a halting hand. "I do not mean to disparage the dead, or minimize the intensity of your friendship with Mr. Tall Trees Magda, but being of a more logical and thereby a more cynical nature than the rest of you, I feel it's my duty to at least put this forward before we go any further on this venture. Now, don't get your knickers in a knot at what I'm about to say Magda, but I think we need to at least consider this possibility: What if Wolf killed the woman and he just told the Sheriff the story of finding the car and the woman to put the law off the track. And this whole Washington thing has nothing to do with you. It might well be another case altogether."

"Ha!" Mitzy jumped in, "Maybe it was an accident, but he caused it, so he planted those clues to lead us off the track..

I mean he'd surely try to cover up any clues that would incriminate him."

Thea reached over and tugged on Mitzy's scarf implying that she'd strangle her if she didn't shut up. "He didn't know anything about US when he wrote those notes. You're letting your imagination run away with you Mitz."

"Besides, he'd never do such a thing! You don't have any idea what he was all about!" Magda dove at Cybil and knocked her into Mitzy and the three of them tumbled into a heap. Thea and Olivia had to pull the pile apart and get Magda to the other side of the room.

Anthea plucked a vial of Rescue Remedy out of her tote; that magical, bottomless satchel which seemed to contain whatever Anthea wanted, whenever she wanted it. Right now she wanted Rescue Remedy and she insisted they each take the maximum dosage. "Calme, calme amigas. A little love vibe, please," Thea said in her most honeyed tones.

Cybil apologized to Magda. "I honestly didn't mean to upset you. You're right. We didn't know him. I just think we need to seriously consider other possibilities."

Mitzy confessed she didn't even know what happened to her. She just got caught up in the moment.

But the incident made one thing abundantly clear to Magda. Even though they professed to have seen the light, she had to show Cybil and Mitzy how wrong they were. "I'm not sure you two should take part in the ceremony. How can you honor a man you so quickly accuse?"

Calzona threw her hands up in frustration. Mitzy did the flag-waving with scarf bit and Thea realized it was meant as much for her as for Magda.

"*Anthea Calzona,*" she launched into a little self-lecture, "*do not let her addiction to negative energy drag you into that whirlpool. It's your turn to calme, calme.*" Somehow Spanish seemed more soothing than English. She took several deep breaths and turned to her friend.

"Magda, mi amiga, you're clinging to those nasty vibrations like they're some kind of life-line. I'm here to tell you it's just the opposite. Here, let me show you something. You've heard of kinesiology, right? Well, hold your arm out and see what kind of energy your inner self really believes Mitzy and Cybil are emitting. Not what your mind is telling you, but what your inner self knows."

Thea pulled Magda's arm gently up to perpendicular, "Now, resist my downward pressure. I'm not putting a whole lot on it, just a little."

Thea tested her for something negative first: "Think about your next door neighbor and how much you just <u>love</u> that dear man." Anthea gave a nod, applied two fingers and pushed lightly down on Magda's arm, which collapsed immediately. "Hah, not true. It's telling us there's so much negative energy attached to that thought that you can't hold your arm up. Now, put your arm back up and we'll see if you truly think Mitzy and Cybil are the enemy. No, wait! I've got to word that differently.....You know in your heart that Mitzy and Cybil are here to help you." Thea applied a stronger pressure, but, Magda's arm stayed right there at shoulder level.

"Now, do you see? Your body knows there is nothing but good, positive energy flowing from these women to you. So, will you please let them help you?" Magda looked sheepishly at the women and shrugged.

Thea got a strange nudge from her intuition to ask

Magda if Wolf was available to them from the beyond and could help them out. But the inclination faded. Almost like a door slamming. Clearly the Universe, or Wolf's spirit didn't want her to go there.

It was just as well because Mitzy jumped up. "Wow! I just remembered – Carmen Solares, one of my girls from the dorm, is a forensic pathologist at the University of Puget Sound in Seattle. I bet she could help us. Isn't that what they do on CSI? Pathologists solve all sorts of cold cases. I'm gonna call Carmen."

"Mitzy, that'll cost a fortune. I don't have that kind of money," Magda moaned.

Cybil intervened, "That little blue book you found says that you do. But it doesn't matter. I've got the funds and I'm itchin' to find out who our mystery woman is. So, lets not hear any of that 'not asking' for help business. Mitzy, you give Dr. Solares a call right now." No one was about to argue with Cybil LaCrosse.

Thea handed Mitzy her cell phone and in no time at all she was busy arranging a meeting with the pathologist.

While Mitzy made her call, Magda softened enough to let Cybil make amends for her dark accusations about Wolf by taking over logistics for the next day. "You can see why we call her the Field Marshall, the way she gets us all organized," Thea explained. And so it was that Field Marshall LaCrosse got a list from Olivia and was soon on the phone arranging for a small collection of people Magda deemed worthy to participate in the event on the bluff. Cybil also called for Jeff to have the plane ready the morning after next.

Mitzy came back with news that Dr. Solares couldn't

meet them till afternoon She was delivering a speech at the UW at a seminar for International Forensics. That did it. They'd head for eastern Washington first, and then they'd go to Seattle.

Chapter Fourteen

The morning dawned clear and sparkling. "Just what I ordered. Thank you Great Spirit. Father Sky. Mother Earth." Magda looked out at the cerulean sky with just a few pristine white cumulus clouds puffing here and there.

As they finished breakfast and began the clean-up, Magda informed her friends that she was going to ride out and bring back Wolf's friend, Grandmother Strong Feather, to conduct the ceremony. Thea and Cybil took Mitzy aside and encouraged her to plead with Magda to please let her ride along. "You've always wanted to go on a round-up. Pretend this is your dream come true. You always wanted to act. Act like this is really important to you. This is your chance. I know you can pull this off," Thea urged.

Mitzy growled a low growl, "You are so full of bull, Calzona. What I want is to go to a dude ranch and watch the cowboys from a fence rail. Not saddle up and ride out to work on a collection of saddle sores."

Cybil gave her a little nudge in Magda's direction. "You don't want her riding out there all alone, do you? I can't go. Look at this list of chores I've got lined up."

"And get the frown off your face. You know it makes wrinkles," Thea reminded her. Mitzy put on a happy face and went over to where Magda was doing the breakfast dishes.

"You wouldn't be up for some company, would you? I've always wanted to see the desert from horseback and this looks like a beautiful morning for a ride." Mitzy put on her consummate actor guise to say this.

"Mitzy, you are as full of bull as they are," Magda tossed her head toward Cybil and Thea, "but sure. You really think you can handle an hour in the saddle?"

That did it. Mitzy was nothing if not prone to thwart challenges to her physical capabilities. "Just lead me to my pony pod'ner."

They saddled up Wolf's pony, Buck, for Magda and Lady, a lovely gray mare for Mitzy. They also took Serenity, a pack mule with a comfortable riding gait. This was just in case Grandmother Strong Feather could be inveigled to ride. As that was highly unlikely, at least they could use the mule to carry Grandmother's medicine bundle. Again highly unlikely that she'd let them; but at least, they would be prepared.

"We'll be back by noon. That's when you're telling folks to be here, right Cybil?" Magda said. Cybil nodded the affirmation, and with that Mitzy and Magda rode out into the sage brush to bring the aged one back to lead the ceremony. It took them about half an hour to get to the little cluster of teepees in the lee of a bluff. A stand of cottonwoods rose as sentinels to mark the spot. On the east side of the encampment there was an artesian spring flowing clear water that created a tiny stream for about 15' and then sank abruptly back into the desert floor.

Grandmother was out tending her chickens, but the way she greeted Magda made it clear she already knew why Wolf's friend was there without him. In fact she had her medicine bundle ready to go. And Magda was right about the mule. Grandmother walked the red path back to the ranch. So Mitzy and Magda followed suit.

It took an hour to get back but it was an homage to Wolf every step of the way, and so time stood still while the three women stirred the dust. Well, Mitzy and the horses stirred the dust. Grandmother and Magda seemed to progress without leaving any sign of their having been that way.

While they were gone, Doc and the Sheriff arrived and took care of the manly stuff. They dug a pit big enough to accommodate the footlocker, the urn, which they retrieved from the Pontiac, and Wolf's memorabilia. The men laid on some good, aged pine for the fire and placed the footlocker and the urn at the end of the rectangular cavity. They'd gotten little to no help from Mayor Simpson, who was there with his wife Bella. But Ed Smiley of the Gazette pitched in, making sure his picture was taken by his paper's photographer. Gillian, Olivia and all of the other women from the Ranch were gathered around as Grandmother and company made their auspicious entrance.

The Juicy Crones had decided to let the Sheriff and Doc think they'd given up on having an autopsy of the aged body out of deference to Doc's sensitive nature about the issue. What they'd actually done was place a few limbs of some big old sagebrush in the trunk to approximate the heft of the body. The real remains were packed and waiting in the back of the van in a wooden crate, lined with a lovely satin shawl Olivia gave them, ready to go to Seattle.

Grandmother Strong Feather asked all of the guests to stand in a circle about four feet outside of the pit and then she turned to Magda and nodded her head. The plaintive shrill of Wolf's flute soared on the air as Magda eased her breath through the sacred bone. Wolf had decorated it, like his Wikiup, with images from nature in brown and green stains, for Mother Earth and light blue for Father Sky. Cybil began to tap lightly on the deer-hide drum which he had dressed in the colors of inner spirit, purple and lavender. Mitzy began shaking the gourd rattle as Strong Feather invoked the four directions and the elements.

She asked the participants to face the East as she called up the Grandmother Watchers. For the rising sun's direction, she waved a yellow ribbon on a sunflower stalk, and held a piece of citrine to help clear and protect the body/mind/spirit, to transmute any negative energy that might try to enter the space or disrupt Wolf's travels. She chanted, "Energy of Grandmother of the East, thank you for being here watching with us as we send our brother, Wolf Tall Trees, to join you."

Strong Feather had them turn to the south. As she held up her citrine, she intoned, "Grandmother of the South, your color is green and we thank you for all of the energy of growth and exploration you shared with our friend, Wolf Tall Trees."

Taking another turn to her right, Wolf's friend intoned, "Grandmother of the West, with these ribbons of night-sky blue and black we thank you for the introspection, the turning within of Tall Trees' sun-down years, his mature growth."

With one more turn, Strong Feather invoked, "Grandmother of the North, old age, endings, we salute you with this white scarf to help us all be ready for new beginnings. This is a time of letting go and of moving on to a new life."

This done, Grandmother Strong Feather invited the gathering to begin to walk, spiraling in toward the pit as she addressed the four cardinal points of the compass with her own rattle. "We come in the beginning with yellow and gold, we walk on the Red Road of Life. Now anyone who would like to share stories of those parts of Tall Trees' walk on the Red Road, please do so."

As Wolf's friends slowly continued to spiral in, two of the women from the Ranch had tales. Mostly these involved him teaching them new ways to look at the situations that had upset them, connecting with Mother Nature, asking for guidance and offering an act of kindness to someone, anyone, not necessarily the person who had upset them.

Anthea realized that Wolf had been teaching aspects of the Law of Attraction, of the Secret, of Deliberate Creation vs. creating our lives by default; of living in a gratitude attitude, for as long as these people had known him. Not many of them really understood all of this information, but it amounted to a nature-focused course of reprogramming neuropeptides and healing wounds of the spirit to release dis-ease from the body and mind. Everyone who was there that day had experienced the results of his knowledge, whether they truly understood it or not.

Sheriff Willery told of Wolf's incredible tracking abilities and how brave he was when coming up against the worst of society's criminals. In spite of the huge successes he'd had, all the crooks, a few killers and prison escapees he'd brought in, the stories Wolf kept in his heart were those of lost children.

Not a child but a child-like rescue had taken place when Mayor Simpson asked for help. It was back in '75. The

Mayor's wife, Biddy hadn't paid attention when Grandfather Simpson apparently walked out into the night. Well, she'd been watching Dick Van Dyke reruns and the old man kept interrupting her with stupid questions. He was senile (that's what they called it in those days). Her response was to lock him in his room. When she went to check on him after the show, he was gone. Sheriff Fox sent out a search party but nobody found any trace of Gramps, and now here it was morning, the old guy'd been out all night in just his jammies and a terry cloth robe and slippers.

It took a lot of grumbling before Sheriff Fox asked for Wolf's help, because of course no self-respecting Sheriff could ask "no 'injun fer hep," as he put it. But the Mayor insisted. He himself was suffering guilt pangs since he'd been away till one in the morning playing poker.

Tall Trees had a challenge getting started since the official search party had fairly well trampled away any viable tracks near the house. He did find out that the clever old man had climbed out on the roof and gone down a sycamore tree. But from there the tracks were pretty well stirred up.

Tall Trees refused the aid of the camping and tracking equipment the Sheriff insisted he'd need, it would just slow him down. Besides he didn't need it at all. Everything he needed was out there. The job took some doing, as old man Simpson didn't go about things the way a normal white man would. First he'd spent the night with the Cooper's dog, Boomer, curled up next to the chicken house. He apparently ate the raw egg Henny Penny had been sitting on for his breakfast, and then lit out across the desert in some kind of loop-the-loop. The old man was far more capable than his son and daughter-in-law gave him credit for. But he wasn't up to trying to sustain himself on grubs and shoots the way Wolf did. After three days, his tracks made it clear the old man was fading.

That particular tale turned out well, as Wolf found Grandfather Simpson before the coyotes got him. The Indian carried him back to town and put him gently in his bed at the Mayor's house. When Willery finished the tale, a chagrined Mayor felt he had to defend himself even at this late date, and with the Indian no longer around to make any bones about it he put his spin on it. "Hey, I was a young guy back then. We didn't know about this Old-timers disease. We just thought he liked to make Biddy crazy. I mean the old geezer kept yelling at her to get his supper and he'd already 'et. Then he hit her over the head with her own purse and all the stuff fell out on the floor behind the couch there. He got quiet for awhile and she watched her show. But he musta got bored and started up again. That's when she found out why he'd been so quiet . He'd been using her lipstick to draw on the wall. She just kinda blew her stack and locked him in his room. Who knew he'd climb out the window and shinny down a tree? Help me out here, Doc. You got some good stories 'bout ol' Tall Trees."

"You're right, Mayor. I know what you mean to say is this community owes Wolf Tall Trees plenty. My first real encounter with his special way of fixing up sick folks came about a year or so after I got back from med school. The two of us were out huntin' when the Tolliver boy came lookin' for me. Guess Sheriff Fox sent 'im out. Anyway, his pa was pretty much disabled, been hurt in a mining accident. That left everything up to the mom, Maybell. And now here's this kid Adam, 'bout seven-years old, tellin' me his ma's sick and dad's drinking and Carey, she's all of ten and she's tryin' to take care of everything but its hard with pa rantin' and crying that ma's dyin'.

"Before the kid finished tellin' us what happened Tall Trees had his medicine bundle wrapped and was up on his horse with the kid behind him and they were headed toward the Tolliver place. I had to slap leather to get to 'em before they reached the cabin."

"While I was inside trying to calm down their pa, Gunter, and get Carey busy boilin' water, (that's an old trick to keep the nurse types occupied and out of the way,) anyway she was doin' the water, and Wolf was busy showin' Adam how to talk to the mice. He figured out long 'fore I did that Maybell'd, that's the mama, got herself a case of Hanta Virus. I don't even think us pale faces knew what it was in those days. 'Course Wolf didn't call it virus. He just said the mice had to go. He drew a perimeter outside the cabin and sat down on the ground and had Adam with him and they chanted, and he played his flute and pretty soon he says its all clear."

"He comes back in the cabin and sees my hang-dog face and pats me on the shoulder and says not to worry. But I said, how'm I gonna tell these kids their ma's not gonna make it? And he says, 'who says?' And then he asks the girl for a mug of fresh water, and he dumps some gray-green powder in it and swishes it around, and gets a rag and dips it in the stuff and puts it up to Maybell's lips, and shows the kids what he's doin'. Then he tells them to keep that up every hour. They can take turns. And they should keep her forehead cool with a cloth. And most important of all they gotta start remembering how much fun they have with her when she's feelin' good. And close their eyes and picture doin' all that stuff with her, climbing trees, building a fort, swingin' on a rope and such. He had 'em practice by tellin' her what they'd all be doin' in a few days.

When they said that she couldn't hear 'em, he said she could, even if she didn't act like it. Sure 'nuf they calmed down and got into it and were tellin' her all the stuff they were gonna do as soon as she was up and around," Doc shook his head at the memory.

"So? What happened?" the query came from several directions at once.

"Well, he was absolutely right. She was good as gold in a few days. The kids invited us to go on a picnic with the whole family."

"Wait a minute Doc. What'd he give her? How'd he get some kinda medicine you didn't even know about?"

"I asked him that very question. He told me it was just some herbs he kept in his pouch. That the powder had nothing to do with her healing. It was kinda like what we call a placebo effect nowadays. He said it really happened because the kids were so sure she was gonna be fine. He said it was all about being connected to Mother Earth and trusting that the human body will heal itself if it truly is in tune with Her."

"That's a hard act to follow Doc," Mme Olivia offered. "Let me just say that I can't imagine how our world is changed with his passing. But the warm place in our hearts, the gratitude we all feel for how he looked after the lot of us for most of his life, will be with each of us for as long as we live. And, while we'll miss him, I have every confidence he'll continue to watch over us as long as we need him."

And then Magda told the story of the flute she'd been playing. Wolf had made it to honor a bird shot by a poacher, not long after she came to the Ranch. He spoke with the eagle's spirit and the bird asked to continue to soar on the earth plane even as he did in the spirit world. Wolf was then guided to use the bird's thigh bone for a flute and to decorate it with three feathers from the regal one's wing.

But before he got to that Wolf tracked the eagle's killer, found him, hauled him in and explained to Sheriff Fox that the man might just be a spy for a foreign government. Even though the eagle was not yet protected from hunters by law, (this was before the Endangered Species Act of 1973), the one who needlessly killed the eagle was incarcerated. "You see, Wolf pointed out to the Government Agents that the poacher had been on Federal Land that was posted and fenced and was an area of high security. If they wouldn't protect the symbol of our nation, they sure as shootin' would protect whatever secret they had goin' on out there. Wolf, being a tracker for the FBI, had the clearance to be there that the poacher didn't. Once the man was locked up, Wolf was able to fulfill his promise to the bird. It would soar again in the music played on the flute," Magda came out of her reverie just as the whole group arrived at the edge of the pit.

Thea, in the soothing voice of her meditative invocations asked them all to lend support for a moment during which she encouraged Magda to connect with Wolf. "Visualize him showing you what to do, where he would go next in this search for your past."

"I can't do that. I never see anything when they tell you to visualize."

"Okay, so think about what you would see if you could. Let it come to you. We all ask Wolf Tall Trees over the coming days, show us how to go. Guide our foot steps; help us to move forward with your spirit leading the way. Help our friend Magda to be open to your guidance. Magda, you already know what to do. Now your friend will give you the courage to move on."

Magda opened her eyes and looked out into the darkening desert sky. Suddenly, she gasped. When Thea reached out to steady her, she pointed the flute. Everyone turned to follow her direction and there he stood, a lone gray wolf at the end of the butte. He bayed at Father Sky, then turned and trotted into the desert. The collectively held breath sighed after him. Grandmother smiled, looked at Thea and nodded. "He is with you."

Doc Willery would never admit it but he was spooked. "That can't be a wolf Magda. We don't have wolves round here any more. They got bounty-hunted to extinction. You know that. We've got coyotes but not wolves. And wolves have a more soulful, longer howl, more eerie." He was trying real hard to convince himself that the creature was a coyote.

"Anyone think that wasn't a wolf?" the Sheriff asked. There was utter silence. Anthea recalled the day Raelene told Magda she'd seen a big silver-gray dog with yellow eyes behind her. Yes, Tall Trees was definitely watching over his friends.

One by one, Wolf's friends carefully chose an item from the basket Cybil and Thea had brought to the ceremony. They dropped these items onto the pile of brush and cottonwood Doc and the Sheriff had gathered and laid earlier. Flames were already licking at the footlocker, which supposedly contained the bones of the old woman Wolf had communed with for so many years. The fire would send the mementos, along with Wolf, on his new journey.

Magda had brought his deerskin leggings, wrapped in a buffalo hide she'd taken off the wall of his Wikiup earlier, and let the bundle drop into the pit. When the fire banked down,

Magda placed the urn in the pit and then Doc and the Sheriff, the Mayor and Smiley all shoveled the red dirt into the pit and that was all there was left of Wolf Tall Tree's earth journey. Grandmother Strong Feather had already begun her walk home. She had her own way of communing with the Wolf she called friend.

The guests made their way back to the Ranch House where Magda stood tall, squared her shoulders and felt quite strong saying good-bye to Doc and the Sheriff.

Then the Juicy Crones returned to the Wikiup. They were indeed going to follow Wolf's guidance and track where he'd gone. They would find out what Wolf had found out about Magda's origins and the identity of the woman in the trunk on the luggage rack of the car.

The search began with a re-visit to Wolf's notes. Amongst the spiral binders they found out that the young buck, (for that was what he was in those days), had talked to the car, asking for guidance while he worked to restore it. It led him to faint tracings of the name Magdalena on one door. This he re-painted in gold leaf in letters reminiscent of the period of the vehicle. The car told him it belonged to the old woman, but the girl was Magda, too. This was a piece of the puzzle he worried over for years. Reading this, Magda became even more introspective. Was the woman her mother? And was she then named after her? But according to Doc she'd have been too old for that — Grandmother? Who was she?

Magda placed the evidence box on a shelf next to the stack of notebooks and headed for the door. It was time to prepare for their journey the next day. As they left, Cybil pulled out a small wooden crate they'd stashed under some bedding and, with reverence, she carried it to the car. After the

Sheriff had left the day before, they had taken a sampling of Wolf's ashes from the urn and placed them in this small crate. The plan was to fly them, along with the purloined little skeleton, to Seattle. They had already stashed that in the van.

The first thing they'd ask Dr. Carmen Solares for was a DNA match with Magda. And then they wanted to see what other information the forensic pathologist could ferret out about both of these people who held clues to Magda's past.

Chapter Fifteen

At 4:30 the next morning the tracking party, with the crate and the box in the van, was ready to head out. Of course, Magda had gotten up about half an hour earlier to fix a selection of breakfast burritos which she packed in a hotbox. That, and two extra large thermoses of Fair Trade Guatemalan coffee, along with some raw cream and some chocolate sticks for dipping, completed the repast.

Cybil did a thorough pre-departure check of the vehicle, including the satellite dish. When she was convinced it was ready for take off they loaded up, this time with Thea at the wheel. Once they were under way Anthea had a contribution to the morning's festivities: she'd had another vision, very different from the rest. "No girl, no body, no car."

"What makes you think it's connected to the others?" Cybil wanted to know. "The period. It looked the same as the others – late '60s." Thea told them what she saw: *"Two boys standing next to a work bench, in a chemistry lab with gurgling retorts, over Bunsen burners, and then slow drips from the distiller into a cup."*

While she was explaining it Cybil's right brain grabbed for a logical handle, "Maybe its got something to do with the pathology tests we're going to have done? They use those retorts, those glass bowls, don't they?"

"I don't think it was Dr. Solares. Remember what I said, two boys, '60s' era, not CSI."

As Thea drove, Cybil pulled out her laptop and googled the area where they were headed and put through a text message to a car rental company in Twisp, WA. The map indicated this was the closest town to where they were headed. Cybil found the town website and perused the latest news, if you could call it that. Fiddler's End had a population of 872 if you didn't count the county. It was situated on Hwy 20 up along the eastern side of the north Cascades.

Posted on the town's web bulletin board Cybil read out for the others to hear: "Cowboy extravaganza fund raiser, Sat. at Hatton's barn. House sitter wanted, must love geese and goats, 555.2160. Husky needs home without chickens, call Sammy Gloor. Good talker needs ride to Seattle next Wednesday, josh@fiddler.gov. Quilting Bee will be at Bertha Coe's this week due to Charlotte Schmidt's gotta go baby-sit the grand kids in Selah. Propane stove cheap, see Zeke at Schmidt's Variety Store. '62 Harley in a basket – free to loving home, call Chris. 555.7143.' Well, there you are ladies. Fiddler's End in local blog speak. Somebody up there is a farmer/webmaster."

At 6:30 in the morning, Las Vegas was as quiet as it ever got. It took no time at all to get through the city to the airport. Jeff was there, the plane was all checked out and ready to go. As they flew out of Las Vegas North, Cybil headed the Cessna for the Pacific Northwest.

Magda was still trying to figure out how a chemistry lab had anything to do with her. But then she didn't know if she'd had chemistry in school, or if she even went to school.

Her frustration set Thea thinking how grateful she was to be able to recall her own early years. To hear her grandmother Brigit, whom she called Gran, tell it, Anthea's mom, Fiona, was a winsome Irish, upper-class lass who ran off with a tall, dark and dashing young gypsy named Rory. He was Brigit's son, Thea's Da. Fiona was disowned by her family for this irrational act.

In due time, Rory and Fiona had fraternal twins, Iona the wee one, and Anthea, like her Da, was quite the big one. When the babes were born, in the fall of '38, the snobbish upper-crust Grandmother, Branwyn Sullivan, deigned to allow an audience. Looking down her patrician nose at the babes, she deemed Iona acceptable. After all she looked just like Fiona as a babe. But Anthea appalled her delicate sensitivities. "Must take after that thieving gypsy who lured you off," was her pronouncement as she glowered at Fiona.

Everything was going along merrily for the little vagabond family, right smack up to the day that Rory decided to cut across an open field in the territory about 30 miles south of Belfast. Rory had no truck with either side of the 'troubles' in northern Ireland, but when he entered that field, both sides decided he was fair game. Brigit had warned him the fae folk couldn't protect him with all those bullets flying about. But he was a stubborn one where his girls were concerned. He had some fine tin-ware to sell in Glen Ivy, and he wanted the money for his wee lassies. Wouldn't you know he'd step right into the line of fire.

With Rory gone, Fiona had no intention of staying with the gypsies. She took tiny Iona to help her wedge her way back into the Manor house. As she left the camp, she told

Brigit she'd send for the "other one" when the time was right. That time never seemed to come, which left Anthea, much to her delight, to be raised by her Gran. Brigit was not only a gypsy, she was totally involved in the other world: faeries, elves and "the knowing."

Despite her precarious upbringing with her gypsy Gran, Anthea had one oddly sophisticated entertainment. She would sneak into the motion picture theater in whatever town they camped near. Many's the time she stood, looking pathetic, outside the theater, and told the kindhearted theater goers that she was waiting for her "mither" who had gone to see the movie but didn't have enough money to take her in, too.

As the Irish tend to be kind hearted souls, the gangly girl with the mop of carrot-colored curls, always found someone who would pay her way. She would go into the darkened theater, sit down next to some unsuspecting woman and pretend to be so glad to be with her "mum." Thus, she learned all about life outside the gypsy camp from Rosalind Russell, Kate Hepburn, Betty Hutton and Lucille Ball, amongst others. Men were all modeled after Clark Gable, Spencer Tracy, Gary Cooper, Lawrence Olivier, and David Niven.

Thinking of the memories that made her life so rich, Anthea could only hope that uncovering Magda's youth would prove as nourishing for her. Whether it was positive or negative though, the only way to help get her new friend out of the morass of her misery was to find out what her blocks were. Even if it was horrific enough to have caused her to lock it away, they would all be there to support her as she shed light on the black hole in her memory. Then again, Anthea knew she had to tread lightly as the choice had to be Magda's.

Their flight took them over the east side of Mt. St.

Helens. Captain LaCrosse directed their gaze to the wisps of steam coming from the great crater and then she had Jeff take over the controls. "Hope you don't mind if we veer off just a mite. I can never resist takin' the scenic route."

Shortly they were passing west of Mt. Rainer over Washington's capital, Olympia, and on out over the Puget Sound, Alki point, Elliott Bay. Cybil pointed off into the distance, "Mt. Baker and the Canadian border. And just this side of Baker is where we put in our pre-fab houses to replace the homes that washed out in that horrible flood we had last fall. We got 'em all up and folks living in them in two weeks. The stick and mortar contractors are still working on theirs."[10]

To the west ever so slightly lay her beloved Whidbey Island. "Just up island about ten miles is The Eyrie. That's what I call home when I'm up here. Totally green. It's even got photovoltaic panels for windows and sky lights so we get sunshine, and electricity at the same time. And we've got a garden on the roof. You'll all have to visit when this over." And then they headed east over the Cascades.

Shortly, Jeff was making contact with the tower at Methow Valley State airfield, some 100 miles north east of Seattle. They cruised down the 5000' runway to the hanger where they were met by the car rental guy, Ken Knightly. Leaving Jeff to mind the plane and the two precious containers, they made their way toward Fiddler's End.

Knightly instructed them to take Highway 20 past the welcome sign reading: Farmer's Market Saturdays May-Oct. 10-3, Rotary, Kiwanis, Elks etc. meet in Twisp till Oct.; Church Services at Fiddler's Grange, non-denominational, Sundays, 11 a.m., testimonials Wed. 7 P.M. Before they drove off Cybil asked the rental agent if he'd seen an Indian with braids, about 70-something, on an Indian motorcycle anytime in the recent past?

"Sorry Ms. LaCrosse. Sounds like a standup kinda guy, but I don't recall such a fella. Howsomever, I'll ask around and let you know if I find out anything. Got your contact info right her on the contract." Knightly was clearly proud of his ability to text message. He tipped his cap and sent them off down the road.

In no time at all they were driving into Fiddler's End. As they rode into town Cybil took note of a Honda Civic with an Early Bird Real Estate sign on the driver's door, parked in front of the Two Toad Café.

"Hah, that's the cafe I found when I Googled Fiddler's End this morning. My farmer friend, Roger, told me if I wanted to find the locals, look for the place with the cheapest coffee."

The parking spaces were filled with pick-up trucks, some mud-spattered, some shiny and bright. They were all pulled up to a hitching post that ran along the boardwalk from one end of town to the other... all of about seven store fronts. "Looks like the northern version of Dos Lobos," Mitzy laughed. Cybil pulled into the spot right next to the Early Bird.

"Why on earth would you want the cheapest coffee?" Magda asked indignantly, her sense of culinary perfection gravely bruised.

"Like Roger said, find the farmers hang out, it'll be the most likely place to find out what we want." As usual, no one was going to argue with Cybil's logic.

They got out of the car and stood surveying the establishment. The swinging doors beckoned. They stepped inside and Cybil was proved right, they'd found the spot where the ol' timers hung out. A whole flock of 'em roosted at one round table, all gettin' their refills, probably number three or four, from Earlene, or so it said on the name tag pinned to the starched hankie on her equally starched apron. The women found themselves a four-top and sat down.

Next to the window, there was a book case with well-worn copies of western classics and a sign that read "Use 'em, don't abuse 'em" which Cybil took to include the stack of local Fiddler's Gazettes she leafed through. She pulled out a copy of the local paper with a amused look on her face, laid it flat on the table and began going through it.

As Earlene handed them menus Mitzy couldn't resist asking: "Why Two Toad?"

"Tourist," Cybil hissed at Mitzy.

"Goes back 'bout 42-years to be sorta eggs-act. Sissy in there," she pointed to the pass-through and into the kitchen where a gnarly-haired little bird of a woman was banging pots and clunking dishes. "Sissy's kids wanted a pond and some frogs, so she dug a hole out back there. This here was her cabin. Wasn't so grand back then."

The women looked around at the hewed plank tables, the second hand captain's chairs, the nicked counter, well-worn hardwood floors, the walls covered with pre-fifties posters. Oh it was grand.

"Anyways, Sissy went out back and dug a trench to the River there and the hole for the pond and then she says to the kids; 'Ok, you guys get the frogs.' Well, they come home with buckets of frogs and the place was ahoppin'. And Ol' Man Kitchen says something about them Frenchies he met when he fought in the big war; they'd a loved to eat all them frogs. That's why they called them guys frogs. Anyway, the next thing you know Sissies got herself a recipe and she's cookin' frogs legs, and the kids managed to hold out the two toads that got mixed in with the frogs and there you are."

While Mitzy was getting this lowdown Cybil had been listening in on the morning catch-up conversation amongst the cover-all contingent. She reported to her friends, "The fellow standing off to the side of the table tellin' the story, that's Turly Early. His brother, Clem Early, over in Twisp, was trying to help the trash collectors with that new-fangled fork thingie and his pant leg got caught and he went flying up into the truck. Clem's over in Wanachee at the hospital for x-rays. As for Nestor there, his grandkids are getting him all hooked up to the internet so's he can keep track of the commodities, know how to price his crops. Banger got a new John Deer, well not really new, but '85 which is almost new for him."

"I'm so glad we're up to speed on the locals Cybil, but none of that is helpin' us any. We need to zero in on this place where Wolf was trackin'. See if there's a link to Magda's origins," Thea insisted.

Just then there was a little ruckus at the round table and one of the John Deers shooed the Early Bird off. "Go on, gurly, shouldn't you outta be over with the ladies?"

With as much dignity as he could muster, the dump-truck story teller sauntered over, pulling his business card from his breast pocket. Where in heaven's name did he find a seersucker suit in this day and age? wondered Cybil.

"Howdy, ladies. Turly Early's the name. Folks call me Burly," he grinned and gave his abundant belly a little Oliver Hardy riff. His nails were polished. His hair well coifed. "You just drivin' through or you come to check us out? If it's the former, you have a nice trip. If it's the latter, I'm your man. Early Bird Real Estate. I cover the whole Methow Valley and I always get the best places 'cause I got connections to all the old timers here-'bouts," he nodded toward the round table. He did a double take when he spotted Mitzy, "Hey, aren't you? Naw, you can't be. Too young. But you sure look a lot like Grace's mom on Will and Grace." Mitzy preened appropriately at being taken for Debbie Reynolds. "Jack's my hero. He gets away with everything," said Burly.

Anthea tried to sidle back to the subject, "Well, as a matter of fact," but before she could finish her sentence Burly had plopped his brief case on their table, opened it out, and ordered: coffee and Sissie's giant cinnamon buns with extra maple topping, lots of raisins and walnuts, heated, with butter. "They are simply divine," he said as he indicated 'all around' to Earlene and pulled a pad of tear-off maps of the local area out of his case.

Just what Thea wanted. Thank you Universe. In that moment of gratitude, she asked for inspiration on how to further pursue their quarry without causing a stir. After all, if Wolf had been onto something when he came here, if indeed this is where he landed, well then someone around here might have been responsible for that body in the trunk. She did a BrainGym doodle on her napkin and inspiration flowed right to her: "Yes, a friend of mine was up here not long ago crusin' on his motorcycle. He told me this was a good area for some people I know in California. They live on the land and do organic farming. They like to say they've pulled together an anti-retirement community. They're thinking of franchising." Thea was pleased that she hadn't even had to shade the truth.

Not too much anyway.

"Hah, you mean what they're callin' a eco-village these days?" Turly laughed.

"I guess you could say that," she responded.

"We already got it. Your folks down there are a little late comin' to the party for a buncha Californicators." Earlene smacked him with a menu.

"So, Mr. Early," Anthea urged him forward.

"You can call me Turly, or you can call me Burly, just don't call me Surly," He laughed a hearty belly bouncer.

"Okay," Thea went on, "Turly, would it be okay with you if I marked on that map?"

"No problemo, little lady," he tore one off the pad and handed it to her. She promptly drew lines across it in the now familiar pie pieces, and then took off her pendant and held it over the map. A quiet settled over the hustle and bustle of the Two Toad Café. The farmers all pretended not to be the least bit interested. The pendant swung out over the map and settled into a north-east swing or the south-west if you looked at it that way. She zeroed in on the north-east. Next Thea held the pendulum over the end of the line. It swung out and then started doing a sort of mobius swing. "Great goddess, I've never seen it do anything like that before. So, what's this area out here?" she said pointing at the place where the pendant continued its odd looping.

"Hah! There's two places in this valley nobody's ever gonna sell and you picked 'em both. Funny thing. That's the spot where those hippies had a real commune back in the '60s. The ones that stayed are the ones I tol' you about. The ones doin' this organic stuff and sellin' big time to the high-end restaurants all the way to Seattle. They built up a buncha these eco-cabins. SIPs I think they call 'em." Cybil's ears pricked up, but before she could launch into a question and answer, Turly was off and running.

"I was just a little kid back when the big fight was goin' on between the religious kooks, and the hippies right next to 'em. The religious ones, that's the *Shepherd's Flock,*" he looked around to make sure there were no *Shepherds* around now. He tapped one area where the pendant quivered, "It's writ big in valley history. But lemme give you a little local color first."

Cybil stopped him before he launched a recap starting with the Mastodon bone and a tooth that were the centerpiece of the museum display (said museum being the back wall of the coffee shop). 14,000 years was a little further back than they needed to go. Besides, Earlene brought withering looks to their part of the room from the Oshkosh brigade when she said everybody knew Clem brought that stuff from Sequim, out on the Olympic Peninsula. They were supposed to be on loan from his brother-in-law, but they'd been in Fiddler's End for 35 years. Now, they were considered local artifacts and they even used the Mastodon theme in the town logo, so they could hardly take them back.

"Would you be kind enough to show us the way to this place, Sunny Acres it says?" Turly was quick to nod in the affirmative to Thea's request. While he gathered his briefcase, Anthea made a check motion to Earlene followed by a little come-hither gesture with her fingers as she stood up and tried to head her friends out of the Two Toad Café. As they left Cybil sauntered over to the round table and asked if any of the gentlemen could tell her how to find the Mayor. There was a shift in the atmosphere.

"That'd be Warren Oakley, the guy in the John Deere cap," Turly said. They all had Deere caps. She guessed the one who tipped his head her direction must be the Mayor. Cybil folded the Fiddler's Gazette she'd picked up earlier from the free-be pile to feature the half-page photo of the Governor and Senators' Patty Murray and Maria Cantwell with Cybil. She placed it on the table virtually in their faces. The headline said <u>LaCrosse Supports the The Real Kinder/Gentler Government.</u>

It tickled Cybil because she knew that these men were the very sort against whom she'd been doin' political warfare for twenty years. Power is power, and she loved wielding it any chance she got. She'd already admitted it was one of her addictions.

To the Mayor she directed, "You be sure to take good care of Turly here. The Governor and I will be keepin' our eyes on him. He's a real asset to your little community. You should be proud of him." As she passed Earlene she dropped a $100 bill on the waitress's tray and quietly said, "Give the gents our cinnamon rolls. They look terrific, but we ate on the plane. Tell the boys it's Turly's treat... and keep the change." She put her arm around Turly's shoulder as she voice-dialed on her cell phone, "Margot, Cybil LaCrosse here. Yes, would you be a darling and have Sean sign an 8x10 glossy from Will & Grace. Yes: To Burly, any friend of Cybil's is a friend of Jack's. Thanks ... you just ship it to Turly Early c/o Early Bird Real Estate in Fiddler's End, WA.

By then they were out the door and headed to where "X marked the spot" on Turly's map. But not without Magda and Mitzy stopping short to ask, "How the hell did you do that newspaper thing?" Cybil looked knowingly at Thea, "It's what she's been saying all along, Mags. It's your energy at work. You made your intention known, you got clear that you wanted to follow through on Wolf's tracks and were willing to go where that led."

Thea intoned, "You had no idea how to do that but you've kept that in mind, even if its on a subliminal level, and Source is showing the way. Every step of this journey is about your willingness to be led. And gratitude, Lady." Thea flipped the heartful-of-gratitude pendant[11] Magda had worn faithfully since she'd put it around her neck at the start of their journey, "Doesn't it feel terrific?"

"What I loved most was the date," Cybil grinned, "November of last year. Believe me, I was as surprised as you when I opened the newspaper and that was right in front of my face. I wasn't about to let a good thing get away from me. Now Turly, you going to take us out to this farm?"

"Well, it's not any commune you'd imagine. There's only three of the original bunch left, but new folks seem to come and go. Co-operative 'stead of commune. That's all I know about. And, like I said, they've built it into a kind of little village."

"Shouldn't we call first?" Magda was starting to get a little edgy.

Turly flipped open his cell phone and did the speed dial bit. "Hey Terra, that you? Course I know it's you 'cause I'm the one that called. So this here's me, Turly Early. Sounds like you're out on the tractor," he shouted. "Yeah, well, I got some folks'd like to see the place....Yep, just to get a gander at your operation... Okay, sure 'nough. We're just leaving town. Meet ya at the barn." He flipped his phone closed. "Terra's sorta the boss out there. Least wise she's the most bossy. Anyway she's just headed in from the field for lunch. We're all invited. You best not be too full for Allegra's victuals. They're all mighty proud of their harvest. Follow me, ladies," he instructed as he ushered Cybil into his Honda with the Early Bird Special magnetic ad on the side, and drove off down the road.

As the other three were getting into the rental car, Mitzy mentioned to Thea, out of Magda's hearing, that she felt like they were being watched, "and I don't mean by the faeries or the Universe." Thea nodded in acknowledgment but kept them moving.

"By the way, wasn't the word 'hippies' on Wolf's map?" Thea asked.

Chapter Sixteen

Within ten minutes Turly pulled off the highway onto a side road and a few miles beyond that he turned down a long dirt drive. Just as he'd said, like a mini-village, a cluster of little cottages, each with its own yard and garden stood off to one side of a pond, a large out building and a gigantic barn. A Volkswagen van and a VW bug with flower-power and psychedelic paint jobs paid homage to the Love Generation. A big red Super A International tractor came charging up from the back forty and headed straight for the equipment shed which stretched along about 100' next to one of the fields.

As the visitors got out of the cars a pack of dogs greeted them with barks and wiggles, a cock crowed from his perch on the barn's roof, and a pygmy goat 'goosed' Mitzy, if a goat can goose, that is. A tall fellow in the ubiquitous John Deere duck-billed gimmie cap, a plaid shirt, cut-off jeans with room to spare in the tail-gate department, and well-worn handmade sandals, came out of the barn to see what the commotion was all about.

Turly started the introductions, "Tranquill Seaforth, these here ladies come up from California," but before he could finish, the Juicy Crones were totally distracted as the tractor maneuvered its cultivator back into a small space between two other pieces of equipment. A fellow ran over out of another building and disengaged it. The tractor pulled forward and deftly eased into a space between two other tractors. They watched as the driver dismounted and strode lithely across the drive, taking off her work gloves and stuffing them in her jeans' back pocket.

With a few swipes at the dust on her thighs she stuck out a friendly hand, "Howdy, I'm Terra. Welcome to Sunny Acres."

The women introduced themselves and when Quill shook hands with Magda Lindal and heard her name Thea noticed a look of puzzlement crossed his face, but it passed as quickly as it had come. "Call me Quill."

Then began an odd duet with first Quill and then Terra filling in a sentence, each finishing off for the other.

Quill: "You're just in time for supper."

Terra: "Quill's wife Allegra fixed up a big batch of ratatouille today. We get the farm team leaders together…"

Quill: "…once a week to talk over what's going on. Grow everything we eat 'round about here. Well, not the olives and olive oil.

Terra: "That's from a sister co-op farm down in Temecula, in California…[12] in your neck o' the woods. The goat cheese comes from a joint-venture dairy down the road, and cow's milk from across the way."

Quill: "We do an exchange. They get grain from us, we get carcasses for the compost, along with other cow stuff, cheese, milk, butter and ice cream."

Terra: "That long burm out there behind the tractor shed, that's the compost." Terra indicated a mound about 200' feet long and about three feet high.

"We're headed over there." Quill pointed to a sturdy farm house. "We use it as a meetin' hall and there's extra rooms for visitors and hands. Alli still can't cook for less'n 50, so we got plenty," he said, making sure they understood they were invited to join the farmers' lunch.

"'Course we've got the boys up in the hills back there. We usually fix up a batch of left-overs once or twice a week and mule-pack it up in to 'em. They're some of the fellas from Viet Nam that just never quite made it all the way back." Terra explained.

"You'd be amazed what they set up for themselves back in there. Now they got a whole new batch filtering in from I-raq. So young. So wounded. It just breaks your heart. Alli'd like to take 'em all in. Thing is, they don't want to come in... even here," Quill shook his head.

By the time the duet had finished their routine, Quill was ushering the covey of visitors past a sage-green cottage with lilac shutters and window boxes full of cascading snapdragons and pansies and petunias. It had a beautifully painted little sign that said "Sage Cottage."

At that point Turly excused himself to head back to town. He wanted to think about how he could maximize his new relationship with the Mayor and the town council. And he wanted to figure out just the right place on his office wall to hang his much anticipated 8x10 Jack glossy.

The group arrived at the farm house, "Built in 1872," said a little marker sign. Everybody left their dusty work boots or sandals, as the case may be, in the mud room and entered through the kitchen. Thea took note of a pair of boots looking very much like the one in the trunk. She elbowed Cybil to check it out.

Their timing was perfect. Allegra Seaforth came out drying her hands on her apron. She matched her surroundings to perfection; plump, cozy, bubbling warmth, dressed in classic hippie tie-dye, fringed and embroidered, rings on her bare toes. She was directing the various crew members, handing out tasks for getting the big oak table ready for them all to sit down. While Thea and Cybil joined in to dole out the silver-ware, Mitzy and Magda put the plates and napkins out. Terra washed up in the mud room sink and was ready just in time to join the circle and offer gratitude for all who helped provide the bounty and especially to their favorite cook. Cheers for Alli brought a blush to her already rosy cheeks.

"Eating is a celebration of our connection to Mother Earth, and to each other, so everybody better dig in and show your appreciation," Terra invited the guests to toast with wine from home-grown grapes.

Quill spooned a mound of sweet brown rice onto each platter and handed it to Alli who ladled on the fragrant stew of vegetables.

"Mmmm, zucchini, eggplant, bell peppers, onions and tomatoes; a nice grassy green olive oil, salt, garlic, oregano, turmeric, tarragon? What am I missing?" asked Magda.

Alli smiled, "just the dill and marjoram. That's amazing. You make it too? Where'd you get your recipe?"

"As a matter of fact..." Magda began but didn't finish. An odd buzz washed over her as she sat amongst these people, in this setting and tapped into a deeply buried memory.

Thea recognized Maggie's reaction as the queasy one she'd experienced earlier when the questions touched on something too close to the truth. She went inside her psyche and asked her guides what to do. *'There is an energy here that is too much all at once. Distract her, generalize,'* is what Anthea got. She turned to Quill and asked him to tell them about the origins of the place.

Quill started, "In 1872..."

Terra jumped to interrupt him, "I think they mean our history, not the whole place, Quill." She took over, "We'd all opted out of the so-called civilized life of the big city. Allegra from Chicago, me from Portland, Quill from Atlanta. Birch Farber found this place. The Lowes who owned it were gettin' along in years and needed help. Birch figured out a way to let them stay on and we'd farm it and make payments to buy them out along the way. He was from Boston I think. Birch that is. No Cambridge. One of those brainiac places. He took care of all the business around here back then."

Quill resumed, "Anyway, we met up when some of us were living in a commune in Portland and came up to Seattle for what was probably the first Love In in the Pacific North West. Met some other kids camped out on Mercer Island. You could do that in those days – camp out in the forest I mean. There was a lot more forest back then. Anyway, Birch got this idea when he read 'bout this place in the local alternative newspaper. How the couple were trying to keep things going with just the two of them since their son died in Korea." Quill clearly loved his role as story teller.

As so often is the case, his spouse wanted to make sure he got it right: "So a bunch of us piled in his flatbed and drove out here. It was a lot longer drive in those days, but it was spring time. We fell in love with the place and moved right on in. Birch took care of the paper work, like Terra said. Some of us wrote to friends, and pretty soon there were about 20 of us. In a sense we saved the farm for the Lowes." Alli blushed to have been so bold as to claim credit.

"Anyway, the Seattle Post Intelligencer did an article on us." Quill was back on task, "We were pretty full of ourselves. A bunch of us kids were about four months into trying to figure out how to use a hoe, let alone a tractor. And then this older woman shows up. She'd seen the article and hitched a ride out. Like I said, she was older than any of us, but she had spirit. Fit right in. Had lots of know-how about communal farming. Built the first yurt any of us ever saw. I don't recall a last name, just said her name was Magdalena."

Magda did the "deer in the headlights" look, her eyes rounder than silver dollars. "Magdalena?" she whispered and flopped back in her chair.

Mitzy grabbed for the scarf at her neck but found she hadn't worn one that day, so she did the next best thing and grabbed for the scarf around Thea's pile of curls. The scarf came right off. And along with it came her hair piece, a cascade of curly extensions. Thea leapt out of her chair and made for Mitzy who in turn leapt up and started to run around the table. "Of all the nasty little twits, you take the cake, you clumsy, dunder-headed," Thea ran out of expletives as she began beating Mitzy over the head with her napkin. Mitzy swooped down, plucked Thea's red mop off the floor and plopped it back on her friend's head. "Oh, that is such a totally metaphysical response Calzona," she said sarcastically. "What would the Dalai Lama do in a case like this?"

Thea looked around the room. They all broke into whooping laughter, and she couldn't help but join them. Sucking up her diaphragm, standing tall and straight, she settled the combs to once again hold her hair firmly in place, and with all the dignity she could muster, she turned to Magda, who was still in a state of shock, and began to intone: "Take a nice deep breath, let it out, breathe again, slowly, keep going, you're doing fine," Anthea lulled her into as relaxed a state as was possible given the circumstances.

"Uh-huh, she said she was a Hungarian freedom fighter," Quill confirmed with pride, picking up where they'd left off.

"Hungarian, like goulash?" Mitzy asked softly.

"And *paska*?" teased Thea.

Maggie weakly stirred out of her dumbfounded state, "My god, I killed a Hungarian freedom fighter."

Noting her pale look Allegra got up and poured some tea for Magda, "It's chamomile. Are you sure you wouldn't like to lie down? We've got three bedrooms upstairs. It can't have been the food." Poor Alli was clearly a mother hen with a chick in trouble. It would have mortified her if her food were responsible for this distress.

"No, no, thank you. I'll be all right. It's just all this information and confusion. Please go on."

As Terra continued the farm hands quietly cleared the table and dispersed.

Picking up the story tentatively, Terra kept an eye on Magda to see how she reacted to each step of the tale. "Once she got here she said she felt like she'd finally come home. It took a long time to get all the pieces of her story out of her.

But if you could get her going she was a great tale teller. So, like Quill said, she was an escapee, which musta been hard 'cause she sure wasn't any spring chicken."

Quill moved over to sit closer to Magda, wanting to somehow comfort her. "She said she was a writer back there, but everybody had to put in their time on the commune. She and Janos, her second husband, chose the farm rather than the factory and she was glad they did. At least it meant they got better food than the people in the cities. Besides, it was only for two weeks out of every four. The rest of the time she was in Budapest doing her journalism thing."

"By the time the revolution came she'd become proficient in hand-to-hand combat and the use of firearms. Everybody knew some day the real Hungarians would get into it with the army run by the Soviets. Being a journalist she was hooked into the underground, and she and Janos were at Radio Budapest when the students tried to take it over to broadcast their demands about reforms." Terra looked to Alli and Quill to see if she was getting it right.

Quill took over, "Some of them got inside the station, but then the State Police came and fired on the demonstrators. The situation got better for a few weeks when the Russians backed off, but then they came back with tanks and that was when Magdalena's husband was killed, along with hundreds of others. She barely managed to escape." Quill became very pensive as he recalled the evenings when Magdalena told stories that kept the idealists mesmerized.

Alli was pleased to pick up the more pleasant aspect of the story. "The Red Cross and the Austrian Army established refugee camps in Traiskirchen and Graz, Austria. Magdalena was there for almost a year when Mrs. Roosevelt visited. They met and the first lady encouraged her to use her writing skills to tell the world her first-hand experiences. After all she was an English speaking journalist and Eleanor recognized the value of getting the truth about the Soviets out to the world. Magdalena did just that, writing and giving lectures from India to Ceylon and Hong to Japan."

"Why'd she go East? Why not to England or America?" Mitzy wondered.

"After her first husband and her son died in London back in the war in 1916, she'd gone to the Far East to be as far away as possible from the reminders. So the '57 –'58 trip was a kind of touching bases with healing memories," Alli replied.

"She wasn't just telling the story to the outside world, she was keeping her mind busy picking up information as she went. Zen, haiku, feng shui, tantric sex, you name it," Terra explained. "That's how she said she coped with the devastation of her life."

"Whoa, whoa right there," Magda interrupted Terra, "you mean this Hungarian woman, who probably cooked goulash, knew about Tantric Sex way back in the '50s?"

" Jeeze Louise, Mags, you're the one says its been around for 5,000 years," Mitzy interrupted the interruption.

"Go on, Terra," Thea encouraged.

"Well, it fit right in with what was happening at the time for us. You know, The Love Generation and all that. Anyway she taught all us lovers how to make love. And she was not shy about it. She'd teach anyone who might come seeking a 'different kind of enlightenment' as she called it. We were all just looking for a different kind of high. It suited us fine. We never did know much about the little girl, but One seemed to have no qualms about letting her in on the ancient secrets."

Magda nearly leapt out of her chair: "Little girl, what little girl? And what do you mean One?"

Terra apologized, "Sorry about that, but that's about how she turned up. The girl, I mean. Out of the blue. After Magdalena had been here a little while, this kid would just kind of appear and spend the day helping out around here, especially whatever Magdalena was doing. And then she'd disappear. We guessed she was about 10 or 12 years old."

"We knew she couldn't come from next door 'cause they never let the kids out of that place. It was buttoned up tighter than a homophobic preacher's ass. Ooops, sorry for the crude stuff there, but those folks could rile up even a stoner like me... like I was in those days," Quill actually blushed at his confession. "Anyway, we sort of guessed that she was a niece or granddaughter of Magdalena's who ran away from a very abusive father. And hey, some of us could relate."

Alli shushed him, "One day the child just up and moved in with Magdalena and that was it. She called herself Magda Too. That's why Magdalena became Magda One. We all just called the child "Too." Too learned everything quick. She was smart as a whip. And she was a hard little worker."

"Grew up into a beauty too." Quill snuck a peek over at Magda to see if indeed it might be her. Alli elbowed him. Thea recalled his first reaction on meeting Magda.

He went right on, "Everything seemed to be just fine, and then one day when they'd been here about seven or eight years they just up and left in the middle of the night. No good-bye, no nothing. Just gone."

Alli recalled something odd though. "I remember being surprised they didn't clean up where one of 'em upchucked just before they left. They were always such neat-nicks."

"They drove off in that '31 Pontiac One called the Cricket 'cause the door kinda chirped when you opened it.'" Quill said.

"31 Pontiac??!!. That's it! That was <u>me</u> with this Magda One for sure!" Magda was out of her mind with excitement. And then the bubble burst, "so I <u>was</u> the reason she died." Thea watched in dismay as Magda settled back into her old rut.

Mitzy didn't have the heart to wave her scarf.

"Died, what do you mean died?" Terra asked. And then she cut off the potential answer, " Don't be silly. You wouldn't have harmed a hair on her head. You two were close as peas in a pod. If you really are Too. She was like a grandma to you. You were her shadow." Terra was beginning to feel a bit uncomfortable.

"Didn't anyone go after them? Try to find out what happened to them, us?" Magda tried not to sound too accusing.

"Remember, those were footloose days. Everybody did their own thing. If they wanted to leave, that was their option." Quill was a tad defensive. "Why just the week before that, Birch up and left without a word. And he'd been as much a leader of the troops as Magda was. It's just the way things went back then."

Alli became a bit dispirited as she admitted,"We knew enough about how to keep the place going, but after Magda and Too, left and with Birch gone, things did sort of fall apart.

For a long time it felt like the soul was gone. The whole Love Generation was already on the verge of a kinda melt-down. Some of us stayed, sorta slid into a half-assed version of middle-class-in-funky-clothes. We were able to buy out the Lowes and let them stay on. They've both passed now. And you can see we sort of regrouped."

But Magda was not about to be sidetracked, "My god, could I really be this Too? I must be." She fell back into her chair in a stupor once again.

Seeing the concern on the faces of their hosts, Thea realized it was time to explain how they had come to show up that day.

As she told the story they sipped wine and nibbled on cheese and apples so crisp they spurted juice across the table. She related it all: the car, the body, the name on the car, the pendant, Magda's amnesia, how Magda came to call herself Magda and where they were now in the whole situation. And of course, Wolf. "Wolf Tall Trees. It was his notes that led us to this neck of the woods, so to speak. So the question is did he come here?"

"Wolf Tall Trees, sure 'nuf, 'bout two weeks ago.. On his motorcycle. Nice o' Indian. The bike. Well, him too. Said he was just crusin', lookin' to work for his keep. Helped out for a few days. Really good hand. Asked if he could camp out back in the woods. Did some scouting around out there in his spare time. Took his meals with us. Real quiet. Mostly just took it all in. Seemed to like helpin' Alli in the kitchen. Not many of our itinerants do that," Quill observed. "they all wanna work the land."

Anthea noticed a slight blush rising on Alli's cheeks. "Did he talk to you when you worked in the kitchen, Alli?"

"Well, now you mention it. Didn't talk about himself at all. He was downright neighborly, asked lotsa questions."

"Do you remember what he asked about?" Thea didn't want to make her defensive.

"Mostly what was it like when we started? I s'pose I did tell him pretty much like what we've been tellin' you." A worried looked crossed Alli's face. "Was that wrong? You said he was a friend."

Magda piped up at that, "Of course he's a friend. Was. He passed day before yesterday."

Now Alli was all atwitter. "Oh heavenly days. I meant no disrespect. Oh, I'm so sorry to hear."

"No offense taken, I assure you." But Maggie couldn't look Alli straight in the eye as she said it.

"He was trying to find out what happened to Magda. Like I said, his trail led us to you. It had taken him decades to get the pieces together because there really wasn't anything to go on. We think he was on the verge of finding out not only who Maggie here was, but who the mystery woman in the car was. Now it looks like we know where Magdalena met Maggie." Thea said. "There's still the question of where Maggie came from before she came from here?"

"The bigger question for me is why would I want to kill her?" Magda just couldn't let it go.

But Quill couldn't stand that. With a farmer's practicality, he put it rather bluntly, "What does it matter? She'd be long gone by now. Well over 100."

It was an awkward time. Nobody quite knew where to go next.

Chapter Seventeen

Thea suggested a nice tour of the grounds might help them all sort things out a bit; get some fresh air, a little exercise. What she really wanted was to see how Magda reacted to the place that most probably had been her home and the place where something happened that caused her friend's death and her own loss of memory.

In a twinkling, Quill and Terra were up and out the door leading the way and doing their little alternate story-telling bit. Cybil delighted to find that so much of what was going on on the farm fit right in with her current project -- the eco-village on the Olympic Peninsula.

Allegra was torn between finishing up in the kitchen and playing hostess to her guests. The latter won out and she trotted along with the parade of visitors.

When it came to the practical aspects of organic farming, Quill was pleased to explain it all really began with the hippie movement. Despite the drugs and sex and nudity and all that stuff that middle America was up in arms about, the Love Generation was majorly into loving, not just each other but the Earth. They were the first to farm without pesticides, "Well, that is the first since the chemical companies started the whole 'kill the pests' concept of farming. We were into Health, Nature, and Nurture, and One taught us a lot about how to get the most out of the land with the least amount of heavy machinery and chemicals."

Allegra had a niche for herself when their mentor, Magdalena, left. The current mother figure for the farm had done her studies at Findhorn in Scotland back when it began. She was totally in touch with the garden devas & faeries. "I try to schedule tea with them daily to find out what they think needs doing around the place."

"She's kidding about the tea, but she does come up with some good info which she insists comes directly from the elementals," Terra acknowledged.

"Some of these kids that are comin' along now are terrific. They're really connected to the earth and they're showing us new ways to do things – like Josh. He's a horticulturist, does a lot of what I call bio-magic – finding and protecting heirloom seeds, stuff like that. Has a whole side business. We've got patents on our spinach and one of our carrots. Have to do it to protect 'em from the big boys. They'd like nothing better than to buy 'em and destroy 'em all. They don't want folks being able to propagate from their own seeds. GMOs are basically dead seeds. Can't reproduce. No life force." Terra glowered. "That's one of the few remaining problems we have with the folks next door. They're all into GMOs and their pollen drifts over here and ruins our heirlooms. And their pesticides kill off all the beneficial insects. We're having to fight to save our bees right now between the pesticides and the cell tower that's throwing the wild life's navigation systems outta whack. But I'm trusting these kids to come up with the answers. We just gotta hang on till they do. "

Quill beamed. He loved sharing the place with visitors and they all looked like they were as delighted as he was.

Except Magda, whose brow grew deeper and deeper furrows as they walked. When they passed the compost burm she literally shivered, even in the warm glow of the afternoon sun. Thea took note. It was a little hard for a city girl to think about the animal carcasses that might be part of that pile. Best not to dwell on it.

Pointing off to the west, Quill explained, "That little barn is the garage. One of the fellows from the lunch group is working on a '20 Ford pick-up. Came with the place and it still runs great. One used to take care of it back in the early days." Magda blanched again and rubbed the goose bumps rapidly rising on her forearms. Some flash-back to an event she recalled but couldn't get ahold of sure had a hold of her.

Thea was getting squiggly feelings of her own. She took Quill aside. "That wouldn't happen to be where Magdalena kept her Pontiac would it?"

"You hit the nail on the head Thea. That's the very spot it disappeared from."

"Let's not say anything to Magda just yet. She's got a lot to process already."

They joined back up with the rest of the group. "As we drove out here we passed huge fields that I thought were part of this place. It looked endless," Thea said.

"Ah, well, a lot of the land you passed is wet-lands. Bought by US Fish and Game. It's great for us because it'll always be protected. No developments."

Alli had been watching Magda out of the corner of her eye as they went and it was evident that the woman was distressed. "Are you all right Maggie?" she asked.

"There's just something about this barn that's giving me

an uneasy feeling." Maggie rubbed her goose-bumpy arms.

Alli patted her shoulder. "How about we have a spot of tea, eh? We can take it out on the deck. We'll let Thea round up some of the fae folk to join us," she laughed.

Terra took her leave, needing to get back out on the soil with her cultivating crew. Thea danced around, singing a little bit of *Toora Loora Loora* to call the fae ones to gather. Alli mother-henned her little clutch of guests back to Sage Cottage. She showed them inside the little house -- as cozy inside as out, a storybook quality about it, despite being basically one great room that went clean on through to the kitchen. The décor was well-chosen: from Pier One Imports, bamboo, willow and batik.

Everybody carried something out to the deck. They all sat down to chamomile tea and chocolate chip cookies, making sure to leave plenty of cookie crumbs for the elementals.

Magda was still having a hard time adjusting to the tremendous amount of input. Her mind was whirling. She asked Thea about her last vision again, and then she homed in on the young men aspect. "Were there any boys who might have been close to Magda One? They might have been trying to protect her, to stop me from killing her."

"Why do you insist they were trying to stop you from some evil deed? Maybe it was the other way around. Don't forget the part about the chemistry lab," Thea reminded her. "It was boys in the lab after all."

"But we don't know how that connects to the trunk and Magda One." It was weird to say that name with the whole truck-load of history it carried. A truck-load of history that apparently was hers.

The Seaforths conferred and couldn't think of anybody in particular. Lots of the local boys wanted to have One teach what they thought must involve some kind of magical sex potion. Maybe that was what they were concocting in the lab? Quill once overheard a few of the boys in town, "If it works for old folks like her – jeeze, figure what it'd do for us."

"Crap, would yer ol man whup the tar outta ya if he ever found out you was tryin' to get some outta that ol' hippy sexpot," his pal replied.

As for the boys living at Sunny Acres, there weren't many. "We were all young , but not kids, not in school any more. Not till the next generation came along. And they'd 've been little kids. Besides, everybody loved One," Quill said. None of them could think of how any of the guys who were part of the commune would have had anything to do with a chemistry lab. They were all into Ag classes and pretty much anti-chemical. After all, it was Monsanto, Dow and the big fertilizer companies that were poisoning the soil, the water, the air, the seeds. "And we knew that no matter how much they were trying to tell us they were just making farming more affordable, less labor intensive, truth be told, they were destroying everything — the plants, animals, ultimately people. We knew we were right. Just look at the nation's health stats."

"Ok, course-correction time. We're drifting here," Cybil raised her napkin like a surrender flag.

"So, where would Too have to gone to school? Maybe they were boy-friends from school. Do you remember anything like that?" said Mitzy for the hormone department.

"Nope. She went to Cleveland High School over in Winthrop. The girl was pretty shy and stayed to herself. I don't mean she was rude or weird or anything, she just didn't reach out. But she was quick as a flea, let me tell you. She caught on to everything One showed her. Always had her nose in her homework. Really good student."

Allegra mused over a new take on their conversation. "You know, it's odd to think of her as a child. We weren't much older than she was and by now, if you're really Too, well it seems like you've sorta caught up with us."

Before they could go anywhere with that thread Quill piped up, "Hey wait! I just remembered. The girl was really a terrific musician. Had a natural talent. Led the school orchestra to a National competition. Everybody did music in those days, but most of us were just fakin' it. She'd play that old upright in the gathering room like she'd been born to it. And then later she came home from school one day with a cello," Quill was very pleased to shed this brilliant light on the mystery. "She took to that cello like it was a lover. You could see ecstasy glowin' on her face when she played. And for all her shyness it took nothing to get her to perform. She did classical concerts, she did pop stuff, folk, country, you name it. Boy she made that thing sing. And she sang along with it. Real pretty voice."

Magda did her quiver thing, her teacup rattled, tears formed. The women all started to get up and move toward her, but she waved them away and motioned Quill to go on.

"Nowadays I'd say she was either channeling some famous cellist or it was a past life thing for her... she just knew too much about it right from the git go." It was all coming back to Quill now.

"Yahoo. We've got our next clue. The music department at the school," said Thea.

While this was going on, Cybil spotted a local phone book. She reached for it even as she asked Alli, "May I?" Alli nodded, Cybil leafed through the pages, pulled out her cell phone and dialed. "Hello, yes, may I speak with the person who would keep the back issues of the high school year book, or anyone who can tell me about students back in the '60s?... Oh, I see. Well thank you."

"So?" Magda sat on pins and needles.

"They had a fire in '73. Burnt the administration building. Class rooms were okay, but the records and the year books are all gone. And all the old teachers have retired, moved to warmer climates."

The pins and needles Magda had been sitting on totally burst her bubble.

"Okay, so that's not getting us anywhere. Let's go over what we do know." Right-brained Cybil was quick to pick up the pieces and get them back on track.

"We've all pretty much accepted that the remains of the little lady we're taking to be examined by Dr. Solares is Magdalena One. And you are Magda Too. I'm assuming that's Too as in 'also', not 'two' the number?" Anthea teased as she made air quotes.

Magda was more prickly than a Saguaro cactus. "Hohoho. The thing is, she must've had some kind of passport or visa, or something. This Magdalena, I mean."

"We just figured she took it with her, wouldn't you?" Quill looked a tad sheepish, as though he should have known what he couldn't have known.

"Didn't either of them leave anything that would be a clue? They didn't have anything in the car. Or so the Sheriff says. So they must have left all their stuff here."

"You gotta remember back then nobody really had stuff. It was just whatever you needed. People were coming and going, and if stuff got left it went into the pot, so to speak. I don't remember anything standing out especially."

"And nobody ever came looking for this little girl?" Magda clearly wanted someone to have come looking for her.

"Not then. Well, several years after they left, if that counts, there was a young woman. Colleen Collins came in about the mid-70s, I'd say. Asking for a friend of hers who had disappeared seven years earlier. A girl named Mary. From the compound next door. They'd been told by the one they called the Prophet that Mary went crazy and had to be put in a mental institution," said Alli. "But Colleen says she never believed it."

"Hah!" said Quill, "So you're saying Too _was_ from next door? Boy, I was really spaced out. Never put that together. Amazing that she was able to get out. Did you guys get that connection?" He turned to Alli.

"Yes. When Colleen came calling. But by then it didn't really matter much, did it?" Alli admitted. "We did have to confess to Colleen that nobody knew where the girl and Magda One had gone. We always figured if Magda needed us, she'd get in touch."

"Mary, I can't be a Mary. It's so not me. There's got to be another girl that was Mary. I want to be Magda. I've always been Magda. This Colleen will be able to prove I'm not someone named Mary," Magda blurted out.

"Calme, calme, caro. You are and always will be Magda to all of us." Thea tried to soothe Magda yet again.

Allegra suggested they might want to talk to Colleen.

"Might?!!!" yelped Magda. "We <u>have</u> to talk to her. Do you know how to get in touch with her? What's her last name? Oh, you said Collins. Oh my god, someone who knew me. I was real. But wait, I'm not Mary. We've gotta find out who this Mary was, and who this 'Too' really was, er...is. We haven't gotten anywhere. Where does she live? This Colleen Collins?" Magda was running on high test fumes now. Once again, Monkey Mind was swingin' in the rafters.

"Oh, that's a nice affirmation Ms. Magda." Anthea was clearly edging beyond perturbation at how easily Magda slipped back into her low vibrations. She had to remind herself that people often got their validation in life from the degree of their misery. The Crones needed to keep going till Magda found other ways to self-validate.

Alli poured another round of chamomile. "Colleen did seem to enjoy our company and over the years she's sent us post cards from her travels. Even came back to visit once or twice. Anyway, the last I heard she was retired from teaching up north and lives in Wallingford."

"You don't suppose you could give this woman a call? See if she'd let us visit her?" Thea didn't want to push too hard. She knew that Alli was a sensitive and would be very concerned about putting Colleen in an uncomfortable position. "But of course I will. I think she's going to be thrilled, once she gets over the shock of finally finding her friend, if that is true."

Alli dug through an old roll-top desk and found her address book, pulled glasses out of the pocket of her apron and flipped through the pages.

Magda literally held her breath while Alli got Colleen on the line. When Alli indicated the phone, like, do you want to talk to her, Magda frantically waved no. Alli did her best to explain what she could with all of these eyes and ears focused on her. In the end she assured Colleen that they were lovely women and she was going to enjoy them as much as the farmers had. With that, she wrote down the address and a few brief directions and slipped into a bit of a lilt, "yes, soon. We'd luv ta hae ya cume and stay fer a wee while. Harvest time would be too looverly. Ta, luv." She hung up with a slight blush, "All that time I spent at Findhorn. I pop out in a bit of brogue now and then. I know its Scotland not Ireland, but the faeries were my teachers and they ALL seem to have the Irish lilt when they talk, so it all gets mixed up. Sometimes Scots, sometimes Irish."

Alli handed the card with Colleen's address on it to Cybil. "You know how to get to Wallingford?" Cybil assured her it was no problem.

Hugs were distributed all around. Alli handed Mitzy a huge basket, "a snack for the road." Quill added a few bottles of their very private stock of Merlot, and again they were off.

Chapter Eighteen

As the Juicy Crones drove back to the highway, there was a glint from up on the nearby foothill. Mitzy nudged Thea. They both took note of that, and of the odd fence on the far north side of Sunny Acres made of crosses, and here and there reflections from what seemed to be mirrors and shinny rocks across from some of them. A moment later someone was watching them with binoculars from a lookout tower as they passed a virtual fortress protecting the ranch next door, which seemed incongruous with the name carved into the cross beam: *Shepherd's Fold of Eternal Light.*

As Cybil headed the car toward Highway 20, Thea turned back to see how Magda was doing. Her look was one of perplexity: excitement at getting closer to her identity, but a soupçon of fear at the same time. Thea herself could only think of gratitude for the progress they were making.

Meanwhile, Cybil was in Heaven, multitasking: driving, on voice-activated cell phone and turning on the GPS locator. The first call was to Cleveland High School in Winthrop. "Yes, this is Cybil LaCrosse. I called earlier about school records. I wonder if we could find your music teacher? ... Mr. Fallow... busy getting ready for summer class? I see.... Taking the kids for pizza. Would you be kind enough to ask him to hang around a little longer? We've come a very long way. We'll buy the pizza if he'll wait and order it delivered. We'll be there in about ten minutes... Yes, thank you so much."

As she drove on, Cybil dialed up Jeff at the airstrip. "Hi pal. We're almost on our way back to you. Our passengers giving you any trouble? All quiet, eh? Have the plane ready. We're headed to Boeing field for our rendezvous with the forensic Sleuth of Seattle. We should be back where you are in about an hour. And will you please call ahead and have Natasha and Reneé get things ready at The Eyrie and meet us with the Dragon Fly. We'll stay over tonight and head back to California tomorrow afternoon, unless something else comes along."

Looking at the others, she checked to make sure she hadn't spoken out of turn, "That is okay with all of you, isn't it? I mean, we may as well stay at my place on Whidbey. That way we've got plenty of time with Colleen tonight."

She snapped the phone shut then focused on the GPS, touching the screen and asking for "Cleveland High School, Winthrop, Washington," she enunciated clearly. A map adjusted itself and gave her the most direct route while a woman with a French accent spoke the directions. "Don't you just love these things?"

They entered the red-brick building and followed the signs to the Admin. Off. There the woman behind the counter said Mr. Fallow couldn't possibly help them when Cybil explained what they'd come for. "He's too young to know anything about the 1960s." She herself was probably all of 30. Fortunately she was fairly astute. She took note of the crest-fallen look on Magda's face and had a thought; "We do have a trophy case over in the arts building. Its got photos of kids who went to Nationals with the orchestra back then. Tell Mr. Fallow that's what you want to see. You go out the side door of this building, across the quad. The big red-brick building on your left is the where the music department is. Just go down the hall to the end and you'll hear him in there clumping around with some of the band kids. Like I said, they're getting the instruments ready for the new kids coming to summer session. The trophy cases are along the walls."

The little band of Crones crossed the quad as directed. It was evident the main building was much newer than the one they were about to enter. Finding the band room was no problem: follow the cacophony. The kids were definitely trying out the drums and a trumpet. As they got closer, it was clear that Mr. Fallow, a somewhat sallow fellow, in a blue and white striped, short-sleeved shirt, tan slacks and a red and white bow tie was not exactly in charge. There didn't seem to be anyone in charge in the room. Just rampant chaos. The frazzled teacher looked grateful for the interruption... and the pizza offer. When he heard what the women were after – late 1960s National Competition, he had one of the boys call in the lunch order while he led the women down to the end of the corridor.

The group stood, looking at a glass-front case with trophies and photos... and there was the girl with the cello. "Oh my god, National High School Orchestra Competition, 1968. Winning Orchestra. And that's me. I really did exist before 1969." She laughed a tiny laugh when she saw the name below the photo... "Magda Too, boy, I sure was good at keeping the secret about my name." Magda gushed a water-fall of tears. The poor teacher didn't know what to do. Cybil asked if it would be possible to get a copy of the photos.

Fallow opened the case, took the pictures and led the group to a kind of communal utility room. Deftly he scanned the photos, handed them to Magda, accepted Cybil's gracious laying on of enough largess to pay for plenty of pizzas, and dashed off to quell what sounded like a battle of the bands.

As they left the building, Magda clutched her new-found treasures and mused to Thea that "I guess I have always had a musical ear. That must have been why my first film was about the girl cello player in the orchestra with the conductor who, well, you know, seduced her. I always wondered where that came from."

"I'm getting the feeling that we need to talk about your movies," Thea said. "Right now, let's just get back to the airport and head for Seattle, leave off our packages with Dr. Solares and find this Ms. Colleen Collins. That is what Alli said her name is, right?"

On the flight back to Boeing, Cybil actually let Jeff fly. She wanted to get on the internet and check out Magda's filmography. While she did that, Magda went back to piss-and-moan mode, "I still wonder about the body in the trunk? Why the visions? What did I do to deserve all of this?"

Thea held up her hands to still the storm. "I keep telling you, if there was any killing, you didn't do it."

Cybil interrupted. "I've searched everywhere I know to go but I can't find anything under Magda Lindal. Did you use another name?"

Magda bowed her head to avoid their looks of curiosity. "Actually, I did. I wrote under the name Lena, just the one name. I didn't really want publicity, didn't want the press hounding me."

"I thought you said you took the producer's mother's name, Lindal." Cyb was confused.

"That's what's on the contracts. The name I used on the credits was just plain Lena."

"Lena, you're that Lena." While she was talking Cybil was tapping away at the keys. "Ah hah. Here we are. You made it sound like you just wrote some little C grade movies — just one step up from home-made videos. These are classics. You've got a whole cult following."

"That's amazing. I've seen all of these films," Mitzy turned the laptop so they could all look at the list. *A Taste of Love, The Scent of Money, Blinded by Beauty, The Sound of Passion, A Touching Tale.*

Anthea perused the list, "The theme is always pretty much about the woman learning to believe in her self. Interesting. I hadn't put it all together. Saw them over the years, but it didn't connect the way it does now. I find it so intriguing that many writers who teach profound lessons with their work are unable to walk the talk."

"Oh, get off her case Anthea. Magda, I'm a big fan. They're all such nice, old-fashioned love stories, on top of having that shero kind of message." Mitzy gushed and then slid into embarrassment when she realized she had not gotten the connection between her new friend and the famous underground film writer either.

Magda shrugged. "They were just B movies. No big deal. My whole movie career was a fluke."

"Don't you say that. I loved that one, especially," Mitzy moued, pointing at *A Taste of Love,* "Well really, both of them, all of them... my kind of movies. But *A Taste of Love,* with all that food. No wonder you're such a terrific cook. Did you have a professional chef make all that fantastic food? Is that how you learned to cook such exotic stuff? No, wait. Madame Olivia said you cooked at the Ranch right from the start."

"Actually, before I wrote that movie I went to the Cordon Blue and then I interned at the Tour d'Argent and that's when I got the idea for the film. Or did it go the other way around? I don't know. That's what happens to me. I'd do something, get into it over the top, meet all the right people, everything just falling into place, and then it would stop. Blam! And I'd put my tail between my legs and limp on back to the Ranch. "

Thea didn't want to say anything in case it caused a relapse, but Maggie had just recalled a whole chunk of her life without any coaching. Not only that, but there were huge phases of success which Magda seemed fully capable of wiping out of her memory bank, totally discounting not one, but several remarkable careers. The others were still looking at the computer.

"This is my favorite," Cybil indicated *Blinded by Beauty*. "I mean really fantastic. She wouldn't be stopped even when she lost her husband and her son in that plane crash, which she felt responsible for. Still, she went on painting. And then, losing 90% of her eyesight, she painted from memory by feel and taught young painters to see with their eyes closed. I mean really? That Helen Keller line about losing her sight, but never her vision. Wow!"

"Look! There are reviews from magazines up the wazoo. An interview in <u>People Magazine</u>, no less. Oooh, nice photo of you lady. Quite the glam shot. It says, 'The writer, who doesn't do interviews, much to her producer's annoyance, did agree to sit down with us one afternoon for a cup of tea and cookies she'd made herself, from a recipe that's featured in *A Taste of Love*. (Get the recipe by writing to the editor of this publication.)' And then she goes over each of the films and points out that they all have the same basic theme of a passionate woman overcoming great odds through the love of her art."

Magda squirmed. "When the underground press reviewed my films, they hinted at that theme. I just never thought of it consciously. The stories would come to me, and it was like taking dictation to write the scripts. When they were done I was on to something else. Then suddenly I'd get the itch and I'd disappear and become another person, as though I'd walked into another body. I knew all about cooking, or painting or whatever that body was into. I managed to connect with people who appreciated that particular talent. When I'd achieved some notoriety I'd panic and my memory of the Ranch would come back. It was really odd though, that while I was in that being state, I had no memory of Dos Lobos or my former life. When the pressures of fame got too intense, I'd suddenly remember and run 'home.'"

"Wolf always managed to keep tabs on me, but he never interfered. His spirit guides told him I was on a journey, connecting with my past. He'd fill me in on what I'd done, said he wanted to stimulate my memory cells. He seemed amazed at how some part of me knew how to survive in totally dislocated circumstances. After I'd get settled back in, I'd hide out up in my room and write. One of our clients was Harry Lindal, the producer. He got excited about the first one, and got me help to turn it into a script. And after that he was always waiting for the next one. I just never knew when an event would happen. I never felt connected to Hollywood. Always felt like I was an impostor."

Mitzy waited till Magda seemed to be finished, "There was another aspect to all those films. I saw you on the Oprah show. I can't believe I didn't recognize you all this time. Anyway, Oprah asked if your father was domineering, or abusive. She pointed out that it's in every film, that business about the woman's father telling her it was bad that she was so into her passion, she should be ashamed of herself. He'd say it was ungodly. And then the woman loses everything, like he prophesied. Oprah thought that may have come from having a repressive father."

"Of course I had to evade that question because I don't know anything about him," Magda admitted.

"Well, maybe Colleen will be able to help in that area," Thea reassured.

Mitzy pointed out that all that romance was sure a positive thing. Hot, passionate, exploding in a cosmic orgasm. "And remember, in each film its a burning fire of passion for her art that brings the shero back, redeems her as it were. This reporter pointed that out too." Cybil showed them where the article said just that.

Magda didn't even seem to notice that she moved right into telling a part of the story she claimed to be unable to recall: "I painted when I lived in Arizona. I think I even met a woman who I based the story on. But then no one ever tried to sue me for stealing her life, and I couldn't remember her... if she existed. Maybe it was me. I don't know."

"What about *The Scent of Money?*" Cybil wanted to

know. After all, it was about her favorite topic, money.

"Another idea I apparently got when I lived in Paris. The woman's father tried to sabotage her sense of smell because he thought it was too focused on sensuality. He thought she should use her talents to come up with perfumes that were sweet and homey. Instead, all her famous perfumes were geared at attracting men in a rather feline-in-heat way. They told me later that I was a rising star in the perfume business, but something happened and I stopped, and then I wrote the movie. I remember now, that anosmia part was true. I did lose my sense of smell for awhile. I think it was cooking that brought it back. You can't cook if you can't smell what you're cooking. At least not very well. Uuhmm, I wonder how that worked? What came first, the cooking, or the smelling?"

Anthea sat back and smiled. Magda was breaking through her old blocks. No need to try to outsmart the Source of All That Is. Just stay tuned.

"I still don't get how you managed to be these other personalities while you were 'researching' the films," Cybil asked.

"I told you before, I didn't do any of this consciously. I'd just become this other person and she always seemed to come with a path that I couldn't avoid. I don't even know how I got a passport to go to Europe. I don't recall any of it. It just happened." Magda seemed deeply immersed in shame — she wore it all over her being like a latex glove.

Cybil was immersed in the film concepts. "So, you covered all five of the senses. Each film was about passion. It was about how that sense was the woman's path to understanding life and her own personal power. They were about awakening the self through the senses. Not exactly the usual path to self-awareness."

"Sounds to me like it could be a fugue state, multiple personalities, past-life bleed-through, or parallel life interface... it could be all of them combined." Thea busily analyzed.

"I wonder where this Tantric Sex Goddess phase comes from? Dr. Phil should love you," Mitzy teased.

"Oh, that's a great help." Magda wrapped herself further into her own encompassing arms.

"So what happened? You haven't done anything for a long time." Cybil closed down her laptop.

"I met Tran and we bought the place in Bonsall. Wolf came down and put in the sweat lodge and life settled down. Every once in awhile Wolf'd show up to do a sweat with us. It's been pretty tranquil up to now. There haven't been any incidents in almost fifteen years. I've tried not to think about all of it. It's too stressful. I'm always afraid I'll wake up in another one of those episodes. Or after one."

"Well, none of that matters now. You're on your way to knowing who you are, and we won't leave you until you're secure and centered in this new state of beingness." Thea hugged Magda.

"Who I really am is a quiet woman who just wants to use my horses for therapy for people with challenges, like me. I only do the Tantric stuff because I need the money."

"Guess again, woman. The cards, your chart, your Oscar." She chided Magda ever so gently.

Fortunately, they were landing at Boeing before Magda could launch another emotional downdraft.

Chapter Nineteen

The passengers were astounded by the reception that awaited them. The landing was another of Cybil's choreographed performances, with a van marked Puget Sound Forensics Labs, pulling onto the tarmac alongside an '86 Suburban wagon, and a cobalt blue Suzuki GXXR 1000 motorcycle gliding in beside it. All the vehicles came to a halt. A trim Versace-suited woman with Sassoon cut jet black hair, got out of the van, along with two college students who looked to have taken their dress code cues from CSI. Out of the Suburban and off the bike came a pair of nymphs dancing, or rather skating on the rollers imbedded in their shoes... making the asphalt look as smooth as a lake of ice. The bike rider peeled off her leathers to reveal an outfit matching the one on the girl who got out of the Suburban: Cybil's Great Goddess brand boy boxers and workout bras in vibrant colors clashed electrically with their hair.

"What did you do, hire the Cirque de Soliel to meet us?" Mitzy giggled.

"The one with the spikey burgundy cellophane do is Natasha. The wheat-colored dreds belong to Renée. They're student caretakers at my place on the island. They brought the Suburban over for us."

"Great Goddess, it looks like flow yoga on ice skates

with a bit of stompin' thrown in. I can't wait to hear the music they're tuned into." Anthea practically pushed the door open she was so excited to get to the scene below. As the hatch lifted the music coming from speakers on the motorcycle proved to be an extremely exotic combination of Celtic and Caribbean, steel drums and bagpipes. Anthea was with them before she hit the ground.

Meanwhile Cybil organized the move to the Suburban. The dragonfly-logo matching the one on the jet, floated on the iridescent tequila sunrise paint job. Cybil had the driver of the University van pull up next to the baggage compartment of the plane, while Mitzy did an extremely emotional reunion dance with Carmen. The CSI wanna-be's were a trifle confused at the professor's non-academic behavior. Introductions passed all around, Dr. Solares and her assistants, Cybil's team, Renee and Natalie. Mitzy explained a little further what they wanted; Dr. Solares took a swab to Magda's mouth; Thea gave the doctor her card: "Just give me a call as soon as you have anything interesting. And you can send the report to that email address."

Cybil gave Dr. Solares her card. "Send the bill to that address." Thank you's all around, the forensic assistants took custody of the box with Wolf's ashes and the crate with the skeleton in it, and then the pathologists drove off.

The kinetic girl's slid into their Icon cycle gear and Darth Vader helmets and zoomed off on the bike while the Juicy Crones were herded to the Suburban. The whole operation was executed in under ten minutes. "They could use you to handle Navy Seal Operations, Cyb." Thea wasn't joking.

Thea noted the bumper sticker: Beyond Biodisel.

"Check out the solar panels," Cybil did her Vanna White presentation of the top of the car. "And the baffle to maintain our aerodynamic integrity. It's got a conversion kit to handle biodisel, the solar panels give us electricity. My friend Noel, the one who runs my construction business, did the conversion and restoration. Juicy Crones, I give you the future." But she was anxious to get going. She stuffed them all into their seats and beamed as she drove out of Boeing Field headed for I-5, north past beautiful downtown Seattle, with Elliott Bay glistening, the snow-capped Olympic mountains in the distance and the ferry boats gliding past each other across the water. They drove past Lake Union and up North to the Wallingford exit. It would have been a wonderful drive if it weren't for the commuter traffic and the low-pressure zone that was hovering over Magda's head.

Using her GPS Cyb quickly found the address and eased the big vehicle into a small space in front of a typical urban Seattle frame house, with a drive that went down a slope to the garage which had been converted into a charming cottage. As soon as they got out of the SUV and started down the walk the door popped open and out stepped a woman to warm Mitzy's heart. She was no more than an inch taller than MacDonald and since she wore flat loafers, Mitzy actually towered over her by the two extra inches she gained in her own 4" platforms. Their hostess had stylishly cut short hair with golden highlights on a wheat-colored base. She bubbled a great laugh that made them feel welcome immediately.

"Helloooo, I'm Colleen Collins. Please come in, come in. Which one of you is Mary?" Magda froze, creating a jam up of women eager to get this show on the road. Magda cringed back and hid behind Cybil. "You can't imagine the shock I was in when Alli called and said Mary had turned up," Colleen laughed. What a joyful punctuation, thought Thea.

Cyb reached around and pulled Magda back to the fore.

"Mary, is that really you? Sorry. I'm blathering. But I've been going crazy since Alli called. Trying to figure out what to say, where to start. Do I hug you? Do I jump up and down and scream like a kid?" Realizing that they were all still standing there Colleen stepped aside and ushered them into a single large room with a Pullman kitchen off to one side and a round oak table next to that. Wooden chairs all around, with Laura Ashley print cushions which matched the pillows on the over-stuffed couch, which in turn sat in front of the fireplace. Through the window boxes, spring flowers lit up the panes like stained glass. There were fresh flowers on the dining table and on an end table by the sofa. Lavender and chamomile wafted from a diffuser on a shelf by one of the windows. Pale blue chalcedony and howlite stones clustered on a little table by the door. On the ledges beneath the windows clear crystals refracted rainbows all around the room. The whole place just reeked esoteric TLC and a good eye for the perfect. Gentle lute music lingered in the background.

"Please have a seat. Actually, have four seats," Colleen laughed at herself. Another very good sign, thought Anthea. They all managed to fit comfortably around the table which was loaded: paté, a baguette on a board with a knife for cutting, olives, marinated artichoke hearts, crackers, pita wedges, hummus, crudités with ranch dressing, a couple of bottles of robust looking red wine and all the appropriate glasses, plates and cutlery.

"You didn't just <u>happen</u> to have all this on hand?" Mitzy nudged her new best friend. Colleen laughed that warm laugh and urged them all to fill their plates. Thea was pleased to see that, "at least we don't have to worry that we're intruding."

"My God, intruding? Are you kidding? This is the most exciting thing that's happened to me since I ran away from home, which, as you can imagine, was a few years ago."

She caught herself staring at Magda, who still hadn't said a word. "Excuse me, I'm just not used to the idea that you might indeed be Mary. Are you really you?"

"I don't know. I can't imagine being Mary. Didn't Alli explain to you that I don't remember any of my life before somewhere about 1968? And that I've been Magda most of the time since then."

Thea jumped up and pulled Magda out of her chair, "I don't know why I didn't think of this earlier. Here, hold your arm out," she said pulling Magda's arm up. Turning to Colleen she asked, "You know about kinesiology, don't you?"

"Sure. I use my pendulum to test supplements and vegetables. But what has that got to do with whether she's Magda or Mary?" Colleen was puzzled.

Thea addressed her cohorts, "You three've heard me talk about Dr. Hawkins. He's figured out how to use Kinesiology to test all sorts of issues; emotional frequencies, locations, the truth."

"Yeah, sure," said Magda, holding tight to her position as titular queen of cynicism.

"Let's start just seeing if it works for you, Magda. I'm going to press down lightly with two fingers on your outstretched arm. You resist. I'll make a statement which will either register as true or not true in Magda's body." She turned to the others to see that she was connecting with them. "Her vibrational frequency will tell us what is." She addressed Magda, "we are in the home of Colleen Collins. See, I push down and her arm stays firm. <u>Your</u> name <u>is</u> Colleen, isn't it?" Maggie's arm went right down to her side. Anthea laughed. "That was a question for Colleen but Maggie's body responded truthfully. It knows a false vibration when it's presented. So lets go for it. Repeat after me," she said looking Magda straight in the eyes, "My birth name is Mary. Now, you say it."

"My birth name is Mary." Thea gently pushed down on Magda's arm but it held firm.

"That can't be. Try me again, Thea. I wasn't paying attention."

"It doesn't matter whether you're paying attention or not. It doesn't matter what you think. It's the vibration of veracity." Oh, that sounds good. I do love alliteration, thought Thea as she adjusted Magda's arm to shoulder level, and applied two fingers. "Repeat after me, I was named Mary when I was born."

Magda complied. "I was named Mary when I was born." Her arm held steady until her psyche forced a whoosh out of her lungs and she collapsed into Thea's arms, sobbing, whether with joy or despair no one was quite sure.

Thea settled Magda on the sofa, pulled the sobbing woman's head down on her shoulder and did a little motherly patting. Cybil passed the wine around as they all found seats in front of the fireplace, which was filled with a huge bouquet of pale pink peonies and blowzy, soft peach colored roses. It was beyond decadent.

Thea pointed at Magda's head snugged into her breast, encouraging Colleen to take over: "So tell us about your career, Colleen. You seem a little young to be retired. Didn't you like teaching?"

"Ah well, in fact I did, still do, I substitute here in Seattle. But out there, it was just getting a bit restrictive. You can see that I'm pretty well into an esoteric life style. Honestly, most of the kids enjoyed it, but more and more often they were giving somewhat slanted reports to their parents... I suspect it was a way to earn points at home."

"What?" Mitzy, ever the politician was on the alert for some form of infringement of Colleen's rights. "What did you do that they could possibly find fault with?"

"Remember, we were out there in cowboy country and the *Shepherd's Flock*, that's the religious compound where Mary and I grew up, well, that was spreading, attracting new followers. Converts — and you know what they say about converts, just a hair more 'devout' shall we say? Back when I started teaching things were okay. But then along came what some of my friends call the 'funnymentalist' explosion. It gave the *Fold* group the notion that they were meant to take over the whole valley, eventually convert everybody. They figured if they had control, they could pretty well decide what would be taught and how and by whom. One of the brightest kids in our school set me up. He asked me what evolution really was, like he was curious.

"I told him to think about the word: evolve. Things change. I showed them pictures of how animals have changed over centuries, especially dogs and horses, even their own herd of prize Short Horn cattle. How they'd bred them to refine certain characteristics. I reminded them that farmers had been hybridizing crops to make them easier to grow and transport. And their moms worked to get that prize winning rose at the county fair. That's all evolution is.

"We were okay up to the point when I showed them that back in the times of the knights, whose armor you see in European castles...those warriors that went off on the Crusades were mostly five foot, five foot two. Short little guys. Now we've evolved to where lots of people are over six feet tall and even seven feet. And the pioneers had families at 15 and 16 and were dead at 35... and now people live to be over 100 and that's evolution."

"How could they argue with basic evidence?" Mitzy wanted to know.

"Hey, you know as well as I do, this argument is going on in courts and state houses and schools all over the country. People demanding that Intelligent Design replace science in the schools. They didn't want to hear that I think Divine Intelligence has room for both Evolution and Intelligent Design. For all we know, those seven days were actually millions of years long. We have no idea what time means in the realm of the Infinite.

"That was it? That drove you out of work you must have loved? You really know how to make it interesting. That can only come from passion about your subject."

"Well, it was just getting less and less fun. Having to be careful what I said, and wishing I could really tell it like I see it."

"Go on. Give us another example," Cybil prodded.

"Halloween. I couldn't resist. They got off on the burning of witches. One of the kids actually took pot shots at an old woman's black cat, saying she was a witch, look how old

she was and with that cat, — 'you just know she's one of
Satan's whores.' That got me going on witches or Wicca being
Wise Women back in olden times. They were revered. Women
who knew how to heal with herbs and potions. But that pissed
off the barbers, the guys who done did the doctoring in those
days, 'cause that took away from thar leeching bidness."
Colleen couldn't resist shifting into a sort of home-boy way of
talkin' when she got into her story telling. "And these here herb
women kept cats to keep the mice 'n rats away from their drying
sheds. So the barber/doctors got the clergy to say the women
were evil and their cats were tools of the devil and they killed all
the cats and the rat population exploded with no cats to eat
them, and so the 'doctors' blamed the witches for the plagues
that followed. They didn't have a clue that their cat killing was
the cause. They just had to have someone to blame and why
not those meddling women who kept curing people so they
didn't have to get bled. And that, children is when they took to
burning women at the stake."

"Then, for good measure, I quoted them Jim
Stafford's poem, 'Swamp Witch'. I'm sure you remember it
from the old 45 record. It shows a more modern form of the anti-
witch mentality." And with that she launched into a recitation in
a Cajun accent with all the flare of a master story teller:

> "Black Water live back in the swamp where
> the strange green reptiles creep,
> where snakes hang thick from the cypress trees,
> like sausage on a smoke house wall.
> And the swamp is alive with a thousand eyes,
> and all of 'em watchin' you.
> Stay off the track of Hattie's shack,

back in the black Bayou.
Way up the road from Hattie's shack
lies a sleepy little Okachobee town.

and on the teacher went telling the tale for nearly two
minutes, never losing a beat, never slipping out of her Cajun
accent all the way to the end when it turned out,

"They never found Hattie
an' they never found her shack.
An' they never made a trip back in.
'Cause a parchment note they found
tacked to a stump said,
'Don't come lookin' agin!'"

Colleen took a breath and then smiled. "Then we
discussed why Hattie lived in the swamp, and why she played
on the town's superstitions to keep them away. They knew as
well as Hattie did that the next time anything went wrong, she'd
be blamed and her life would be in danger."

"And that's what got you fired?"

"Oh, no, it was when I got into the other holidays, like
telling them that Shepherds in the fields would only be out in
the spring time when the ewes were lambing so Jesus couldn't
have been born in December, and that was really just the
church using the old pagan holiday of solstice to get the people
into the church and distract them from going out to celebrate
the pagan way."

"The congregation would have loved to burn me at that
point. And then I told them the Easter egg was a fertility right
that was borrowed from the pagans. The church just cut out
the Beltane fires, but they kept May poles, cause its purty. It

also reminded them that all cultures had creation stories and good-versus-evil and apocalypse stories. It was the Council of Nicea that created the Bible by picking the stories that supported what they wanted people to believe, what they could use to frighten people into thinking they could only be saved by the church. They perverted the beauty of a loving Mother-Father-God into a stringent patriarch who only cared for those who believed what they said. In other words, man re-created god in his image and voila, organized Christianity as we know it today. I just don't think that's the way it started out. I think it was about Love, and compassion for all, no mater what your belief system."

Anthea reached over and took a deep whiff of the lovely peach-hued roses. The fragrance lingered on her finger tips when she drew back. "I can see how that would rock the creation ark."

"They didn't want to hear that I felt the stories, and Jesus' teachings are wonderful and valid — but not because Reverend Jonas said so. And not the way he twisted them. They're wonderful when they make your heart sing... when you feel the light of their truth shine, no matter where they come from."

"That's when I was called into the Principal's office and it was hinted that I might want to consider alternative occupational options."

"Good heavens!" The four women said in unison.

All of this had thrown Maggie deep into thought. "Those quotes, all that poetry, how do you remember it all? It doesn't seem fair that I can't even remember who I am."

"Hardly anyone can remember things like you seem to

Colleen. That's quite a talent." Mitzy was totally impressed.

"Oh, that's not a talent. It's because the leader of the *Flock*, Father Jonas, made us all memorize and recite the Bible. And then, when I was too old for the school at the compound, they only had up to the 6th grade, I was allowed to go to the junior High School in Twisp. But I was forbidden to go to the gym classes because that required shorts. Big no-no to the Prophet Jonas. So I spent my time 'studying' in the library. What I really did was speed read all the books forbidden by the Good Shepherd. And I'd memorize as much as I could, so I could study it all in my head later."

Cybil poured more wine all around. "My goodness, after all that, if we weren't already full from your lovely repast, I'd say we should take you out to dinner."

Colleen laughed. "Good lord. I've used up all this time on my story and haven't even told you anything about... can I say Mary when I'm talking about the girl I knew?" she looked soulfully at Magda. "I mean, it's hard to call her anything else. I'll tell you what, I'll call <u>you</u> Magda, but when I talk about then, I'll call her Mary. Does that make any sense?"

Magda nodded her head tentatively.

"Yes, I do think we need to get some of that history cleared up," Anthea said, patting Magda on the arm.

"Of course. I mean that is what you came for. Let me see, where shall I begin? I think I already mentioned I grew up on what's called the compound of the *Shepherd's Flock of Enduring Light*. It's next door to what was then the commune with the hippies, where I went looking for Mary and met Alli and Quill and Terra. She had been gone seven years before I managed to get over there. My parents kept a tight leash on me. I'd been about eight and Mary would have been eleven when she disappeared."

"Did she ever tell you why she went there?" Magda longed to remember what had compelled her.

"She'd come back from visiting and tell me she wanted to tell me things. Things that went on, not over there, but with the Prophet. But she said I was too young, and anyway she was afraid I'd get in trouble if I knew about it. I think that's the reason that when she disappeared, Jonas told the 'family' he'd had to put Mary in a mental home. He said she'd conspired with the devil and was a very evil child. But I never believed it. I knew Mary and I was sure she had escaped. I just never had the courage to question the Founding Father of the Flock."

Colleen told them about Nora and Brian OBrien, Mary's parents, who went to the big city for their monthly shopping in a converted school bus painted red and white. In bold electric blue letters it proclaimed itself to be the vehicle of the *Shepherd's Fold of Enduring Light,* Fiddler's End, WA. And the rest of the space was taken up with the pitch; *Saving the Flock One Lost Lamb at a Time; Jesus Saves* (several times), *Praise the Lord; Let the Son shine into your life; Saved by the blood of the lamb* and best of all, *Heaven Bound,* with a great red arrow aimed at the clouds.

Brian was the designated quartermaster in charge of provisions for the family. Nora was allowed to go with him because she could keep him from temptation should any wanton harlots approach him, and because there were certain female necessities he couldn't deign to select. Besides 'groceries were woman's work,' and most importantly, she could hold up the cross in the window to protect them as they drove past what Prophet Jonas called Lucifer's Lair. That was the commune I mentioned, the one I knew *you*," she looked straight at Magda, "went to. It was a lot like our farm, but it was run by what Jonas snarlingly called Hippies, Pagans, Heathens, Witches, Wild Men, Women and Children who wore as little clothing as the weather allowed, and cavorted around, dancing in the fields, singing licentious songs while they planted and harvested. Can you imagine that sweet Allegra as a wild woman? Well, maybe back then she was a little less fussy, but so what? It all sounded wonderful to me and it sure did to Mary." This last part of the story was told even as Colleen was putting on a pot of water for tea, getting out cups, the pot and cozy, and two platters of homemade cookies. She kept putting things out as she went on with the story.

"Mary told me that as soon as her parents were gone to the city on their buying trips she would climb out her bedroom window onto the oak tree and make her way down to, let's see, how did she put it?, uhm, to 'Let her bare toes tickle Mother Earth's sweet face.' She knew she wasn't supposed to run around barefoot, wantonly showing her naked toes, but then she wasn't supposed to leave her room either."

By this time, Magda finally began to thaw. How could she not like this brave little girl named Mary? "You say she went to the commune when she got out of her room? She sounds plucky for a young girl. Especially if this Jonas character was making it sound like the pits of hell." It didn't occur to her that the "she" of this tale was her own self.

"I'd say she was just filled with anticipation. She said she'd give the tree a hug and skip off across the lawn, past the garden shed and then make a run for the hedge that kept the heathens from view. She'd work her way through the boxwood without leaving a trace. Beyond that she knew how to get between the crosses that made the fence Brother Jonas had the clan erect as protection against 'Lucifer's den of iniquity.'"

"She was glad her parents didn't take her to town. Their reason was that they were protecting her from all the temptations the city threw at those who truly love the Lord. It was a testing they didn't think she was ready for. If they only knew. Well, eventually, they must have known, because they couldn't have believed what Jonas said about Mary. I mean that she'd become unmanageable and he'd had to put her in an institution."

"Do you know anything about the time she spent at the hippie commune?" Mitzy took another chocolate chip cookie and poured tea all around. A wonderful lavender and Earl Gray with cream and honey. "I mean, we heard a good deal of it from the sunny farmers, but did you know what Mary was up to over there? Did she talk about the people at all?"

"Oh yes, she'd come back all excited every time she went over there. She talked about one woman who said she had changed her name to honor the woman who'd been abused for centuries by the Christian church."

"You mean Magdalena?" Magda asked.

"Who else?" Colleen teased, happy that Magda was doing a little better with all of this news.

"Then, not long before she disappeared, she got into some serious trouble when she got home. After that she was never herself again. She withdrew. She didn't tell me what had happened, but I knew it was pretty bad. Not over there, but when she got back. Something she did really got her in trouble with the Prophet. I mean more than just the usual."

"What do you mean, just the usual?" Cybil wanted to

hear more of the exploits of this dauntless little girl.

Colleen seemed proud of her friend as she recalled: "She had her own lyrics that she sang while the rest of us were invoking the Almighty. The hippies were teaching her about peace and non-violent protests, so she had a hard time with us all marching into war. One time I remember Reverend Jonas practically turned purple when he caught her singing songs from next door while she was supposed to be practicing hymns. She loved *Mrs. Robinson, Lucy in the Sky with Diamonds, Give Peace a Chance, Go tell Alice, Sounds of Silence,* songs from *Jesus Christ Superstar.* All those 'blasphemous lyrics' made him shudder. Interesting that he knew all the names and that they had 'blasphemous lyrics.'" There was that warm laugh of Colleen's again.

"What about Mary's parents? Didn't they do anything about her being sent away?" Magda asked, still not feeling anything like a girl named Mary.

"You can't imagine how Rev. Jonas was able to shame people. I'm sure he accused them of being in cahoots with Lucifer for having raised such a hellion of a child."

"So what happened?" asked Mitzy.

"Well, after Mary was quote banished, end quote, Nora, Mary's mother, had some kind of breakdown, totally withdrew, didn't talk to anyone. Mary's father, Brian, grew more and more distraught over the years and finally said he had to get away. In 1990 he went to visit another 'brother' in Waco, Texas and was killed in the debacle with David Koresh."

"Do you think Nora is still out there? Do we need to go back to that *Shepherd's Flock* place? Are they hiding her somewhere out there? I'm not getting anything psychically."

Thea didn't want to say that that probably meant Nora was no longer on this plane of existence.

"No, no. After Brian left, they put Nora in an institution."

"You weren't still around then though, right?" Thea was calculating.

"You're right. I'd gotten the courage to leave. I secretly kept in touch with my mom at the compound though. You should have seen what we went through to keep our connection. She's gone now, and so is my dad. But it felt like he died a long time ago. After I got out he was one of the ones who tried to keep my mom from calling or writing to me. But he's passed over now."

"All we like sheep have gone astray. Turning everyone to his own way. But the Lord hath laid upon Him the iniquity of us all." This time Magda was aware that she'd quoted the Bible and was quite puzzled that she knew the phrase. "Where the heck did I get that?"

"You've done that before, Maggie," Mitzy tried to be gentle with the notion that she did this bible quoting without seeming to be aware of it.

"I do not... Couldn't... I don't know Bible stuff like that."

"Do you think it wasn't drummed into you like it was the rest of us?" Colleen countered with a quote of her own, 'By his stripes we are all healed.' Believe me, The Prophet made sure we got all the stripes we needed if we didn't learn the Good Word."

"Enough with the biblical reminiscing ladies. We need to hear the end of this story," Cybil directed firmly.

"Well, like I said, I stayed in touch with my mom. She

kept me up to date. I was always sure Mary had gotten away. I wanted to hear that she was outside somewhere. I had a dream that one day I'd find her."

Colleen looked at Magda for a reaction and was still kept at arm's length by the woman's confusion. Then she threw them a totally unexpected bouquet. "Over the years, I'd go to visit Nora at the home where they'd stashed her. Now she spends her days singing, dancing and fiddling, and talking to the faeries. That's what gave Rev. Jonas the ammunition he needed to put her in that place...when she started talking to faeries."

"You mean Magda's mother is accessible? We've got to see her. Where is she?" Thea nearly knocked her tea cup over. Magda recoiled, either at the thought or at Thea's reaction.

"I don't know about Magda's mother, but Mary's is. Oh, I'm sorry. I don't mean to sound snide. It's just, there's a lot going on for me here too, you know. I want so much to believe I've found you," she looked fondly at Magda, "but then you sort of put up this wall that makes me hesitate. And I surely don't want to do anything that will upset Nora. She's been very close to me for all these years. Give me a minute." Colleen got very still, closed her eyes and hummed a little Ooohm. Thea matched her Ooohm for Ooohm. "I'm getting that the time has come. That, whether you believe it or not, Nora is your mother and the faeries will protect her from whatever shock might arise from your resurrection. It feels good" Colleen reported. Thea nodded in agreement. "I'm getting the same feeling."

There was no getting around it for Magda. "Tomorrow!" Thea announced, and Maggie realized that the very next day she was going to meet her mother. No amount of trepidation on her part was going to counter the formidable force of the Juicy Crones. Resistance was out of the question. Her head was abuzz with questions she had been avoiding for decades. Thea picked up on that thought, "You're magnetizing the information you've asked for Maggie. The Universe is complying with your desires, even if you think on a conscious level that you don't really want to know all of this, that its too fast, too soon. You are ready my friend. Gratitude! Think gratitude."

"My gosh! Its almost 10:30. If we don't hurry we'll miss the last ferry." Cybil was organizing things and getting collected to get out the door. "Colleen, pick you up at ten or so? I'll call when we're in the ferry line tomorrow morning." Like a sheep dog Cybil herded the women out the door, with quick hugs from all for Colleen.

"I'll meet you there at noon. No sense coming all the way down here. Its about half way between here and Mukeltio." Colleen couldn't resist a final comment, "It's going to be wonderful Magda. I've wanted to know where you were and what was going on with you for forty years. And to be able to introduce you to Nora... even if she doesn't recognize you and you don't remember her, it's a link, a connection. As much as I always knew you were out there, I know that its all coming right. I'll see you tomorrow." Colleen shut the door before she got caught up in prolonging their departure, a habit she always chided herself for indulging, but all too often did anyway.

Chapter Twenty

Wallingford was cozied down for the night. All except for one of Cybil's favorite little detours. She pulled into the drive of a 24-hour espresso stand, Buzz Inn for a Brewed Awakening, jumped out, ran around to the back and opened the rear hatch of the Suburban. Out of curiosity Thea got out, joined Cybil and watched in amazement as her friend opened a refrigerator, "Remember, this whole rig is run by solar electric panels and flex fuel. That way I can have this little convenience all the time" Cybil beamed. She pulled out a jug of raw milk. Out of another cupboard she extracted a bottle of something dark brown and creamy looking, "76% Columbian Chocolate and our own raw honey. Thea, toss everybody an afghan and a pillow from that stash on the side there while I get our drinks. I'm about to one-up Magda in the phenethylamine department."

Another car pulled up behind them, and Cybil gave the driver a sweet smile as she mouthed "almost through" while Thea did a cheerful tweedle of fingers acknowledging the presence.

In moments Cybil pulled forward to the order window with Thea trotting along behind, tossing afghans and pillows across the seat backs at her friends. By the time Cybil was at the window, Thea climbed back into her seat, carrying her own mohair throw and down pillow. Cybil assured Thea the "bees," as she called the kids in the hive-shaped hut, were used to her strange orders. She handed over her liquid cocoa and raw milk and asked for three straight hot chocolates, heavy on the steamed milk, and one with a double shot of Fair Trade Peruvian espresso."

LaCrosse paid generously, even though she'd supplied most of the ingredients. She also told the girls to take the order from the car behind her out of the $50 bill. "Pay it forward... or backward in this case. The rest is for you kids," she smiled at the girls and pulled on around the little building through an archway of huge fir trees with plants hanging in baskets, a pond with a rock wall and waterfall, and burlap coffee-bean bags on the wood fence at the end of the drive. It felt like they were driving through a fairy land. Thea felt right at home.

As she pulled out on the road Cybil voice activated her cell phone, "The Eyrie" She got the house voice mail, where she made arrangements for four breakfast burritos and chai matés in the morning so they could sleep till it was nearly time to go.

Moments later, with everybody snugged into place and sipping on their orgasmic cocoa, Cybil eased out onto the I-5. By the time she'd passed the second exit marker Mitzy had finished her elixir and was sawing logs. Magda attempted to cozy in, but basically tossed and turned, trying to catch up with all the new information that was flooding her psyche. Thea graciously tried to keep Cybil company, but the conversation was more garbled than coherent: "Such connection... Source guiding... wish she could let go... wish I could... judgment such a nuisance..." which segued into a snore, snore, and a snuffle.

Cybil sipped her mocha supreme and thought about how blessed she was to have these dear friends. She mused over their last escapade, when Thea had a week-long workshop in the San Bernardino mountains and they had gotten snowed in!! Snowed in in southern California? And not one but two of the attendees ended up dead. And what was that all with Will, Anthea's long-time and ardent suitor and what he did to Anthea's organic honey? Lacing it with thorazine so her visions would be garbled and she'd finally be dependent on him. Of course that never happened. They figured out what was going on and Will was still somewhat in the dog house. Not that Thea held a grudge, but that it cooled her ardor a tad.

There were other adventures, and at some point Mitzy, having become a big fan of Dr. Jean Bolen, had taken to calling the trio the "Juicy Crones." That was about when their friend, Burgess suggested they open a Detective Agency since they seemed to keep falling into situations where they had to solve some very curious mysteries. But Thea had said, ever so firmly, that it would have to be "Investigations" because that was what they were about — investigating the mysteries of the universe. It just happened that sometimes that led to adventures on the dark side. Of course, they were all too busy to actually open an office, but they did seem to keep coming up with clients, if she could call them that.

With all of this buzzing through her brain, Cybil was on the ferry bobbing across the water before she knew it. From there, it was an easy ride up the hill and out to the point where her glorious Whidbey Island Eyrie overlooked the Sound. Lights twinkled on her little bay below the house as she pulled into the portico. Natasha opened the front door and bounded out to help guide the sleep-walking women into their respective bedrooms. Not one of them seemed to need the chamomile tea or the valerian caps René had arranged for their bedside tables.

Despite their late night and exhaustion from the infusion of information the day before, anticipation woke the three Juicy Crones early the next morning. Mitzy hit the trail down to the beach in her platform cross-trainers, Anthea found a spot on the lawn overlooking the water for her meditation and flow yoga. A doe and her fawns watched from the shade of a stand of fir trees. Cybil did a quick stint in the infra-red sauna and then a Pilates work out before a session of water aerobics in the pool. For the first time in as long as she could remember Magda had sunk into a deep sleep and didn't awaken till everybody was indulging in burritos and Yerba Matés on the deck over-looking the water. Rubbing her eyes like a toddler, Magda stumbled into the morning, mumbling what it was that had her mind in such a whirl: "What if she hates me? I don't know what I did that she didn't try to get me back. It must have been something horrible."

"What if you ran away because of something she did?" Cybil was ever on the look out for the logical alternative.

"Do we really have to do this?" Magda nervously twirled her spiky hair.

"I've got an idea. Let's go shopping. Nothing takes a girl's mind off her troubles like a shopping spree for some nice naughty undies." Cybil picked up a walkie talkie, "Hey, kids, get ready. I'm coming over with some customers."

Knowing Cybil as they did, Thea and Mitzy began to follow her, only to find Magda hanging back in utter confusion. "How can we go shopping? We have to be at the Institute at noon. Shouldn't we get ready?"

Cybil was still talking into her Nexus, "You've got Thea and Mitzy in the Laguna data bank. We'll have to do some measuring on Magda. Here we come," and she danced down the steps and out across the lawn, past Cynthia Thomas's bronze sculpture called Motherhood,[13] with its one side bear mother and the other human. None of the Juicy ones could resist giving her a rub on the way to the studio. "Ta da, my lair! Welcome to the heart and soul of Great Goddess Lingerie."

Light spilled through clerestory windows into a high-beamed room. Natasha was at the computer printing out data, while Renée whirled around, pulling things out of drawers. She did a little stomp dance over to Magda, took her gently by the hand and led her to a dressing room while Cybil began holding up bras and camisoles, boy briefs, boxers, hi-cuts... all manner of color combinations, tossing them around the room like so many flower petals.

"Let's get into some Gratitude Attitude here women?" The heart full of gratitude icon was everywhere... batiked into silk, embroidered on silk, labeled on green organic cotton.

Indeed, they immersed themselves in an orgasm of luxury. "This'll up your vibe Magda!" Cybil sang. She put a heart-full of gratitude key on a lovely golden chain around Magda's neck.

Chapter Twenty-One

It wasn't until they drove away later that morning that the women got the full vista of Cybil's Eyrie. The house, the studio, the barn... all timbers and aged siding to blend with the little forest that eased down to the water's edge, with terraced garden roofs and solar panels. They wound down the drive through fir trees. Everyone was eager to come back, but right at that moment they had a reunion to attend.

The Suburban hummed along a meandering corridor of cedars and ferns in Alden, north of Seattle. The lane had the feel of English countryside. Around a curve they came to a low, moss-covered stone wall that ended at a pair of stately pilasters, complete with guard house and wrought iron gates that swung open when Cybil announced they were "the expected guests of Dr. Furbelow". That was the name Colleen had said to use and it worked like the proverbial charm. Up the drive they went, around a corner and came to a halt. *Serenity Manor* was breath-taking. A huge Tudor mansion set on a rise. Half-timbered, its wooden-frame spaced out with wattle and daub, it was the picture of the famous 'black-and-white' effect of the period from whence it came. A propitiously placed plaque informed them it had been moved (down to the last pebble and splinter) from Lowfall, Middlesex, Great Britain in 1883. The sloping lawn led down to a pond.

And there, dancing lightly across the green at the top of a knoll was a veritable sylph of woman, playing a fiddle as she dipped and swooped. Her gown appeared, from their vantage point, to be of soft turquoise voile with a scarf-tipped hem, giving it a lyric edge that flowed to perfection with her movements. She had a flower wreath holding her long wheat-colored hair, for the most part, up on her head, though fetching tendrils escaped here and there.

From her perspective, this was just another snorting vehicle with large nosey people invading her sylvan glen. Such invasions threw the faeries, gnomes and elves into a tizzy. They seemed to sense that these large bundles of noise and odd smells were about to bring some sort of disarray to their friends.

For the fae folk did indeed think of the residents as friends. Even Captain Everest, the mountain of a man who loved to fly down the knoll in his wheelchair, thrusting his cane at the heavens and shouting, "Full steam avast!" clearly not having a clue what "avast" meant, and taking great delight in terrorizing Nurse Cogless, whose immense bosom flopped furiously, slapping her in the double chin as she ran down the hill after him, certain that if he splashed into the pond she was duty bound to dive in after him... even though she couldn't swim. It didn't occur to her that she was naturally endowed with the most buoyant of life preservers.

The faery lady danced and played her fiddle. Her little friends, who lived in their nooks in the slump-stone wall, loved it when she played those Irish tunes. Even if they were indigenous faery folk with origins in the North American traditions, there was still some spark that lit up when those

Celtic tunes wafted on the air. They danced around her, somehow knowing that changes were about to take place. They could feel the energy in the ethers. And so could Nora. She didn't know what it was, and she didn't know if she liked the feeling — if it felt good or if it was uncomfortable. But it was coming and that was for certain. It was driving toward the main building in that big, colorful vehicle, so she played louder than ever. Somehow she felt like playing and dancing joyously. For so long her music had been lovely but lonely. Now it was buoyant. And the fae folk felt her exhilaration.

The dancing sylph was none other than Nora O'Brien. And in case they hadn't yet guessed it, Colleen, who met the Suburban at the portico, announced to the Juicy Crones and Magda, that this was indeed Mary's mother.

Magda began to feel a bit odd. How does one react upon meeting with the woman whom Colleen insisted was her mother, a mother who had let her 11-year-old daughter run off to live with a bunch of hippies. Was she angry with this woman? She was definitely in the midst of conflicted emotions. And she knew that feeling as one that had led to fugue episodes in the past. She clung to Anthea like kudzu to a swamp oak, fearing that her mind could whisk her into some bizarre neverland. What might she become this time? But then, as they drew closer to Nora, Magda relaxed noticeably: "That can't possibly by my mother. She's not a day over 40."

Colleen urged them to move on into the main building, "Ah, well that's another part of the tale of Nora O'Brien. Before we try to meet her, maybe we could go into the salon and have tea and get Dr. Furbelow to tell you a bit about what's going on."

Anthea turned back and waved to the woman, "Did you

all see them? She attracts faeries in droves. They're all over the place. I mean, I can well imagine this is a place they'd love. But they seem to venerate her as though she's fae royalty. Oh, I can't wait to have her introduce me to them." She waved again as Nora fiddled and danced on into the woods. She was too far away for any of them to recognize the tune, and that was probably just as well, for had Magda heard it... well she was under enough stress already without that little piece of the puzzle being thrown into the pot at that particular moment.

Serenity Manor seemed like a nice, peaceful place. Clearly, a great deal of money was spent to keep up the ambiance, but Magda was having none of it. The tension of her vibe could have suspended a tightrope walker over the Grand Canyon. As they reached the entrance Magda drew back. "Just to be sure this is what I should do," she asked, holding her arm out for a quick energy test.

"It's a tad late, lass," Thea muttered but obliged.

Magda's arm held strong despite the weirdness of what she was about to do... confirm that that strange young woman was her mother, whom she hadn't seen in nearly four decades. So far the evidence was far from convincing to Magda.

Opulence was definitely the keynote to interior design. Someone had been very careful to maintain the Tudor theme, from the stickback love-seat rocking chair to the Georgian double-bow side chairs, the tables, the sofas. Every detail was seen to with the utmost care. One couldn't help but wonder how Henry the VIII managed to settle his prodigious girth into such delicate seating arrangements.

Colleen led them past the registration desk with a tickle at the air in the direction of the registrar and sailed on to the salon. But they couldn't go there. It was filled to capacity with bingo players swatting each other's moves, a gent giggling wildly as he made off with the key piece of a very complex jigsaw puzzle and a matched pair of harried staffers attempting to keep the teacarts from being toppled.

"This is where the stragglers begin to form up for the second sitting. Usually they're aren't so many of them. Must be a special on the menu today. It pisses them off that they didn't get in there first when there's a special," Colleen tried to make it sound perfectly normal.

Next they passed what was surely the dining hall. They couldn't help but notice that lunch was stirring up a bit of a ruckus. Somebody didn't like rutabagas and somebody else felt she should "shut up and be grateful they're mashed, you old ninny. You can gum 'um "

"They're excitedly awaiting mashed rutabagas?" Mitzy was definitely puzzled. But she also felt a twinge of an urge to get in there and throw mashed rutabagas at the scrawny one that was laying down the food rules.

Colleen pointed at the menu board: Tiramisu for desert. "No wonder," she read: "<u>With</u> genuine brandy <u>and</u> imported rum." She urged them to come along with her so "we can beard the lion in his den. I've always wanted to say that. Know where it comes from?" They all shook their heads wondering what pearl of wisdom their new friend would bestow..."Neither do I. If you ever come across it, let me know." They all laughed heartily.

As they proceeded down an appropriately long corridor, Thea was twitchingly distracted by cross-vibrations she was getting just walking down the hall. Little fuzzy electronic tickles resulted in involuntary tweaks to various parts of her anatomy. ElectroMagnetic frequencies abounded. She raised her arms up and out in front and began waving her open palms in a frequency scan which tended to make her appear to be a potential resident. She whispered to Cybil, "I'm getting that the place is alive with video scanners and laser beams."

"Aren't you the one who talks about 'pronoia'? The antidote to paranoia. Remember, the whole world is conspiring to shower you with blessings?" Cybil taunted Thea for forgetting what she taught. So it was a character flaw of Cyb's, gloating over her friend's lapse. She had to have at least one imperfection.

"Sometimes you really are being watched. Anyway, its not the watching so much as the invasion of our biofields with all these micro-waves" Thea hissed back. Just then they reached their destination and Colleen knocked on Dr. Furbelow's door.

After appropriate introductions, Dr. Cuthbert Furbelow danced a veritable minuet on oddly tiny feet for such a large man. It was as though parts of him were completely at odds with the establishment's theme, starting with his Victorian partner's desk. If he weren't the doctor and, therefore, supposedly vetted as sane by the powers in charge, the Crones might have wondered if he weren't at the very least a dual personality. He couldn't decide which side of his desk to sit on. Which partner should he be? The relaxed and confident Cuthbert in the three-piece dove gray suit, with the huge picture window framing his profile in front of a lush garden vista. Or the tightly snugged up Dr. Furbelow, with his jacket buttoned to match his demeanor, not to mention his lilac button-down collar Arrow shirt, sitting on the side that would put his books, plaques and awards behind him as backdrop.

Colleen had apparently been through this dance

before. Applying her natural aptitude for controlling adolescents, she guided the ladies to a seating arrangement of mini sofas and arm chairs, thus requiring the good doctor to abandon his dance around the desk and join them in the pseudo-casual seating arrangement.

It only took about twenty minutes of verbal folderol before they managed to get him to talk directly about Nora O'Brien, and her passive behavior. She'd come to them not long after her husband had gone to Texas to visit some fellow in a symbiotic ministry and met an untimely demise. Maggie turned a pasty white. The concept that her father was killed in that debacle was another boulder on the pyramid of information about her past that was accumulating. It just hadn't sunk in when they told her about it at Sunny Acres. After all, the notion of her being from next door to the commune, raised in a religious community, didn't register at all. Now she had that, in addition to the mysterious woman who was apparently her mother. Not the freedom fighter she'd grown to hope was her progenitor.

Furbelow didn't really know anything about the Texas part of the story. Just that after it happened the people where Nora lived wanted to find a place for her to have peace and quiet. Apparently the press had been swarming around when they found out about Brother O'Brien, and the elders felt a need to "protect his widow," as they put it. They assured the Institute she was totally benign, just a little peculiar. All of her needs were to be met as long as her presence was kept top secret. That was the last the Institute heard from the *Shepherd's Flock,* except to get quarterly payments that assured Nora's upkeep. She'd been here fiddling away, speaking only to the faeries, ever since. Furbelow smirked. The only thing the staff ever heard out of her was that annoying tune she sang when she played her violin, something that sounded like *Amazing Grace* on speed, and the only word the staff understood was Mary, so they figured it was some kind of religious thing from the *Shepherd's Fold*.

If she wasn't one to be concerned about what people would think Maggie would have flopped on the floor in a faint. Thea sat beside her and attempted to do a little Reiki, drawing on her own soothing energy.

Mitzy had clearly been thinking very single-mindedly about only one aspect of the whole Nora puzzle, "So if that woman we saw with the fiddle is supposed to be Maggie's mother, how come she doesn't look a day over forty?"

"Oh that," Thea chuckled. "It only makes sense. If she's been waiting for Mary to come to her, she's stopped her internal clock. It's something I've been working on for years, but this is the first real case I've seen. I can't wait to get to know her."

"Good luck," Cuthbert chortled. "Nobody gets to know Nora. Not even the people who dropped her off knew what was going on with her. They said she'd been like that since her daughter had to be put in a looney bin by the Prophet of their Family. That was part of why her husband went to Texas. He couldn't bear it any longer. Like I said before, the Flockers couldn't either. We've seen neither hide nor hair of any of them since they brought her."

Cybil glared at Furbelow, "You mean to say no one ever visits her, checks on her?"

"Well, of course Ms. Collins here..."

Cybil sat back and cogitated. Ms. Collins on the other

hand was ready for a breath of fresh air. Anything to get them out of Furbelow's oppressive presence.

And that was when Magda, Colleen, Thea and Mitzy went to meet Nora O'Brien. Cybil excused herself to take care of some business. "In fact," she turned to Colleen, "could you get them back to my place on Whidbey after they've had a visit with Nora. This is going to take awhile. You're welcome to stay over. There's plenty of room. Then we'll all come back tomorrow for another visit on our way home."

Mitzy and Colleen saluted Cybil and turned to join Thea, who was dragging the reluctant Maggie down the sloping lawn, toward the pond where Nora stood on a large rock and played to the water nymphs darting amongst the lily pads.

Cybil went off on her mysterious errand while Thea and Colleen played mediator between Maggie, who didn't want to go too fast with this business of meeting her mother, and Nora who paid no attention to the strange collection of women. Nora clearly had the edge. It's difficult to take a stand with someone who has the ability to make you feel non-existent. Although Thea could usually metaphysicate herself out of a such a bog, Colleen had years of practice tilling in the hazy tangle of Nora's social skills and Magda hovered in her own version of a blue funk--that left Mitzy wanting to give the reunion some space.

She found herself a nice little bench under the wings of a spreading oak and fiddled in her own way, playing the ring tones on her cell phone. It was when she hit Lulu Haynes that the brilliance of her own mind zapped her. She hit "send," and held a brief conversation with the voice in the ethers.

Meanwhile, either Thea had gotten the fae folk to kick

butt, or that dose of metaphysics had taken hold. Nora was doing that thing Cuthbert said she did, playing a whirling variation of *Amazing Grace,* but then, for no seeming reason, she slowed down to lilting strains. Just when she got to the third time through Magda peered out from under her funk and sang along in a voice so sweet it made them all tear up:

"'T was mamma taught my heart to sing,
And she who played my game,"

Nora replied:

"How quickly does my girl appear,
When err I call her name."

In harmony the duo sang:

"Through hedges thick, cross fields so wide,
she's on her way to me;
I hear her laughter dear, and I rejoice,
For in my arms she'll be.

"I'm waiting here in patience still,
because I know that she,
Will dance and sing and she will bring
her sunshine home to me."

Nora looked at Magda and clearly saw the child she'd been waiting for all these years. "Did you have a good time next door, little one?" Not a shred of anger or retribution for having in some way broken a rule. Not confusion. Just utter joy to have her child come when she was called.

Magda went to Nora on the rock and, with frogs leaping, dragon flies buzzing, and, though only Nora and Thea were sure, faeries singing and dancing up a storm, Nora and Magda embraced and Gaia let out a sign of relief.

Mitzy was on the verge of explosion. How do you interrupt a scene like that? But she couldn't hold back. They had work to do. She pulled Thea and Colleen over and explained her plan. Hah! Why not? If they could deal with Hortense, they could certainly deal with any challenges this place could dole out.

In Nora's room, Mitzy and Magda folded her skirts and dresses and unmentionables (they'd have to get Cybil on the job in that department), into the suitcase they found under her bed – a vintage 1970 powder-blue Samsonite.

Outside, Thea pushed Mitzy up and over the stone wall to emerge through the hedges out on the road. She checked her watch and her cell phone... and waited impatiently while Thea went back to see to the final touches on Nora's packing.

The first thing they had to do was make it down the stairs and past all those security cameras Thea had noticed earlier. Calzona sent Collins (detective books call their operatives by last names a lot) off to the kitchen pantry where she was instructed to tell the staff that she needed some aluminum foil to help one of the residents make a gift for her great-grand-child. That was how they managed to rig deflector hats to disrupt the laser sensors as they worked their way along the corridor with Thea dowsing for beams of red light. Then they came to the part where they snuck Nora, her suit case and her fiddle case, (though why she had a case when she never let go of the fiddle was beyond any of them), out through the laundry and down some strange arrangement that might have been a coal chute back in England.

Before they did that, Nora had asked to be able to leave a note for Dr. Furbelow. Now that she was talking she seemed to have a strong sense of propriety. She wanted to tell the Doctor not to worry about her as she was going to join her daughter and friends and was sure she'd be eternally happy where she was going. She did want to make sure he explained to the fae folk, and took good care of them. Colleen, with her experience in dealing with humorless bureaucrats, talked her out of it. As she pointed out, it was best to leave the institution to what institutions like this did in cases of disappearing patients. Sweep it under the Aubosson carpet.

Meanwhile, Mitzy was hiding in the hedge, fidgeting her way into a royal tizzy, which, considering what she was planning to do was probably the state she needed to be in to pull off her part of the caper. Finally it came, a nice little "rent a wreck," per her instructions. It hadn't been easy to find such a plum amongst the upscale connections where Lulu Haynes did business, but the entrepreneur had called someone in Bellevue who knew someone in Queen Anne who knew a woman in Renton who had a connection in the University District and voila. Mitzy gave the driver a $20 to hang out, she'd be back within the hour, and off she went.

Just inside the guard gate she pulled forward about 15' before she stalled out the engine and came to a sputtering halt. She got out, popped her bubble gum, popped the hood, poked around and got a smear of grease on her cheek, (too endearing,) and turned to share her pathetic self with the guard, whom she had so artfully enticed away from his post with her "breakdown."

Mitzy under any circumstances was an eye-catcher, but Mitzy in her lipstick-red spandex toreadors above stiletto heels, and her shirt tied up at the waist but unbuttoned down the front to said tie, artfully revealing her Great Goddess enhanced endowments, her carrot top sufficiently fluffed out and frazzled, and a little Japanese fan fanning furiously to ward off the heat of her frustration...? What was a self-respecting retired cop-cum-security guard to do when she began to sob, "Oh thank goodness, a man in uniform. You'll know what to do. I'm supposed to pick up Momma right now. We got reservations at the Benaroya to see Tom Jones. He's her favorite in the whole world and she's losing it... there ain't much that gets her goin' any more. I got to get this thing on the road. Can you see if you can figure out what's wrong?"

While Mitzy kept him thus occupied Colleen's Toyota pick-up whizzed past and out into the metaphorical 'setting sun.' Actually they just went down the road a half-mile and waited till Mitzy's uniformed man managed to detect that the distributor cap was loose and got it snugged down. (Thank the Goddess he hadn't been close enough to see her loosen it before he arrived to save the day.) In no time she was giving him a thank-you kiss on the cheek with enough Goddess-enhanced hug to keep him confused so as not to notice that she swung around and drove off, apparently forgetting about Momma and Tom Jones.

Mitzy gave the clunker back to the kid from the rental lot with another $20, and, with Thea's help she clambered up to join Magda in the truck bed which, thankfully had a camper shell and a couple of sleeping bags to pad the hard bottom. As Colleen drove get-away Nora rode shotgun, her fiddle at the ready.

Chapter Twenty-Two

Back at The Eyrie Cybil was more than astounded to see the group arrive with Nora. After greeting the unexpected guest, she had to laugh at herself. And then laugh at her friends. They'd been double teaming each other without knowing it, just because they each had an idea on how to help Magda and Nora.

Cybil's project for the afternoon had been to work with her lawyers in Seattle to make arrangements with Furbelow to release Nora into her daughter's care. First, Cybil had a quick session with a friendly judge who managed to arrange papers that agreed that Magda was, in fact, Mary O'Brien, and that Nora was her mother, and that she would be more than well cared for in California and neither Nora nor Mary/Magda was going to say a word to the *Flock*. Cybil pointed out to Cuthbert that it was up to him whether he wanted to spill the beans or not, but it meant that there was now a place for some new paying resident and nobody saw any reason to cut off the flow from such a charitable institution as the Shepherd's congregation.

It was therapy time for Magda. Into the kitchen she went. Renee and Natasha stepped in as kitchen support. Nora asked if she might play her fiddle. Thea quickly acknowledged the wisdom of letting her provide a bit of musical therapy for all of them. "Yes, lovely. We'll dance and sing while they prepare a heavenly feast, if I know Magda." Thea joined Nora and that was when she noticed a colorful piece of paper tucked down inside Nora's fiddle.

"Nora, I think your fiddle will sound sweeter if you take that piece of paper out of it. We'll put it right over here on the counter." Thankfully, Nora didn't resist.

Mitzy put in a call to Carmen. It was time to let her know that Magda had found her mother. No need to pursue the DNA test to link her to the little body they had left with the pathologist. Not that anyone was pushing, but just on the off chance, maybe the call would provide word on Magda One's cause of demise, or on Wolf's ashes. They still felt there was something in his body chemistry that would reveal an unnatural cause of death. And, speaking of Wolf, Cybil decided to call Gillian and see if she would go out to the Wikiup and get the latest of his tracking journals and send them to her place in LaPlaya.

As Colleen and Cybil danced and swooped and sang along with Nora, Thea snuck a peek at the scrap from the fiddle. Her curiosity was immediately aroused. There was something oddly familiar about it. "Nora, do you know what this is?"

"Oh, that's the page Mary left behind when she went away. But I couldn't read it. She wrote it like she did her book. It was her secret book. She wrote in code."

"DaVinci code, I see," Thea pointed at the page.

"Oh my goodness." Magda jumped right off the stool

where she sat chopping onions. " I REMEMBER! That came out of my diary. I covered it with leaves and feathers and bark. Magda showed me how to soften them into almost a cloth -like fabric. I put that on the cover. I wrote all the stuff in there that I couldn't tell anyone else. Magda told me that was a good way to feel better when things got really ugly."

"How the hell did a child know about the DaVinci?" asked Cybil.

"It just means it's reverse imaged. See? backward." Thea held it up to the mirror on the dining room wall. Sure enough, they could all read it plain and clear... "Momma, I love you and I don't want you to cry any more. And I don't want to cry any more. And poor poppy, he cries every time he looks at me. So I will go away and you can stop crying and Rev. Prophet Jonas will let you be happy again once this devil child is gone. I will think of you and sing our song all the time. You do that too. Love, Mary"

Softly, ever so softly Thea whispered, "That journal we found at Wolf's place. It's Mary's diary, not his. We'll have Gillian put it in with the tracking notes when she sends the package."

It was quite a while before anyone thought about the food, prepared before the revelation and getting cold as they all crept inside their thoughts. The mental haze was broken by the ring of the phone.

Cybil answered. It was Gillian on the line. Gillian, a woman known for her self-control. She didn't do frantic, but she sounded on the verge of that very reaction. Not only was there no sign of the tracking notes, but it seemed like someone had been inside the Wikiup after the women had gone north. And worse than that, Wolf's motorcycle was gone from the barn!

Madam Olivia had called the Sheriff's wife and found out that Pete and Doc Saxby had taken off for the back country in honor of Wolf. Gillian and Olivia didn't know what to do. They didn't want to step on the Sheriff's toes by calling in the Staties. After all, if there was a case here it had to be the Sheriff's case. Gillian just hoped she was wrong about this whole thing. She asked if the women could come back and they could clear it all up themselves.

There was only one possible response Cybil declared, "Change of plans. Back to Dos Lobos, ladies. Gillian, we're on our way to you, first thing in the morning. And we'll have two more guests." Because, of course, Colleen must go along as Nora still seemed to feel most comfortable with her nearby. After all, in a sense it was as though Nora was a new-born. She'd spent more than 2/3 of her life speaking only to fairies and dancing everywhere she went and never giving a thought to what came next or how to do for herself. Most of all, there was the issue of trying to sort out this grown woman who seemed to have her daughter Mary stashed away inside of her. She saw glimpses, but then Mary'd disappear. Magda had her own issues to deal with. How does one sort out the business of having a mother who stirred up memories she wasn't used to having. Any... Memories, that is. Let alone a mother.

Chapter Twenty-Three

Before they left the Eyrie in the morning, Mitzy called Lulu to arrange for a van to meet them at the air field in Vegas. And Magda called Hermes to let him know it would be a few more days before she got home with two new members of the household... no not animals, women. One of whom was her mother, Nora O'Brien, and the other, a childhood friend. Yes, she, Magda had been a child, with a mother and a friend. And that launched into an explanation of all that had gone on.

When she finally wound down, she remembered to ask how all the critters were getting along and got a report in return that, "Curry still isn't himself, but the girls from next door come over whenever they can to help out. They seem to have a calming effect on him. They really love the horses. It's too bad they have to sneak around. But hey, they're having lots of fun. Except the one you got into it with over the bike. She's a sneak of a different kind. Haven't quite figured her out yet, but she's not a happy kid."

"Tell them I'll be home and we'll find a way to mend fences with their folks. For now, we're all focused on figuring out what happened to the Magda that I was named after. And who snuck into Wolf's place and stole his journals. We just hope they didn't get the diary that must have been my one and only possession collected from the car crash that started all of this"

On the plane ride back to Vegas, Magda asked Nora and Colleen to tell her more about what she'd been like when she was a little girl. But the only part Nora was willing to discuss was the music. When Mary was a child, Nora played her fiddle and sang and danced with her and sat her on the piano bench and miraculously Mary played whole tunes right from the start. It didn't take long for her to end up being the baby wonder, playing the organ for services. Of course, as Colleen had noted earlier, the only music allowed at the compound was hymns.

"Hah! I remember now. There were serious problems once in awhile because I could never explain what it was that made my fingers go where they went. Something just took over and my fingers played *Ode to Joy*, or something like that. I didn't know what it was. I'd never even heard it before. It just sounded beautiful in my head and my fingers wanted to play it. Jonas came in for the rehearsal and heard it and he stormed down the aisle and screamed at me to 'stop that rambunctious pounding on my organ.'" There was a moment of quiet while the Crones tried to remain appropriately demur.

Magda was like a starved pup, she wanted more information, more, more. "I need to know all about where I grew up. What were those people like? Did I have any friends besides you?"

And Colleen, being the born story teller that she was, was certainly willing to oblige. For instance, there was the way the whole commune did drills hiding out in the caves in the foothills where they had years' worth of supplies and fire arms with ammunition and heavy artillery. They had to be ready when the call came, the trumpet sounded for the battle with the masses of wicked ones. Armageddon was coming closer and closer because of people like those hippies next door.

"Rev. Father Jonas would always complain about the disgrace of those people right out there in broad daylight blasting that nasty music and dancing those grindy moves, their bare muscular arms out there flexing and sweating for all the world to see, while the righteous ones tilled the soil. He spied on them with binoculars from up in a watch tower. The good *Flock* on our side dutifully sang hymns about toiling, and sweat of the brow, as they tried to drown out the bunch over there. Apparently our sweat was righteous while the hippies' was evil."

"The group on the hippy side of the fence surprised us one day when they segued from *Gypsy Woman* to singin' with us: *Nearer My God to Thee*. The Deputy Rev. was thrilled that the heathens seemed to know the song. Nobody ever told them how you can fake it by following along a 1/3 beat behind and it seems like you're right there singing with the group. Anyway, Rev. Solomon had us work closer and closer to the fence to entice the hippies away from their wantonness. He said we would invite them to a prayer and renunciation meeting afterward.

"When they got good and close, the fellow on the tractor, Birch I think they called him, pulled it right up alongside the boundary, with the flatbed trailer next to the little wire fence. The wanton organic crew jumped up on the bed in first-rate circus style, looking for all the world like a scene from Oklahoma, (the musical, not the state). They stacked themselves up in a pyramid. Except for some odd reason they were faced backward. But hey, they were still singing. And then, at the end, for a grand finale, the tractor gave a snort and everybody in the stack dropped their drawers and shined their totally organic moons on us, the till-that-moment-smiling crowd peering over the property line. The next day, the line of crosses went up along the fence."

Chapter Twenty-Four

On the way back to Dos Lobos, Cybil checked her email and found two reports. One from Dr. Solares, and one from Ken Knightly over in Twisp.

Ken's letter was intriguing as it added to what they already knew about Wolf's visit to the area. But this was new information. The Indian on an Indian had definitely been seen in the area. About three weeks ago. Word was he'd been to the *Fold,* and they were madder than the proverbial wet hen about it. Apparently, he'd left the guided tour when he visited. No one did that! The guards at the compound claimed that he stopped at the mausoleum of the Prophet, went inside the chain link enclosure where he stole a pebble from the path in front. (Never mind that they gave away rocks blessed by the Reverend himself before his ascension. The gift shop offered them to all those who took the paid tour. And Wolf had indeed paid his $25.00.) He also apparently took a photograph — but that was with his own camera and film, so how were they considering that a crime? Anyway, according to their account, he took the rock and the photo and then he sat down and had a "conversation" with the Prophet. Then he went to the souvenir shop where he bought a tract of the Prophet's sayings, a copy of the history of the *Flock* and a cartouche of the Reverend's family tree, both coming and going, or rather fore and aft.

And by the way, the town was a buzz now that word was going round that one of the women who'd been at the Two Toad and out to Sunny Acres was the little girl who disappeared all those years ago with the Hungarian hippie.

Once they got over being a little concerned that now people were probably gossiping all over Methow Valley about the return of the mystery girl with the odd name of Too, the women felt they were on a roll. Colleen was as interested as the rest of them. "Sounds like your friend Wolf was onto something about the Prophet. Wonder what he had in mind? And I wonder where those things are that he got from the Fold?"

But Cybil was already onto the email from Dr. Solares. The news wasn't quite as exciting, but it did have one pertinent piece of information. What they found in Magda One's bone marrow were traces of a poison called nicotiana. Normally it shouldn't have still been there, but thanks to the care taken with the body — and the climate control at which it had been kept, much like a mummy in an Egyptian tomb — they were able to run tests that revealed traces of the poison.

"Nicotiana, isn't that nicotine? Of the tobacco family?" Thea said as she read the report.

"Do you suppose that's why we found a tobacco leaf in the Wikiup? I mean, its not exactly the same, but maybe it was some kind of hint." Cybil could hardly stand it. This was hard evidence. Logical. The way she liked. She always went along with Anthea, but give her hard evidence any day and she was a happy camper. "As soon as we get to the Ranch we need to find out where that journal went, even if we have to track the sneak thieves across the desert sands. I think it has to be what he found out about how or why Magda One was murdered using this nicotiana as a poison."

"That must be what I saw those two boys distilling in the vision that seemed out of place with the others — the ones with the girl and the body," Anthea theorized.

Once they had this notion in place the drive from Las Vegas to Dos Lobos would have been rather mundane were it not for Magda's determination that now her life was going to be trebly difficult. For Magda, learning to have a mother and care for one who was quite childlike, let alone learning to deal with the fact that Nora looked so much younger than she did herself, was quite disconcerting. "I just don't get how she does it."

Thea tried ever so hard not to sound exasperated: "Once she turned off the propaganda machine she moved into a non-concensus reality. Without the input from the outside world about the ravages of aging, the deterioration that all of us accept as inevitable, she just naturally stayed where she was. It wasn't as if she did anything conscious. The idyllic life she led, totally stress-free, active, dancing and singing, smelling the roses, left her suspended in the physical form she was in at the moment you moved out of her life."[14]

That brought up another fear for Magda, "My god, does that mean that now, with this exposure to the real world, she's suddenly going to wither into an old woman?"

"You mean a Juicy Crone? Most probably. Not wither, but age appropriately. It's not a curse, Magda. There's a reference in Dr. Bolen's poem, *To Mom on Mother's Day* about Margaret Mead's term, PMZ, post menopausal zest, for the life you are now leading. Enjoy the zest with her."

When they finally got to the Ranch Cybil pulled their rental car, another Mercedes wagon thanks to Lulu, into the clearing in front of the Wikiup and dashed toward the tent, with the others right behind her. Gillian must have been watching for them, because she came running out of the Ranch House.

Actually they were all just two degrees off totally surprised to find that the box with the baggie containing the tobacco leaf they had left behind was still there. Because, like Gillian said, the other things on the list Thea had asked Gillian to send to LaPlaya were gone; the tracking notebooks, the little trophies from the shelves, the things they'd left after they'd put things on the funeral pyre. Things they hadn't thought were important back when they left to fly to Washington. And there was no sign of anything from Wolf's visit to *Shepherd's Fold*. Whoever stole the motorcycle must also have gone through the Wikiup. Cybil had to agree with Anthea -- sometimes there was good cause for paranoia. But they both wondered why the thieves had left the box. An embarrassed Gillian explained, she had taken the box into the house after they left. She'd just brought it back out when she knew they were coming. She was so uncharacteristically rattled she forgot to tell them when she called to report the theft.

That night, Magda, Colleen and Nora slept in the Ranch House, while Thea, Mitzy and Cybil bedded down in the Wikiup. Thea wanted to connect with the energy of whoever had taken Wolf's things. Well they connected with the energy all right, and it was intense. Their sleep was rudely interrupted when a pair of masked men in Ninja gear burst into the structure, one of them tripping over Anthea's portmanteau. It was a toss up who was more frightened, the Ninjas or the Crones? Maybe there were more than two... it seemed like a small army. And they were all bashing away in total confusion. Anyway one looked at it there was a ruckus that was heard all the way to the main house. The women used high kicks, Aikido thrusts and a few good whacks over the head with whatever item came to hand. The surprised sneak-thieves did the best they could to duck and dodge the flying Crones, but they were no match. When gunshots rang out the intruders tumbled over one another as they crashed out the door and ran for the back of the barn. Seconds later a raging HumVee tore out into the desert night. Olivia was the one with the double aught and she didn't hesitate to use it, though without her glasses she was a hair off the mark. Gillian, on the other hand, had a night-scope on her bird-watching digital camera. She got photos of the plates as the vehicle cut out across the moonlit desert. "Did it seem to you there were more than just two of them when they got outside?" Cybil asked. "I thought I saw somebody running off in a lateral direction, around the north of the barn, and someone else headed to the east."

"I only saw the two guys running for the hummer." Gillian patted her camera.

"Well, I thought I heard more than one vehicle start up," Mitzy said.

Back in the Ranch House they were able to pull some nice clean images of the Hummer's plates up on Gillian's Photoshop and call them in to the Sheriff's office... for all the good that would do. At least that was their plan. Cybil tried to get them to notify the FBI or some federal organization. However, Magda, Olivia and Gillian held out for the local troops. After all it was the Sheriff's friend whose home had been broken into, and his friend's bike that had been stolen. They just wanted to give their friend a chance. So what if it didn't make much sense? It's how they felt. And Thea was the one who kept telling Magda to go with how she felt.

Unfortunately, when they called the Sheriff's station, the phone rang through to his house. It was the middle of the night after all. Mrs. Willery informed them, quite stonily that the Sheriff was still out of town with no word of when he'd be back. "You know how it is when men feel the need for a piss-in-woods competition," the wife said. She had not been real fond of Wolf, and wasn't all that thrilled that Pete had gone off with Doc on the pretext of mourning their old buddy. No one really did understand what Pete saw in that woman. But then again, they had awakened her at two in the morning.

When the women hung up they argued once again over reporting... at least to the Highway patrol. But when they called the Staties, they were told there was no reason to try to find any traces of a Hummer in the middle of the night. Since there was no bodily harm done, a car would be sent to check things out in the morning. The patrolman suggested the women all sleep in one room in the Ranch House.

What they did instead was get busy and send the information to Lulu Haynes in Vegas. Because it was clear from the photos that the Hummer was a rental and where else in these parts would it have come from but Vegas? Finally, they turned in. For the second time that night.

By the time they were up and at their morning smoothies, with all sorts of supplemental powders supplied by Mitzy's magic carpet bag, an email came back from Lulu. The i.d. that was used to rent the car from one of her affiliates had apparently been stolen and they were running a trace on it, but it looked like it came from a gang of hackers down in Tijuana.

To Cybil, i.d. theft meant probable drug dealing. She

was hot to trot on a conspiracy theory, and eager to call in a friend at the FDA, until Thea told her to put a little Valerian in her tea and calm down. What conceivable link could there be between a drug and identity-theft gang out of Baja and an old lady who died forty years ago in Washington state?"

At that moment the Crones all had the same thought: Old lady? She would have been about the same age then as they were right right now.

As they were saying good-bye Olivia had a sudden recollection. "Oh good heavens. I don't know if it means anything. I think I told you a couple of men came to see Wolf just before he had his heart attack. I completely forgot all about it what with all the commotion, but they were very strange men. At first I thought they'd come to register for the lodge, so I jumped in and started a card. But they just wanted to talk to Wolf. They were dressed very straight, all in black suits even in this weather. But I couldn't help notice they had wigs and hats. Very odd. Like they didn't want to be recognized, so I assumed they must be agents come about a tracking job. I did take down their auto model and license when I made out the card, but then I just filed it away when they went off to see Wolf."

"Those could have been the intruders from last night. They were probably looking for whatever they couldn't get out of Wolf when then were here before." Magda was clearly on the verge of freaking out, but Thea put a calming hand on her should and whispered to her. "We'll deal with this with the Sheriff. He's got to be back soon. No need to make Olivia feel guilty. She didn't realize it could be significant." Thea turned to the Madam, "Olivia, would you see that Sheriff Willery gets that information as soon as he gets back. I'm sure he'll want a full report on the thefts."

With that piece of business arranged, the women packed their bags. As unsatisfactory as it might be there didn't seem to be anything more they could do in Dos Lobos. That being said, Magda wanted to get Nora settled in Bonsall. It was definitely time to head back to California.

Chapter Twenty-Five

The ride home gave them a chance to look at what the Juicy Crones knew about the situation as Wolf would have seen it. Try to see it from his point of view.

Thea initiated the recap: "One thing I remember is that on the intercom he told Gillian something about Magda's idée. Was he saying he had an ide...a or was he saying i.d. like identification? Either way, he'd gone to Washington and visited Sunny Acres. That trip confirmed that Magda of the trunk had come from there, and he therefore knew that Too did, too. But he couldn't have known that Maggie originally came from the *Fold,* because the farmers hadn't known. Something Alli said in their conversations must have led him to stop in at the *Fold.* Then he collected those things Knightly talked about. I think we need to see if Alli can remember anything more about what she told him. Anything that would have led him next door."

Thea phoned Alli. After greetings and catch-up, she got to the point, "Alli, you said you told Wolf about Colleen and how she came looking for a friend from her days at the *Fold,* right?"

Alli replied a bit defensively, "Well, of course I did. Does that make any difference?"

"Thanks Alli. We really appreciate it. Say hi to

everyone," and Thea hung up.

"So it sounds like he was putting things together that led him to the *Fold*. What we need now is to find out what was in the information he got at the Compound." Thea asked, "What was going on when he got back to Nevada? He called you, Magda, and wanted to see you in person. He didn't give anything away, so it must have been that he'd found out who you were, at least that you were Magda Too from Sunny Acres. And there may have been a link to *Shepherd's Fold*. So does any of this tie in to Olivia's two disguised men?"

Cybil had her own thoughts, "Why would the thieves take those things from Wolf's trophy case? And why did they go back a second time? Hadn't they gotten what they wanted when they ransacked the place and took the bike? None of the things they took seem to connect to anything about you, Magda. It could be that that whole fiasco was about some former case. Some crook who's out of prison and found out Wolf was dead and wanted some kind of revenge, or incriminating evidence that could still be used against them in some case that's still pending... Maybe that's where the heavy guys come in."

Anthea picked up from there, "What we still need is that last tracking notebook. We'll just have to wait to hear from the Sheriff and hope he finds the thieves. Otherwise, we're at a stalemate. I'm not getting anything intuitively. It's as though I've hit a block. I think I need a little R&R. We all do. Let's get out of our intellects, away from all this left-brain-trying-to-figure-it-out. I suggest an intense sensuosity meditation when we get home."

They dropped Magda, Colleen and Nora off at Palomar, where there was a joyful reunion with Tran, who had just returned from trekking in Thailand in time to meet them at the airport. That was when the Crones confirmed what they had all intuited, Tran was of the female persuasion. About 5'4", with decidedly Thai features, a stylish cut on her jet black hair, and a chimsong in a shade of peach that complemented the lilac version Magda wore. Interesting implications for the Tantric Sex Seminar Series. It did help clarify the womens' speculations about the Magda–Wolf relationship.

Magda had so much to tell Tran she hardly noticed when the plane took off, winging the Crones back to John Wayne airport. Besides, Magda needed to get their new family settled in at her place, and try to smooth things over with the Cantwells. Maybe have them over to meet Tran and Colleen and Nora. Oh, that should be a great change of pace.

However, arriving at the house in Bonsall, Magda's anticipated joy was quickly squashed when they drove up to find a fence of crosses between the Cantwell property and Magda and Tran's house.

"Interesting," Colleen mused. "Remember the story I told you about the hippies mooning us? Well, that's just what the fence Rev. Jonas put up looked like."

Magda immediately called Thea, who was just arriving in LaPlaya. The intuitive advised Magda to follow Magdalena's lead and do what the hippies did all those years ago — put up mirrors and black tourmaline aimed at the place next door to reflect the energy back from whence it came. At the Cantwell property.

After she hung up from talking to Magda, Thea asked Cybil to search the internet for more info on the *Fold*. As

Thea put it, "there are no coincidences. Everything is linked in some way." And she was ever so right, for it turned out that the *Shepherd's Fold* was the historical origin of the *Temple at Heaven's Portal*. Quickly she called Magda back with this little piece of information.

"Oh great heavens" Magda fumed, "that's the one we went to with Hortense! The one my neighbors go to."

Thea suggested they combine their sensory intensification with a vision circle. She and Cybil and Mitzy would add that to the gathering in LaPlaya, too. They'd even get Burgess and some of the others to join in. The more positive energy the better. They needed to know: why the fence now? What did all of this have to do with Wolf? What was the link to Magda One, to Magda Too? Not only would they do a visioning, but better yet said Magda, "Tran and I will fire up Wolf's sweat lodge."

Chapter Twenty-Six

Magda asked Hermes, to put a fire under the rocks for the sweat lodge. She and Tran then had about four hours before the coals would be hot enough.

Keeping in mind Anthea's admonition to open up all of their neurotransmitter receptor sites, she asked Tran to put on some Zen-Tango music. Slowly, sensuously, they all whirled and swooped and swayed their way toward the vast kitchen/great room. There they continued to dance from cupboard to sink to refrigerator to stove as Tran started a pot of Grandfather Soup going; thick and rich — to restore them after the sweat. Magda hung her heart full of gratitude key over the sink, and Colleen and Nora joined in, chopping onions, garlic, carrots, chunks of J&R Ranch organic pork, herbs, and artesian well water.

All four of the women worked on the soup and as they did they made sure to breathe deeply and smell each of the ingredients. When it was far enough along, each woman savored what was blending to perfection. It smelled divine and each inhaled a good whiff and then another. Next Magda and Tran created a huge batch of pear, nectarine, lemon, honey and coconut drink to hydrate them before they went into the sweat.

When the rocks were ready, it was time for the women

to don loose cotton shifts. Hermes joined them in his breech cloth and down the hill they went, to the lodge. As carefully and artfully as he'd done his Wikiup, Wolf had woven the lodge out of wicker, fixing it onto a frame about four feet high. A large oval with a door at each end, the frame was covered with canvas.

Hermes, the official tender of the rocks, took a large pitch fork and lifted the rocks out of the burning pit and carried them one by one into the interior. When he was done, Tran, being the closest they had to a healer or a shaman, entered the dark cavern first, then the women filed in and around the perimeter to take seats on the reed floor around the pit where Hermes had placed the rocks. A bucket of water was blessed and then ladled onto the rocks and the steam began to fill the enclosure.

Magda instructed Nora and Colleen in hushed tones, "It's best not to move. It stirs the steam up around you and feels even hotter. If you need to go out, you must ask permission from Tran. Normally, we each take a turn singing about what we want to heal, and when we have finished that is considered a round. We do three of these. But this is a special sweat, so we'll take a few liberties. All the focus will be on connecting with Wolf."

Tran began with a song and that led Magda into the invocation of Wolf's spirit. "Wolf, friend of my heart, please help us to know what to do next. Let us be open to your energy. Give us clarity about what you found in Fiddler's End. Talk to us, Wolf Tall Trees."

The response startled them all. Wolf's voice was so clear it was as if he was right there with them. They all heard it. They all felt his presence. Because he was actually right there.

"Great Grandmother, we've brought him back." Maggie

gasped and grabbed at Tran in horror, or was it hope? She reached for the ladle in the bucket of cold water and splashed a scoop on her face, rubbing her eyes in disbelief, weeping.

"Are you Wolf's spirit? You look so real." Magda whispered in total awe.

"Sorry to disappoint you, but I never went."

"Never went??!!! Don't you play coyote with me you imitation Wolf Tall Trees. Who are you really? And why are you doing this to us?" Magda came out of her reverential state.

The apparition held out a very solid hand to her. "The scar on my hand where you got me when I was teaching you to wield a knife."

"It is you," Magda gasped. "What do you mean, you never went? What in heaven's name happened? What kind of a cruel joke have you been playing on us? And how did you get in here without us seeing you?"

Tran gently eased Maggie back into her seat and spoke, "Please elucidate."

"Exactly, I want to know exactly what happened." Sparks flew from Maggie's eyes. She was totally conflicted between joy that he was alive and rage that he'd let her think he was dead. No more languishing for this lass. She was in high dudgeon. Tran held her back so that Wolf could tell the story.

The Indian got very still and began to sing himself into trance. In a flow of truncated snippets he related the story: "Saliva gushed... spasms erupted... I knew ... poison... be still, body... spirit guide me... focus... shut down... conserve energy... falling... hit intercom... hear Gillian... 'Wolf, is that you? Wolf???...' tried to get her to keep you away... bit about your i.d. just slipped out... didn't mean to lead you on... didn't always have control... the animal guides think different than mortals... in hospital you came ...worried eyes... don't fight ... tried to tell you save energy Sage Blossom... tall gypsy woman protecting you... peace... good energy... in good hands... time to heal... peace."

"But why on earth did you let us think you died?" Magda's Irish was up. After all, she now knew she was an O'Brien. How Irish can you get?

Wolf came out of his trance, "It just sort of worked out that way. When I came around, I was in the morgue. They were getting ready to take me over to the mortuary and Doc was standing over me saying a last good bye. Gave him a bit of a jolt. But nothing like what happened to old Feeny Filbert when he found out. By the way, don't blame him. It was an honest mistake. You know his smeller went out when he hit himself in the face with the peeve pole during the log rolling race at the woodsmen's competition. So there he was celebrating the end of his probation for DUI and that's how he got me confused with Hardy Rockwell. If he smelled Hardy I'm sure he would have gotten us straight. Anyway, I sat up and started talking to the Doc. Scared the bejesus out of Feeny. I believe his drinking days are done. It took some doin' to get MacClennon at the Funeral home to go along with the whole program. He wanted to tell everybody he'd had a resurrection right there in the Mortuary. But Doc and the Sheriff have their ways. Sheriff Willery convinced him he had to keep his mouth shut, and he made him an honorary special deputy in the Home Land Security forces. Not really, but enough to keep his mouth shut."

Magda almost shouted, but quietly as it was too hot in the lodge for any kind of exertion. "Wolfie, someone tried to kill you. We could have helped you." She swatted at him with a eucalyptus switch, "You're still not telling us why you let us think you were dead."

"I realized you might be in danger if the thugs who tried to kill me knew I was alive and saw me talking to you. They might think I told you something that would implicate them."

"I still don't understand why they'd want to kill you?" Magda asked.

"That is what I've been trying to find out. I knew I could only do that if they thought they'd succeeded."

"One thing I don't get, how come Anthea with all her psychic powers couldn't tell you were still alive? She's gonna really be pissed." Magda could hardly wait to tell the intuitive.

"I used a cloaking process, like the one I used to get in here without you knowing I was here. That way Anthea wouldn't catch on and spill the beans. When you explain it to her, she'll understand, I needed you to go on with the ceremony on the butte. And then I figured you'd all go back to California and Doc and the Sheriff and I could go about trying to find out what was going on. I did a spirit travel to let Grandmother Strong Feather know, and to get her to play along with the whole operation."

"And the ashes... whose ashes did we bury? Whose ashes is the pathologist checking out in Seattle. My God, we've got to stop her. Oh, I don't want to be the one to tell Mitzy we've led her doctor friend astray." Magda was in stress mode.

"You buried a dog from the vet. Highway accident."

"OK, next question: Was that your animal guide we saw on the bluff at the ceremony?" Magda was on the case now.

"That was me. I was there but I took on my animal shadow so that I could thank Grandmother without you all knowing what was going on."

"But you disappeared over the edge of the bluff. Where did you go?"

"I went to get my bike to go to Doc's place. I planned to start tracking those two guys as soon as you all left. When I went to get my wheels, I saw you loading that box into the SUV and I knew something was up. I lit out for Doc's and we called Pete. He checked with the airport and found out your plane was being prepped for a longer trip than just back to Southern California."

"Hah! You stole your own bike. AND you were spying on us?" Magda flicked her switch at Wolf.

"Protecting you." Wolf ducked.

"OK, so you knew we weren't going home, but how'd you know where we were going exactly?"

He ticked off on his fingers, "Number one, I figured you'd be tracking where I'd gone before I called you. I did teach you everything you know, didn't I? Number two — Pete called Vegas in the morning, after the pilot filed the flight plan and found out that you were going to the Methow Valley State Airfield. He is a Sheriff, after all. At least we didn't have as far to go as you did. We flew out of the private strip just out of Dos Lobos. The one where Pete keeps his Mooney tied down. It's a forty-year-old single engine so we had a bit of a challenge trying to catch up with you, but you had to drive south first." Wolf ladled water on the rocks, raising more steam.

"OK,' Maggie said, "I'll buy all that. But how'd you get to the Farm? That was you watching us from up on the bluff when Thea and Mitzy saw the flash of binoculars, wasn't it. They told me. We figured it was just the snoopy neighbors watching the goings on at Sunny Acres."

"Oh, they were watching you all right. But we were watching them. I did the same as you, called Ken Knightly car rentals. I had to pay extra to get him to keep his mouth shut."

"And then? I imagine you followed us to Boeing, but we must have gone off to Colleen's by the time you got there? And don't tell me you spirit-traveled, because you had no way of knowing where we were headed."

"The plane was scheduled to return to San Diego the next morning. We hung out at a motel and kept an eye on the jet. We weren't worried. When you didn't show up that day we got a little concerned, but then Willery sidled up to your pilot and found out you were staying over on Whidbey Island. Pete managed to get the location on that Cybil friend of yours and we spent that next night in the woods on Whidbey."

"So you three musketeers were skulking around in the wilds thinking we needed protection." Magda was incredulous.

"Oh, so its okay for a bunch of old ladies to go flying off to face down a pair of thugs you don't even know are lurking out there, but it's not okay for us to try to see that you don't get killed?"

"Don't be a wise-ass, Tall Trees. As far as we knew we were following a trail you left us, just trying to find out who I was. How dangerous could that be? We didn't know about your so called thugs. Now fess up. We were flying and then we had Cybil's car. You were way behind us. How'd you know where we went? I mean besides Jeff rattin' us out. I'll have to have a word with Cybil about that."

"Oh, unknot your bloomers, woman. We'd have found out anyway. Remember about eight or nine years ago, the Ranch had that crazy bomber who tried to blow the place up. The threats and all that?"

"So?"

"Back then, Willery arranged that telephone tap on the phone line. When it was over he left the tap on in case any more nuts decided to wipe out the sex fiends of eastern Nevada — 'sex fiends' being the women of your Spa."

"You mean he's had a tap on the lines to the Ranch all these years. What is he, some kind of Dick Cheney wannabe pervert? Did you all gather round and tap into our calls?"

"Don't be overly dramatic Lindal. We forgot all about it until this thing came up. It seemed like a good idea to crank the system up."

"But we weren't at the Ranch." Magda used her switch to prod him.

"We jacked the system into Pete's wireless. It took a little doing to get it to work from out in the woods. But that way we could be in on the calls you ladies made <u>to</u> the Ranch. Fortunately for us you pretty much laid it all out in your reports to Gillian and Madam Olivia."

"And what about later? While we were being attacked in your Wickiup, you three Lancelots were winging it back in the little bi-plane of Pete's? That's when we could have really used you."

"Well actually, we were there."

"Whoa, wait just a minute. Before we get to why you didn't stop them attacking us if that's true, I think there are some parts of this story missing." Magda was shaking her head.

"Like what?"

"Like I think you know who those guys were, so why won't you tell us?

"I still don't have it completely. Not enough to make a case. But while I was up there snooping around in Fiddler's End I musta spooked somebody. Why else would they try to kill me? And then ransack my place?"

"But there are lotsa guys who hate you for putting them behind bars. Any one of them could have sent some goons to get you. What makes you think they're from up there?"

"You didn't see these guys. No way were they pros. They were just a couple of goofusses who showed up at my door with a lame story about trying to find the old one's sister. You gotta admit it ties right in with the search for your roots Maggie."

"If they think they killed you, why would they come back to your place and go through it?"

"Only thing I can think of is when I was there, at their souvenir shop, I borrowed a pen to write in my Journal, and someone there musta reported that I was asking a lot of questions and making notes about back in the sixties. But they didn't have time to find the book when they tried to kill me. I was already calling Gillian for help. They had to wait till things calmed down and then come back."

"That must have been when Gillian found your place all messed up." Maggie was trying to put the pieces together. "But they didn't find the right book, did they? How'd they know they didn't have the right one?"

"None of the others mention the *Shepherd's Fold*."

"How did they miss that one?"

"It was stashed in a hideyhole I wove into the wall of the Wikiup."

"But you didn't get the book."

"Oh, but I did manage to get it before you clobbered me."

"Wait a minute. Are you saying it was YOU we were battling that night?"

At that point Wolf blushed as much as a par-boiled Native American can.

"Truth be told, yes. I thought we could get back and get the tracking book and with all the other pieces that were coming together we'd finally solve this thing. We didn't want them going after you if they thought you picked it up. We parked out behind the barn and Doc and I came around the back way, so we didn't see your car. We didn't know you were already in there. I admit, we made a total botch of it. But at least while we were all battling it out with you, the other guys never got into the lodge. Pete saw them come up and start to go in, they heard the ruckus and ran back to their vehicle. Doc and I hightailed it back to Pete's truck just as Olivia started taking potshots at the HumVee."

"Hah! Mitzy was right. She said she heard another vehicle out there. But tell us again, what it was they were after."

"That's just it. I'm not exactly sure. Something I came across when I was up in Fiddler's End must have scared them. But I can't put my finger on what it is. That's why I need to go over those notes again. I figured I could do that down here while I keep an eye on you."

As soon as they left the sweat lodge, while they were

eating their soup, Magda reported to Thea. After she got over the startling news that Wolf was alive and on the job in Bonsall, Thea had to deal with a little bit of her own jealousy over the fact that her client had gotten some major pieces of the puzzle without her help. And that Wolf managed to cloak himself so that she didn't know that he was alive — it was good strategy on his part. She had to remind herself what it was all about: Magda learning to trust her own feelings and getting out of the "mire of despond" into a higher vibration. It had nothing to do with Thea's ego and her capacities to find all the answers.

What joy that Wolf was alive! That's what they all needed to focus on now. But there was still work to be done. First thing was to contact Dr. Solares and let her know that she was not going to find any traces of nicotiana in the ashes of the road kill she was examining. Then they had to find evidence relating to the men who'd been after Wolf before they struck again. After all, since they still thought he was dead, Magda would be their target now that word was circulating around Fiddler's End that Magdalena's little Magda Too had been to town.

Chapter Twenty-Seven

Saturday morning dawned clear and crisp and full of promise in Bonsall. Wolf, who'd been up into the night going over Magda's Journal and his own without concrete result, was now down at the stable with Hermes doing horse chores, while Magda had Colleen and Nora busy laying the table for a lovely brunch. She was still in a quandary over what to do next? They planned to spend the afternoon going over the journals together, trying to find the thread that would finally nail down just who those men were.

Then too, Magda had a need to deal with Clelland, next door. The girls were sure it was something he was doing that made Curry so skittish. Wolf planned to do a vision quest to see what was going on. Magda's pondering was broken when a frantic Bonny Cantwell came trotting around the side of the house with five of her girls on her trail and Magda's cat Groucho draped pathetically over her arms. Hysterically she cried, "I was backing out of the driveway, and I must have been going too fast and he darted out and I guess I hit him. Oh please God, please dear Jesus, I don't know what to do Ms. Lindal. I didn't mean to hurt him. He just ran out."

Wolf came up the hill to where the women gathered around Bonny. He lifted the cat out of the woman's arms and Tran began running energy over the ball of fuzz while Magda eased her neighbor into a patio chair, poured her some tea and reassured Bonny that she didn't blame her. But she did wonder why she'd been driving so fast down her own driveway? As it turned out, Clelland had just told her to take the children to his parents and then find herself someplace to stay for a few weeks while he was on his honeymoon with Sissy.

Magda interrupted the story, "Excuse me? Whoa, right there. What do you mean on his honeymoon with Sissy?"

Through her sobs, Bonny related the rest of her saga. "Clelland arranged with Prophet Micah to annul his marriage to me because he says I wasn't a virgin when we got married and besides I've only given him daughters. He needs sons to fulfill his commitment to God. Never mind that the only man I ever slept with was Clelland and he tricked me into doing it before our wedding when we were in high school. It's always been easy for him to convince me its my duty to show how much I loved him. Now, he's told me that after he and Sissy return from their honeymoon he's willing to let me move into the maid's quarters and live in as nanny, cook and housekeeper."

Groucho apparently held no animosity. He'd recovered and jumped up into Bonny's lap to purr and knead.

After she finished exploding, Magda told Bonny and the girls they could bring their gear around and put it in the lanai. "You're welcome here until we get things straightened out."

Bonny was non-plussed. "That is so sweet. After what I did to him," she stroked the cat in her lap, "and you're not even Christian."

Magda smiled and put in yet another call to LaPlaya. "Anthea, you are not going to believe what my idiot neighbor is up to now!" she announced and she told her the whole story. "I know it's a distraction from the investigation about these men who are after Wolf, but we just have to do something about this lame brain next door."

"Trust your gut, Mags. We'll work on this together. When and where is this farce of a wedding supposed to take place?" Thea mentally chastised herself for her sarcasm. There it was again, a nasty attack of judgment. But just as with paranoia, sometimes it's a troubling call when what one person does hurts another. How do you not judge? Where does judgment leave off and discernment begin?

Magda's response startled her out of her self-flagellation, "Tomorrow morning at *The Temple* in Escondido."

"That gives us the rest of today to get the network on it. E-mail me all the particulars. I'll call you back as soon as we've got a plan. Logistics is Cybil's forte."

In no time the Juicy Crone network was indeed humming. Thea's website posted the notice:

Celebration of Gratitude

2:00 p.m., Sunday, July 3rd
Temple at Heaven's Portal, Escondido

Bring your favorite finger foods, beverages,
drums, tambourines, rattles, etc.

Contact Cybil LaCrosse for transportation information.

Everyone, please wear your Heart-Full-of-Gratitude
pendants and bring your Heart-Full-of-Gratitude wands.

This is a festive occasion, so dress accordingly.

All of the gang at MarVista joined in. Mitzy called Lulu to arrange for some of the show girls from Vegas to fly over. A bunch of them who had semi-retired to Palm Springs, where they had their own Follies show, signed on to drive down with their full regalia.[15]

Cybil got on the internet and connected with the leaders of several progressive Protestant Churches. Her Goddess Group got involved, as did Magda's sweat lodge members.

Meanwhile, there was lots of baking to be done.

Chapter Twenty-Eight

As they prepared for Deacon Clelland's nuptial service at the Cathedral, Brother Thaddeus quipped that The Beloved Prophet Micah had ordered the day up special: clear skies, and Heavenly white, puffy clouds.

The usual Temple congregants were a bit startled to see droves of visitors arriving by the bus load. Even more so when they saw the banners where there would normally be crosses on the sides of the buses. These proclaimed Gratitude and Love for All, and were decorated with heart shapes that had an odd circle sort-of-thingy in the middle. How in Heaven's name would they react if they knew it was the logo off Cybil's ever-so-intimate apparel line?

Lots of the arrivals waved wands in the air that had the same heart filled with the gratitude symbol and were decorated with ribbon streamers.

Many of the women getting out of the busses bore platters of fruit and baked goods. They sang *Onward Christian Soldiers* with new lyrics of love and gratitude – no mention of marching or war. Many of the visitors played finger cymbals and tambourines, as they segued into songs like *Getting to Know You,* and *I'm So Excited I Just Can't Hide It.*

The Progressive Christians were thrilled to have a way

to bring <u>their</u> Jesus, who was all about love, not war, into this temple that seemed to need a little enlightenment.

Inside the cathedral the new comers fanned out, causing ushers to run madly off in all directions trying to herd them back outside. Or at least to seats in the rear. This group was just too colorful for their taste. And those cloaks. What were they thinking? It was summer in California after all.

In their own little cloud of ignorant bliss, Clelland and Sissy waited on stage for Prophet Micah, who, at long last and completely oblivious to the commotion, descended on his heavenly platform in a vision of flowing amethyst satin.

Cybil, Mitzy, Magda, Nora and even Hortense joined Thea as she urged Bonny up onto the stage to help celebrate the wedding.

"Bonny is here to give Clelland to you, Sissy," Magda smiled at the bride, making sure that the groom heard her.

At a signal from Cybil, voices all around the perimeter of the cathedral broke into Kismet's peon to lusty love, *With monkeys and peacocks in purple adorning, show me the way to my bridal chamber. Then get you gone till the morn of my mornings, after the night of my nights.* Belly dancers and flow yoga practitioners and show girls dropped their cloaks to better perform their sensuous movements. Exquisite music, exotic lyrics, erotic movements and then, in what must surely have been a stroke of Universally guided timing, Thea got a call on her cell phone. She checked the caller ID, answered, stole a look at Clelland, and asked the caller, "Would you repeat that, please?" She held her cell phone up, and, with flawless placement, aimed it directly into the audio feed for the Cathedral's sound and video system. She motioned for Wolf to listen. The voice came across loud, clear, and amplified to the nth degree. It was Sheriff Willery in Nevada. "The license plate on the car that drove up when the attempt was made on your life, ol' pardner, belonged to one Clelland Cantwell. And the stolen i.d. that was used to rent the HumVee the morning of the assault on the women in your Wikiup? It was traced to the same Cantwell. Is this Cantwell anybody you know?"

Wolf shouted at the phone, "Sure a shootin' Sheriff," as he stepped toward Clelland. "I think we need to have a little talk, Mr. Cantwell. Now that I see you up close and face to face, I remember you. You and that fellow over there." He pointed at Brother Thaddeus. "You're just not wearing those goofy wigs and dark glasses you had on back then." Brother Thaddeus was trying to blend into the crowd on stage. Not an easy task for a man verging on 6'3" and probably weighing in at 300 pounds.

The volume on the festivities had been diminishing and now it dialed down, down, down to a hush. All except for Clelland who screamed at the top of his lungs as he pointed at Thaddeus, "I was just driving for him." The spotlight followed his digit. "He's the one said we had to do it to protect Prophet Micah." He, the digit and the spotlight swung to point at the Reverend, "From the evils of that Whore, Magdalena." Magda stood frozen, expecting the finger to point at her. But it didn't. It pointed up to the heavens, then corrected itself and pointed down to hell. It didn't know where "she" was.

"Do you mean Magdalena One?" Thea asked.

"I don't know what her other name was, but he told me she was Magdalena, the foreigner." Clelland was unstoppable.

"Protect him from what? What the hell could a long-dead woman do to Reverend Micah?" Cybil demanded in teamster cum lawyerly tones. The lighting technician was hard pressed to find the speaker with his light, but find her he did, just in time to have to swing back to Clelland.

"When that fellow Wolf," the spotlight followed the pointing digit to Wolf, "called, trying to find Mary's mother," Colleen pointed at Nora and the spot found her, "and father," the light was at a loss where to go so it just broadened out to catch the ensemble, "Brother Thadd," the light irised in on Thaddeus, "figured out from the way he was asking, that he might dig up something about that evil woman, that Delilah." Clelland rambled on, verging on incoherence. "He told me he and Micah...he wasn't a reverend back then, they were just kids. Anyway the Prophet said the foreign fornicator had to die to protect the movement. She was trying to have our Prophet stopped from his appointed path. Besides, she was gonna turn them in for puttin' that Birch fella's body in the compost heap. The one that stuck his nekked ass in the faces of our flock." The Crone contingent collectively gasped. "God protected them all these years and now that Indian was gonna' ruin everything."

Now, a gasp rippled through the audience, followed by a hush of body-prickling proportions. Even breathing seemed to have ceased.

Brother Thaddeus wasn't about to let Clelland dump the blame on him. "It wasn't my fault. Like he said, we were just kids back then. Rev. Father Jonas told us to get rid of that Magdalena. She was the power that kept them going over there at that communist commune. Father Jonas said that without her, the brothers of the church could drive the hippies out, cleanse the land for righteousness' sake. Remember, she was threatening to tell the police that the Prophet Father was molesting the girls. She refused to believe all those girls just prayed to be the next one chosen. Daddy said God would support us. And He did. All these years. If that story came out, it would rain anathema down upon our beloved daddy Jonas, and on Rev. Micah here." Now he too was babbling incoherently and gesticulating wildly. But the lighting technician was a Hollywood transplant. He was still on top of things. The light found the Rev. Micah attempting to climb onto his cloud.

Clelland reclaimed the spot. "Tall Trees was asking about the girl. The Rev. always thought she died when the car went over the edge. We needed the indian to tell us where she was. For all we knew he was in cahoots with one of those investigative reporters wanting a story about our beloved Prophet Father. When we got him in that teepee of his he refused to give up that notebook he wrote at *The Fold*. We were just trying to get him to talk so we could figure out what we needed to do to protect the congregation from his lies. Brother Thaddeus put Rev. Micah's truth drops in his water. It didn't work. He just got sick all over everything."

"You tried to kill me." Wolf was in Clelland's face. The spotlight loved it.

Prophet Micah felt the fervor, the call to stand and show the sheep of his flock the true path to understanding. He intoned in his most stentorian voice, the lights and television cameras full on him, "God told me we needed to protect YOU," he waved his arms over the crowd, "protect all you who had worked for so long. Way back when Brother Thaddeus sent the car over the edge of that cliff I knew it was the hand of God working through us, calling us to cleanse our Nation. We had to get rid of that foreign sex fiend and the girl. It was divinely inspired."

Thaddeus, getting into the God-as-divine-director theme turned and shouted louder and louder, the purple rising in his face as the spirit moved him, "Young Micah was guided by the Right Hand to distill some herbs. HE prepared the way and directed Micah to put it in the lemonade. The old woman went to Hades, where she dances and burns yet with the devil. But then, the girl came upon us. She found out what we'd done and she fought us. We were just trying to clean things up, put the body in an old trunk and get it on that car of hers. And then the other hippies started coming toward the barn to do some evening chores, so we just bopped her on the head to shut her up. We put her in the car. You see? It is the duty of the sons to protect the Daddy."

"Daddy, as in your father?" Magda squeaked.

"Of course. We're all of us the Blessed Ones. Jonas had been led by God to get children with his own pure little girls, just as he had with our mothers." He turned to look at Magda and saw Nora there, looking just as she had all those years ago. And he saw the child Mary in Magda's face. Thaddeus's inspiration fled in a whoosh. He didn't know whether to shrivel or attack.

Stunningly, Nora spoke in tones so sweet and gentle they could have been channeled from an angel, "He wanted my daughter Mary as soon as she came ready and I refused. She was just eleven then, and he was her own father. I guess I went a little crazy and I beat on him and sent her through the hedges to hide with the foreign woman."

"You see? Now you understand. We had to get rid of them. Both Magdalena and Mary." Micah shouted in righteous indignation.

Magda clung to her mother, trembling. It was all she

could do to stay upright. "Oh my dear, just when I was getting an image of Brian O'Brien as my father, you're telling me he wasn't. That evil man Jonas was." Suddenly, beyond Nora's words, Magda remembered. Recognition dawned, an epiphenomenon was upon her. "That's why you let me go." She embraced Nora. "He tried to make me the mother of the next holy child. Oh my dear heaven!" pointing at Micah, she announced, "You're my brother and you killed Magdalena and you tried to kill me!"

"Well, so did he," Micah said truculently as he turned and directed the spotlight at Thadd.

Magda's reaction at first was rage and horror, but Mitzy waved her gratitude wand, "Just remember what Thea taught you. He's here to allow you to learn forgiveness and kindness."

"Oh stuff it, MacDonald." Magda wheeled on Micah.

Thea picked up her queue, "Re-create your reality.... Gratitude, gratitude, great heartfuls of gratitude." She waved her own wand.

By the time Thea finished this snippet of a sermon, the congregation was in total confusion. What had they been hearing? Could any of it be true? They were horror-struck on one hand and exhilarated on the other. They felt a welling up of joy and an urge to applaud, but they didn't do that sort of thing at their services. And who would they be applauding? The visitors were all doing it -- clapping, rejoicing, singing, playing their instruments, waving their wands and dancing. Totally pissing the great Reverend off. He had lost control of his followers; they were listening to that wild woman. He wanted to strangle the lot of them; to rally his army of Shepherds and attack the violators.

Thea was still sermonizing to his people: "Give gratitude to the Universe for the clarity we've been shown about our selves and our own participation in all of this. The law will deal with the details."

Magda turned to Micah trying to figure out how to react. Propitiously, Nora shined her gentle smile on him. Her loving sweetness was too much for him. Filled with a purple rage, he began to lunge across the stage toward them.

Just then, Hortense slammed her cart into high gear and rammed across the stage. "You're not going anywhere you coward. Not till you heal me or gimme my two-hunnerd dollars back." It didn't occur to her that she'd never paid the $200. "Elsewise I'll have you hung on your own petard."

In yet another act of heavenly timing, Micah's cloud began to lift and swing, scooping him up and out to catch on Hortense's oxygen line. Thadd leapt across the stage making for the exit, only to be hit by the swinging platform, jarring it and knocking the Prophet off his perch and into the pit. Thaddeus, caught by the back swing, was sent careening after him down onto the organ to land splayed across his brother as the pipes resounded in thunderous discord.

Chapter Twenty-Nine

It took the rest of the day for everybody to be interviewed by a team of astonished police detectives and FBI agents, and then it was time to reconnoiter. A small group of the instigators gathered at Magda and Tran's place. Under Magda's guidance and with everybody pitching in, they pulled together a huge fruit salad, brie en brochette, bread from the freezer ready to bake, and an amazing ganach cake with walnuts.[16] Out by the pool, with a CD of sensuous middle-eastern-Caribbean music playing, Magda, Tran, Wolf, Hermes, Cybil, Mitzy, Bonny and her girls all gathered round so that Thea could explain the meaning beneath their whole adventure of the last few weeks. Magda asked for a moment to get a tape recorder and a notepad.

"But before you get into that, Thea, I want to know why you didn't just ask your inner spirit who I was, and get the answers when this all began?" Magda sounded a little on the peeved side.

"That, my dear sister is what I am about to reveal."

Magda got the recorder and sat down with a plop. "Ok, let's do it," she said turning on the recorder, pen poised.

Thea began, "You see, none of this is about _me_ doing it _for_ you. It's about _you_ letting go of past concepts that have kept you locked into the low vibration of your 'don't wants.'

The things I did see were because you were putting it out to the Universe that you were ready to find answers to your life quest, and were open enough to allow me to see what we needed to lead us on."

She went on, "Your reactions and thoughts along the way drew us toward the solution. It's all about the process of allowing the secret to work for you rather than against you in your life. Recognizing that you are always attracting what you create, what you project mentally and emotionally in your concept of life. Obviously I'm not talking about just you, but about any and all of us. It may be in obscure ways that we do this, and in most people's lives it's a matter of functioning from the 'don't wants,' because if you're not clear on your 'wants' and giving them lots of energy, then you create the 'don't wants' by default. It's what you're focused on that is what you get. And the majority of us focus 95% of the time on things we don't want."

"Give me a break Anthea. There is no way you are going to convince me that I drew all that misery at *The Shepherd's Fold* into my life. I was just a little kid."

"But you were programmed by what was going on with your folks before you were born. Like my friend Linda Logan says, you had a *Womb With a View*,[17] you picked up the energy that vibrated into that fish pond you were floating in and that shaped a good deal of what you expected. It created the vibrational frequency that then attracted people and experiences that matched the frequency you were holding. It sure explains why you've had addictions to feeling unworthy, harboring misery and expecting disappointment. That was what the good Shepherd convinced you was your role in life, to supplicate and agree that you were what the quote loving

Father unquote told you you were: unworthy, a disappointment to him, a miserable little wretch."

"I can't believe I'd do something that horrible to myself."

"I'm not saying you did it to yourself on purpose. It was all part of the way in which you were able to live a path of sheroism.

"Why can't you just explain it to me now?"

Anthea resisted the temptation to say, *that's what I'm trying to do,* and got on with it: "Think about it. You and Tran were led to agree to appear at the *Esoteric and Faerie Festival.* Then Tran got the offer of her dreams. You felt bereft and abandoned before she even agreed. You put on your martyr hat," Mitzy twirled her scarf as Thea continued, "and you thought of her desires first, sending her off, even though you were miserable about doing the seminar by yourself. It fit your disappointment addiction, but your psyche knew you needed to be vulnerable so that you would connect with me and allow the process to proceed. Normally your pattern has been to bear up under pressure, do it all yourself and live totally in the now, which meant no digging into the past, no calling new friends to come to your rescue. Living in the now can be very effective. Affirming your desire -- as Louise Hay teaches; as Matrix Energetics teaches,[18] -- but for many of us, we are tenaciously clinging to our subconscious addictions, little habit patterns of thought we don't even know we've filled our neurons with. You learned not to ask for help because your psyche had some serious blows. From your perspective it appeared that your mom and dad abandoned you. They weren't able to protect you the way parents should. When you turned to Magdalena, she was killed. You assumed it was for helping you, when in fact, Jonas and his boys were after the 'licentious Witch' who was going to expose their earlier crimes."

"You mean killing Birch and putting him in that compost heap? That one sure gave me creepy feelings when Thadd let it out of the bag. No wonder I felt so woozy when we walked past that burm at Sunny Acres. My head has been spinning with the things that have been coming back in bits and pieces all afternoon." Magda was almost jumping for joy. It was as though all the revelations were peeling away layers of a life she never felt quite at home with, leaving her almost childlike. "I'll tell you about some of it in a bit, but first I want you to finish, Thea."

"Calme, calme, Magda. All right, here we go, Clelland told us how Thadd and Micah killed Magdalena and tried to get you out of the way. You lived, but they didn't know that till Wolf turned up at Sunny Acres. When he took that tour of the *Shepard's Fold*, they alerted Thadd about the tracker and his notebook."

"And the visions of me struggling with Magdalena's body?"

"You're jumping around, but all right. I was just picking up on what you were going through psychologically. It was your spirit energy I was seeing. What your psyche wanted to do: rescue your friend," Thea said.

"OK, what about Wolf? Why did he get pulled into all of this? I mean I get it on a reality level, he's a tracker, he tracks. But what about on the soul level?" Magda was writing furiously now.

"You can call it whatever you want — karma, past life connections, entanglement — he was playing his role in your drama, and it so nicely fit a niche in his own unfolding."

"So his finding me all those years ago, then finally

tracking me last month, finding my origins, going to the *Shepherd's Fold* and alerting the flock as it were, that was all just our what? I mean I can't believe we planned the whole caper out there in... in where?"

"On the non-physical plane. We don't script it all out, we choose a basic path for our physical experience, and make our debut in conjunction with the constellations. We forget all that prep work; come in with no pre-conceived ideas. Your astrological chart shows you the options you gave yourself."

Magda pushed the micro recorder closer to Anthea: "Go on Thea. This is all good stuff?"

"Good stuff?"

"Yes. Please, just go on? Tell me about my link up with Wolf."

"Wolf, and all of your others. The players in this particular life. Your spirits, your energy sources, working it all out. Enjoying the ride, the super-thriller ride in this gigantic theme park. After we met at the *Faerie Festival,* you got the call from Wolf that he was coming to visit. You're inner being didn't really believe he was coming about tracking some criminals. You had an odd, intuitive feeling. But you didn't pay attention to it. To get it to fit your logic-driven concept of life you jumped to the conclusion that it was about some nameless criminals he'd been tracking. It never occurred to you that it was about you. That wouldn't fit your vision of being unworthy. You wouldn't let yourself think he'd been doing something about your life-long problem."

Wolf thought he better clarify, "I kept a whole separate tracking book over the years, just on this project. It was especially tough for me. I could only work on it between my official jobs. And, I think there was some blocking energy coming from your neck of the woods." He looked fondly, if a bit sternly, at Magda. "I was intending to come down and bring you up to date. See if what I'd found opened any mental doors for you."

"Like he says, you'd subconsciously been blocking any kind of awakening. But by then your energy field was beginning to open up. You attracted a connection to the Cantwells. Clelland suited your needs to a tee. And of course the girls were there to help, even though you had no idea about that."

"And Hortense?" Magda grinned, hardly believing that Tensia had anything to do with her life path.

"Of course Hortense. Our non-physical selves must collectively have a somewhat perverse sense of humor. She played right into the scenario. She got us all to the Cathedral and our encounter with the vibration that was to lead us on. That experience kicked off a reaction. It was a direct link to your past, but again you diligently blocked it out. So it took a few more events to open up those clogged neurons."[19]

"I can see exactly what you're saying Thea. I can use all of this." Magda moved the mic closer to Anthea and urged her on.

"Use all of this?" Anthea thought, even as she determined not to get side tracked by Magda's somewhat odd reaction. "You got a call that Wolf was seriously ill. We all knew that this was our next assignment from the Commander in Chief of the Universal Life Force. That's what I call our inner being, our connectedness to All That Is, to each other. It's that part of the entangled web that becomes the warp and woof of our physical lives. Without these entanglements and physical plane experiences we aren't here. The threads are different for every single being who chooses a physical experience, but they all weave through the whole tapestry.

"Every time we took a step forward your resistance seemed to solidify. I say 'seemed' because it was actually just the appearance at the moment. You were in fact beginning to create new neuro-receptor sites, recreating facets of your brain, so that it could learn a new way to deal with the emerging you. But, out of habit, you couldn't let go of the misery that had been your form of validation for so long. You believed the more misery you appeared to be dealing with the more sheroic you would be to the others in your life."

Magda almost whooped as she made a huge note, "Sheroic, you've all used that term and it zipped right over my head. Now I get it, a she-hero. Terrific imagery."

Now Cybil and Mitzy were starting to cast little glares at Magda. They both wondered what she was up to with these 'use this' comments. Whatever it was she wasn't about to let Thea stop just yet.

"Come on Anthea, keep going. Hah, just got another bit there... I was addicted to misery, but it was really a way for me to appear to be heroic. Er sheroic."

"Right. That was on a subconscious level. On the conscious level, you fought mightily to stay positive, to see the glass half-full. But that stubbornness was a kind of defense mechanism you developed to obscure your past for all those years."

Cybil itched to participate: "Many of us go through stages of validating our existence through misery. Even those who seem the most fortunate get attacked by the press or have miserable love lives or other disasters. Believe me, I've been there."

"We all have. When I was in Vegas I used to see it all the time." Mitzy was not about to be left out. The look she got from Magda settled that question, but not without a last word, "We've been in on these wrap-ups with Thea before." She semi-sulked, but not for long.

Thea proceeded, "It's the hook humans use to keep connected to all of the others on the planet. The way we convince ourselves we're not separate from all the rest of the crowd. Anyway, Wolf 'died.' We went through his things and were led to Fiddler's End. We kept you doing a variety of BrainGym movements to help open up your brain to allow the new information to replace old information. Granted it was information you didn't consciously know you had wired in, but it was there none the less. As you were busily rewiring on a subconscious level, we were all being drawn by your evolving vibration."

"Gee whiz, with all this evolving and vibrating, its a wonder I wasn't exhausted," Magda giggled, followed by clamping one hand over her mouth and indicating go on to Thea with the other.

"We found out about Magdalena and how you were connected to her and you fought harder and harder for the notion that you were responsible for her death. You fought out of a sense of loyalty. And a hint of martyrdom. How valiant you were determined to be."

"Hah, but then I let us find Colleen and Nora. Why do you suppose we were never led to go to the Shepherd's Fold ourselves," asked Magda.

Wolf interrupted, "I did a journey to keep you all moving back to the south. I really didn't want the Shepherds from the Fold to find out about you. But if I'm getting you right, I gather

Ms. Magda was beginning to open up, and that led her to Colleen and Nora."

"You're getting the picture, Wolf."

"OK, I'm getting how all my friends pitched in and participated in this thing I call a life. That was the gentle side of the plot. What about the bad guys?" Magda's pen hovered over her notepad.

"That was inevitable. The life path you designed required partners who would put blocks in your way, so that you could get creative in solving your problem," Anthea reached into her portmanteau, pulled out a deck and turned over three faery cards: The Master Maker, The Green Woman, and the Piper. "All about creativity. When you chose to experience this particular physical script you wanted something totally involved with the way the senses are given to physical beings to allow their spirits to play and really enjoy Gaia. But you also wanted a major challenge, and so you drew Thadd and Jonas and Micah and Clelland in to provide that over-coming, that sheroic part of your journey... you used sensuosity as your modus, and then lined up the opposition — a group of guys who find anything sensuous abhorrent."

"That may work for Maggie, but I'm about as creative as a ... see what I mean? I can't even create an analogy," Wolf said.

"On a spirit level, Wolf, your agreement this time around was to take the hidden-protector role, because she really wanted to do it herself." Thea turned to Maggie, "But you needed some protection." She turned back to Wolf, "You'd forgotten your role, but as much as you wanted to present Mags with a fait accompli, that was not the way her spirit wanted to experience this trip."

"That doesn't sound very fair. It's like I get all the attention, all the help."

"Believe me, we are all the stars of our own productions."

"Well, what about all of you? You seem like bit players in my big drama," Magda sounded a little like her old guilt-ridden self.

Thea looked Magda directly in the eyes. "You were willing to accept us as helpers because, on some level, your psyche was able to relegate us to roles as your sidekicks. We're your second bananas. But we were all in perfect accord with the program."

"Hah. That's a good one. You wouldn't know how to be second to anyone about anything. Any of you." Magda grinned at the Juicy Crones.

"You'd be surprised at what we all do for each other. Often as not without even knowing it. It's called love, and it's the reason we are here."

"So you say Jonas and company were all a part of my play? What have they got to do with love?"

"It's a play we all agreed to before coming. You agreed to play a part for each of them. Human nature uses opposite to teach. The opposite of love is hate. They got to play the villains. And the game is not over. The challenge now is to be grateful for the parts they played in this experience. It's easy to be grateful for Wolf, for Tran, for us, even for Bonny and the girls, but the challenge is to keep finding ways to be grateful for those men. To remember the ways they kept playing their nasty roles so that you could experience your shero part. You did not want a mundane life this time around. And they clearly chose to play the bad guys. They'll carry it through to the bitter end quite dramatically, I guarantee you. It should be something to observe your own behavior as you go through the trials. Because I'm quite sure Micah isn't about to just let it go. He'll want to grand-stand for all he's worth. And that is part of his learning about love...by so totally experiencing its opposite."

Chapter Thirty

Three months later at the MarVista Inn, Magda, Tran, Nora, Colleen and Wolf stopped on their way to LA on business. Magda said she'd explain that later.

"What you need right now is an update," and with that she began to fill them in. They all knew from accounts in the media that Micah was awaiting extradition to Washington state. He was in the hospital wing of the jail as it was clear he would be a paraplegic for life. Thaddeus was also awaiting determination on who had jurisdiction over his various crimes. Clelland was charged as an accessory in the attempt on Wolf's life, along with burglarizing his Wikiup. "It's all pretty complicated, who'll be charged for what, in what venue. But its getting sorted out. And, by the way, the Cantwell girls discovered that Clelland had been feeding my pony loco weed. No wonder he'd been so out of control. At last, Curry was his old peppery self again. The girls are staying with us while their mother does a little R&R at Rebecca Quest's Metaphysical Bootcamp in Malibu."[20] Magda beamed at her progress report.

"By the way, Wolf insisted I use the money in that bank account to buy the property next door and develop it. So we're safe from the cell tower that Clelland was going to put in as an endowment to *The Portal*. I'm sure grateful for that. But

I keep telling the old fart he didn't have to go so far." She gave Wolf a little nudge on the shoulder.

"And I keep telling you, you're as close as I ever got to havin' family. I socked it away from fees I collected tracking for the FBI and the CIA and a few others I'm not at liberty to name. I didn't need it. The Ranch always provided. And now, since we got all this publicity, the Ranch and the website are makin' a bundle for all of us. I've got more money than I know what to do with," said Wolf.

Magda gave him a big hug, "So I insisted that he accept partnership in the Riding Camp. We're using the animals to help people who are either physically or mentally challenged. The Cantwell girls have amazing skills with the animals, and with the clients, so its goin' great."

Anthea beamed, "Isn't this Universe something? The way it fulfills our dreams when we let it. Even when we aren't clear on what those dreams are." That discussion segued right into Thea reminding them all of what Magda had taught them about the power of sensuosity with her movies. She had a motive in bringing it up. "So now, you see why it's time to write *The Sensuous Woman's Guide to Spiritual Awareness*."

Cybil wanted the first book off the presses for her own use, and she didn't care who thought she was being pushy. But then Mitzy demanded her own copy, "And what about Thea? She should get a nice autographed copy." She was trying not to sound too self promoting.

"Sorry friends, it's going to have to wait. That's the big news. We're on our way to LA where I'm about to sign a contract with my old producer. The 15-year writer's block disappeared. Listening to the tapes and reading through the notes I made after the grand finale at *the Portal*," she giggled,

"I got an idea for a new movie and my producer's bustin' to get it out fast. All this esoteric stuff is the new, hot-ticket item. Everything you kept trying to pound into my head, Thea, about the Law of Attraction and Allowing and Creating our own reality... well, it all came through. I got it. Those tapes did it. My whole crazy life story. Including the part that came before this physical plane existence. He's talking big named stars, the whole nine yards."

Thea hugged her. "I think you've found your inner dancing dragon," and they all toasted the newest recruit into the Juicy Crones Sisterhood.

The End

Universal Light Force Enlistment Agreement

I, _____, pledge my allegiance, body/mind & soul to the Universal Light Force. As a member of the Force I accept that my only occupation is a 24-hour-a-day vigilance to see that I stop bemoaning the toil of the soil, human labor, mental or physical, and instead I stand porter at the door of thought. Every time it occurs to me that "I must...", "I ought to...", "What should I...?", "How do I...?", my duty is to immediately arrest that intruder, march it right over and release it to Spirit, who will handle it as only It can. By acknowledging that I can of my own ego-self do nothing to solve the problems of human consciousness, and turning all over to Spirit, I am set free.

Any time fear, doubt, guilt, shame, worry, anger, lack, disappointment or other dis-ease arises, I know it has come to my attention because I have enlisted in the Light Force and it is my job to usher all such dis-eases straight to Divine Wisdom to be dissolved with the Universal Solvent of Love. As I do this for myself I am joining with other members of the Force and together we are widening the beam of Light for all humanity.

I hereby agree to list all of my notions of lack and limitation, my fears, guilts, doubts, desires, goals, all thoughts and ideas to which my ego is still attached, on a piece of paper, and to, with due reverence, dedication and joyful ritual, burn said document in a blaze of purifying glory, knowing once again, it is not I that do the work, but the Spirit within. I will repeat this process whenever it occurs to me as appropriate, knowing that this notion is a prompting from Divine Guidance, my Light Force Commander in Chief.

I realize that this commitment to service in the Light Force may bring up a number of reactions from my ego-self and from others, but I am dedicated to this engagement. I know that the only casualties will be my own worn-out, encrusted old ideas about corporeal existence which, of themselves, are myths of my own creating. It is, from this moment on, my sworn duty & joy to release all such myths and to allow only Truth to permeate my being.

In return for my total commitment to this thought vigil, Spirit agrees to nourish, nurture, and Love me in ways more splendid than I can as yet imagine. And in return I allow Spirit to flow through me freely, manifesting Itself in singing, dancing and rejoicing every day of my life.

On this glorious _____ day of _____, 20__,
I enthusiastically set my hand,

_____.

This commitment is unequivocally accepted on behalf of the Universal Light Force. Acknowledgment by the signatory is in and of itself acknowledgment by Light Force Command.

End Notes

1. With kind permission from Jean Shinoda Bolen, M.D.

2. Anthea uses The Faeries' Oracle by Brian Froud and Jessica MacBeth www.imaginosis.com. *(pg. 4)*

3. Dr. David Hawkins - *Power vs Force* and a number of other books explaining how our energy levels effect our lives. See his website: www.veritaspub.com. *(pg. 4)*

4. Check out www.abraham-hicks.com for more information about this uplifting approach to life. *(pg. 4)*

5. Jean Shinoda Bolen, M.D. *Crones Don't Whine* - Visit her site: www.jeanbolen.com/ This amazing woman will make you feel so good to be exactly who you are. You are going to love her array of titles. Indulge yourself. *(pg. 40)*

6. Crystal or Indigo Children: I suggest googling both. There are some very informative sites out there. You'll start to understand these new generations of kids coming along. *(pg. 40)*

7. BrainGym, a physical technique used by Anthea to unleash the body/mind potential for healing and excelling. See www.braingym.com. *(pg. 59)*

8. Cybil naturally installed a BioPro chip on the dish, and two on the dash board of the car. She's already got them all over anything electrical/wireless including cell phones and such for herself and all of her friends. Once you understand the problem you'll want to BioProtect yourself. See www.ElectroPollutionSolution.biz. *(pg. 74)*

9. Himalayan Krystal Salt... all the micronutrients your body needs in a delicious salt from 2 miles deep within the Himalayan Mountains, so it's pristine and pollution free. Dr. Christian Opitz, biochemist, biophysicist and nutritionist, recommends it for anyone with blood-pressure problems. Order his DVD along with the salt. Please be sure to mention our affiliate #256335. Order from www.krystalwebmatrix.com/ comd.php?af=256335. *(pg. 77)*

10. SIPs = structurally insulated panels. www.SIPS.org for more information about their association and a list of qualified contractors in your area. The one mentioned in the book, Cybil's business partner, is Noel Vangeisen of www.structurestogo.com. *(pg. 116)*

11. The Heartful of Gratitude pendant was inspired by www.gogratitude.com. Get connected to the world-wide movement to spread gratitude. *(pg. 143)*

12. Want to buy some of this incredible organic olive oil? Check out www.awesome-oil.com/shop/. *(pg. 151)*

13. For a view of Cynthia Thomas's awesome work see her website: www.mlce.net. *(pg. 154)*

14. Mary Baker Eddy, founder of Christian Science, wrote of a woman not unlike Nora in the 1860's. *(pg. 237)*

15. Palm Springs Follies www.palmspringsfollies.com. A whole bevy of bolder older women who still strut their stuff. You've got to see their website. *(pg. 262)*

16. A Cynthia Thomas favorite: www.juicycronemysteries.com to get your copy of this juicy recipe. *(pg. 273)*

17. *Womb with a View* by Linda Logan - write to her at lindalogan710@aol.com or coming soon to www.juicycronessisterhood.com/logan for excerpt and updates. *(pg. 274)*

18. To learn more, check out *You Can Heal Your Life*, by Louise Hay at www.hayhouse.com and Matrix Energetics at www.matrixenergetics.com. *(pg. 275)*

19. See www.Whatthebleep.com and www.thesecret.tv to learn more about reprogramming our neuro-receptor sites to change our lives. *(pg. 278)*

20. See the Rebecca Quest novels featuring the 1450-year old Eternalight psychic, trained by Morgan LaFey and Merlin of Avalon fame: www.Rebecca@JuicyCronesSisterhood.com. *(pg. 285)*

21. Write me Hana@juicycronemysteries.com for more copies of the *Universal Light Force Agreement* or for a list of other Agreements with *All That Is*. Also available: certificates celebrating aspects of who you are. *(pg. 289)*

1526519

Made in the USA